the thing about
the truth

the thing about
the truth

LAUREN BARNHOLDT

Simon Pulse
New York London Toronto Sydney New Delhi

SIMON PULSE

An imprint of Simon & Schuster Children's Publishing Division
1230 Avenue of the Americas, New York, NY 10020
First Simon Pulse paperback edition June 2013
Copyright © 2012 by Lauren Barnholdt
All rights reserved, including the right of reproduction
in whole or in part in any form.
SIMON PULSE and colophon are registered trademarks of
Simon & Schuster, Inc.
Also available in a Simon Pulse hardcover edition.
For information about special discounts for bulk purchases,
please contact Simon & Schuster Special Sales at
1-866-506-1949 or business@simonandschuster.com.
The Simon & Schuster Speakers Bureau can bring authors to your live event.
For more information or to book an event contact the
Simon & Schuster Speakers Bureau at 1-866-248-3049 or
visit our website at www.simonspeakers.com.
Designed by Karina Granda
The text of this book was set in Cochin.
Manufactured in the United States of America
2 4 6 8 10 9 7 5 3 1
The Library of Congress has cataloged the hardcover edition as follows:
Barnholdt, Lauren.
The thing about the truth / by Lauren Barnholdt.
p. cm.
Summary: In this story told from alternating viewpoints, seventeen-year-old
Kelsey seeks to redeem her formerly flawless reputation with the help of a
senator's sexy but arrogant son, who has ulterior motives.
ISBN 978-1-4424-3460-8 (hc)
[1. Dating (Social customs)—Fiction. 2. High schools—Fiction.
3. Schools—Fiction.] I. Title.
PZ7.B2667Th 2012 [Fic]—dc23
2011034799
ISBN 978-1-4424-3461-5 (pbk)
ISBN 978-1-4424-3462-2 (eBook)

To the real Kelsey,
who always reads the last page first

Acknowledgments

Thank you, thank you, thank you to:

Jennifer Klonsky, my amazing editor, for her brilliant insight and unwavering support.

Alyssa Eisner Henkin, for being the best agent a girl could ask for.

My mom and my sisters, for being my best friends.

Jessica Burkhart, Kevin Cregg, and Scott Neumyer, for always being there.

And Aaron, my husband, for grounding me, encouraging me, loving me, and making me a better person—I love you, AG.

The Aftermath

Kelsey

I am in so much trouble. So, so, so much trouble. Seriously, I cannot even begin to *imagine* the kind of trouble I'm in. It's the kind of trouble you hope you're never going to be in, the kind of trouble you hear people talk about, and you go, *"Wow, what an idiot. I'm glad I'm never going to be in that kind of trouble."*

I'm probably going to get kicked out of school. My second school in three months. What will happen to me then? Where will I even go? The last school I got kicked out of was Concordia Prep, a private school, so of course I got put into public school. But where do you go when you get kicked out of public school? Reform school or something?

God, that would be horrible. I could never last at a reform

school. I have a pink Kate Spade purse, for God's sake. I got it at the Kate Spade outlet, but still. Reform school would eat me alive. I'd be like one of those girls on those shows on Spike TV, where they take the teen troublemakers and put them in jail for a day to show them where they're headed, and they all break down and start crying and completely lose their shit.

I shift in my chair and look at the clock: 11:27. The meeting with the superintendent, Dr. Ostrander, is supposed to start in three minutes, and Isaac still isn't here. Not that I'm surprised. Isaac is never on time to anything.

The clock's hand ticks over to 11:28, and I start to think that maybe he's not coming. That maybe somehow his dad got him out of it, and that I'm going to be left dealing with this mess on my own.

But then the door to the office opens, and Isaac walks in. His dark eyes scan the room, moving over the secretary, taking in the closed door that leads to Dr. Ostrander's office, and then finally landing on me. Without even talking to the secretary or telling anyone he's there, he walks over and plops himself down in the chair two down from me.

He doesn't say anything, just keeps his gaze facing forward. I sneak a look at him out of the corner of my eye. He's wearing pressed khaki pants, a light blue button-down shirt, and a red-and-blue tie. His black shoes are perfectly shined, his hair freshly gelled. He looks put together, in control, and, as always, completely gorgeous. There's a slight scowl on his face, but it only serves to make him look more in charge of the situation, like he can't believe what a total waste of time this whole thing is.

He turns to look at me, and when he does, he catches *me* looking at *him*, and my heart stops.

"Hey," I say. I'm not sure if we're talking, but the word is out of my mouth before I can stop it.

"Hey." His tone is clipped. He's still mad at me for what happened, still hurt, still upset. Still probably doesn't want to give me another chance.

"I was starting to think you weren't going to come," I say. It's a lame thing to say, but I'm desperate to keep the conversation going.

"Why wouldn't I come?" He looks like he thinks I'm crazy for doubting he would show up.

"I don't know. I thought maybe your dad . . ."

He rolls his eyes and looks away.

"Anyway," I say, "I'm glad you're here."

He doesn't reply, just pulls his cell phone out of his pocket. His fingers move over the screen, checking his texts, reading something, typing a reply. I wonder who he's texting with. Marina? Doubtful, but honestly, at this point, nothing would surprise me.

"Mr. Brandano, Ms. Romano?" the secretary says. "Dr. Ostrander will see you now." I take a deep breath and stand up. I smooth my skirt, a simple black pencil skirt chosen in an effort to make me look mature and trustworthy.

"Here we go," I say to Isaac, and flash him a smile. It's

an attempt to show that we're in this together, that we're both heading into the lion's den, but that maybe we can be okay if we just depend on each other.

But Isaac doesn't say anything. He just turns on the heel of his superexpensive, supershiny black shoe and walks toward Dr. Ostrander's office door. I stand there for a moment, blinking back the tears that are threatening to spill down my cheeks.

I'm upset because Isaac won't talk to me, but mostly I'm upset because I know that this whole thing is my fault. The reason we might get kicked out of school. The reason everything's so completely screwed up. And most of all, the reason we broke up. The reason I've probably lost him forever.

I've spent so many hours thinking about it, going over it again and again in my mind. If I start doing that now, I'll drive myself crazy, letting my thoughts become a tangled mess. And I need to keep my mind clear for this meeting. So I wipe at my eyes with the back of my hand and then force myself to head into Dr. Ostrander's office.

Before

Kelsey

So, my first day at Concordia Public is definitely not off to a great start. First, I spilled orange juice all over the skirt I was wearing. Which was bullshit, since (a) I don't usually even eat breakfast, and (b) I don't even really like orange juice. But this morning when I came downstairs, my dad insisted that I "get something in my stomach" so that I would have energy for my first day at my new school. So I choked down a piece of dry toast and a glass of orange juice, mostly just to please him (that's a whole other story—the doing it just to please him part), and then I spilled it on my skirt. And I had no time to change before the bus came.

Which was another thing. The bus. Riding the bus, in case

you don't know, really sucks. But I don't have a license yet (I'm seventeen, but I've failed my driver's test twice—fingers crossed, though, for my next try!), and there was no way my parents were going to give me a ride to school. They were trying to teach me a lesson, I think. Which makes no sense. How was not driving me to school causing me to learn a lesson? I already learned my lesson when I got kicked out of my old school.

Hopefully, I'll be able to make some new friends quickly. New friends who won't mind picking me up in the morning.

But so far, the prospects at Concordia Public are not looking very promising.

I'm sitting in the guidance office, waiting to have a meeting with my guidance counselor so I can get my schedule and locker combination, and no one here looks even remotely like potential new friend material. I mean, the girl sitting next to me has pink hair and five piercings in each ear. Which is fine. I might be preppy, but I'm not, like, *discriminatory* or anything.

I can be friends with people who have piercings. Not that I ever really have before, but I have nothing against it. I love piercings. I have two in each ear, even. But it's the girl's bag that's the real problem. It's a camouflage print. Which again, whatever. Not my style, but fine. But what *isn't* fine is the patch that's sewn on the front. It says KILL ALL PREPS.

I might not be prejudiced, but she definitely is. I quickly move my Prada shoes (borrowed from my friend Rielle) farther under my chair.

The irony of the whole thing is that I kind of feel the same way she does. Preps do kind of suck. But at my old school, Concordia Prep, everyone was preppy. (Haha, preps at a prep school, big surprise, right?)

Anyway, I was a scholarship student, so I was always trying to make sure I fit in. And that meant having Kate Spade purses and Prada shoes. Even when I couldn't afford it, I would—

The door to the office opens and a boy walks in. Dark blond hair. Sparkling white sneakers. Perfectly faded jeans. He walks with a swagger, the kind that comes from years of being confident. You can't teach a walk like that. Trust me, I've tried to cultivate one. It's impossible.

I make a mental note to stay away from him. He's probably the most popular guy in school, the kind who's mean to everyone, the kind who, for some inexplicable reason, has all the girls wanting him. Why are girls like that, anyway? They're always falling for the jerks. Which is ridiculous. Not that I don't have experience when it comes to that kind of thing.

I mean, I wouldn't be here if I hadn't fallen in love with a jerk. A jerk is the reason I got kicked out of my old school.

But I've learned my lesson.

I look over at the girl next to me, and she's practically falling out of her chair, that's how bad she wants this guy. Poor thing. She doesn't know what she's in for. And besides, I thought she hated all preps. I guess it doesn't apply to hot male preps with perfect hair and perfect—

Mr. Popular is speaking.

"Hello," he says to the secretary, leaning over the desk. "I'm Isaac Brandano. It's my first day, and I was told to come to the office and pick up my schedule."

I almost choke on the peppermint latte I'm drinking. It's this guy's first day? And he's walking like *that*?

"Yes, Mr. Brandano," the secretary says, all friendly. She gives him a smile. When I came in here, she totally scowled at me and acted like I was making her day into a big debacle. "Here you go." She hands him a schedule. What, he doesn't have to sit here and take a meeting with his guidance counselor like everyone else?

Ohmigod. Probably only the rejects who got kicked out of their old schools need to have meetings with their guidance counselors. How humiliating.

Mr. Popular thanks her, then turns toward the door, his eyes running down over his schedule. He frowns slightly, probably because he can't believe they would dare to put him in math or something.

He looks up, his eyes meeting mine. His are dark and slightly brooding, the color of chocolate, and I feel my heart skip a beat. I mean, I'm only human.

"Hey," he says.

"Hi," the girl next to me says, totally butting in.

"Do either of you know where room 107 is?" He smiles, showing perfect white teeth. Real white. Not the kind of white that comes from using those whitening strips or spending hundreds of dollars at the dentist. Rielle has that kind of teeth, along with tons of other girls at Concordia Prep.

"No," I say firmly. I've gotten ahold of my hormones, so I take another sip of my latte and then turn back to the book I'm reading.

"No?" He sounds a little incredulous. I guess he's surprised that I don't want to help him. Obviously, he doesn't know that I'm new and thinks I'm just being a bitch. Which I kind of like. That he thinks I'm being a bitch, I mean. It's sort of amusing.

"No," I repeat.

"I do," the pink-haired girl offers. "I know where it is."

But Isaac Brandano isn't paying attention to her. He's still looking at me. The only reason I've even remembered his name is because he has the same last name as our state senator, John Bran— Oh. My. God. No freakin' way. Isaac Brandano is our state senator's son!

There was all this talk on the news last night about how John Brandano was going to be sending his son to public school in order to prove that a public school education is just as good as a private school one. Of course, I doubt that's really true. I mean, public school is—

"You don't know where room 107 is?" Isaac Brandano's asking me. "You have no idea?" Now his incredulousness makes even more sense. I mean, not only is he gorgeous, but he's a senator's son. Which means he's used to people doing whatever he wants and falling all over themselves to help him. Now I'm doubly happy that he thinks I'm messing with him.

9

"No," I say simply. "Sorry, I don't. But I suppose that you expect me to find out for you."

"No." He shakes his head. "I don't expect that, I just . . ." He looks shocked that someone would be mean to him, and for a second I feel bad. I mean, I *am* being a bitch. And if it were anyone else, I would tell him that I'm new and that's the reason I can't show him where the room is. And let's face it, I'm a little on edge today, which is definitely affecting my mood.

I can't feel too bad, though, because honestly? Probably no one's ever been mean to him in his life. Probably he's used to just smiling at people and having them fall in love with him and do whatever he wants, like he just did with the secretary.

I know his type. I've handled his type. I'm at this stupid school because of his type.

"I'm sorry," Isaac says. He's still looking at me, and he shakes his head again like he doesn't know what just happened, like he wants to start again. "I just—"

"I can show you where the room is," the girl next to me says. She stands up and starts to gather up her bag.

"There you go," I say. "See? It all worked out." I go back to reading my book. Honestly, now I just want the both of them to go away. I need to focus on my meeting and making a good impression on my guidance counselor. Now that I've been kicked out of one of the best prep schools in the country, my college recommendations are going to be doubly important.

Isaac follows the pink-haired girl out into the hallway. Good riddance.

"Ms. Romano?" the secretary asks. Now that Isaac and his good looks have disappeared out the door, she's back to being all frosty. "Mr. Lawler will see you now."

"Thanks." I put my book back in my bag. And then I step into my guidance counselor's office, ready to make a good impression and take the first step toward getting my future back on track.

Before

Isaac

This school is completely fucked up. Seriously, what the hell is going on? Is this how public school is going to be? People just being *mean* to you for no reason? That girl in the guidance office was just . . . I don't know.

I guess I expected people to be a little rude because of who my dad is. At my old school I didn't have to worry about that, since no one really gave a shit. Everyone's parents were important. In fact, there were some kids who had celebrity parents.

But a lot of people get all weird about it. There are people, like that secretary back there, who fall all over themselves trying to be nice to you. And then there are people who go out of their way to show you that they're not going to give you any special treatment. So I knew public school would be different, but I didn't expect to encounter it during my first minute here.

I knew I shouldn't have worn my new sneakers today. Way too flashy.

"So, are you, like, a transfer?" The girl showing me to my homeroom is blabbering on and on, but I haven't been listening to her because I've been distracted, thinking about that girl in the office.

"Yeah," I say, looking around the hallway. "I'm a transfer." Obviously, she hasn't heard about me. Which is to be expected. This whole starting public school thing was a little sudden. My dad's spinning it so that it seems as if he's sending me to public school to make a statement about education or some shit. But the reality is I got kicked out of my last school, and I'm sort of at the end of the line when it comes to private schools. It was either here, or boarding school overseas. And when that possibility came up, I pitched a fit.

The numbers on the rooms are going down as we walk: 119, 117, 115. . . . Hell, if I had known it was going to be this easy to find my homeroom, I never would have even asked for help.

"Where'd you transfer from?" the girl's asking.

"Hotchmann," I say. She looks at me blankly, so I add, "It's a boarding school in New York City."

Her eyes widen. "Wow," she says. "How'd you end up here?"

"My dad thought it would be a good idea."

She nods. She still has no idea who I am, although that's probably going to change soon.

We're in front of the room now. "So, here we are," she says, giving me a bright smile.

I peek inside. The desks are filled with kids sitting, chatting with friends, looking through their bags, texting on their cell phones. There's no teacher in there yet, which is good. The last thing I need is to walk in and have some teacher make a big production out of things. I hate big productions. My life has been an endless string of big productions, and I'm over it.

I turn back to the girl with pink hair.

"Thanks for walking me," I say. "What's your name?"

"Melissa."

"Well, thanks, Melissa." I give her a smile and then head into the classroom. No one looks at me, and obviously I don't have any friends to sit with, so I pick a seat in the middle of the room, deciding that sitting not too close to the back and not too close to the front is a good idea.

As soon as I'm in my chair, the guy in front of me turns around and glares at me. Jesus Christ. People really are not too friendly around here. I might have to go public with this, start some kind of blog or some shit. Tell everyone that public schools really are subpar, that the people here are dangerous. Seriously, the first time I see a knife, I'm writing an exposé.

"That seat's taken," the dude ahead of me says.

"Oh, really?" I ask. "Because it doesn't look like anyone's sitting here." I'm figuring this place is kind of like prison. You have to make sure that you stand up for yourself right off the bat; otherwise these pricks will walk all over you. I put my notebook on the desk, not really able to believe that I'm staking out my territory in a suburban public school homeroom.

He narrows his eyes at me. "Who are you?" he demands.

"Isaac," I say, deciding it's best to leave my last name out of it.

"You're new?"

"Yeah."

He nods like he can accept this. "What do you play?"

"What do I play?"

"Yeah."

"Sports or women?"

He considers. "Either."

"Lacrosse and basketball."

He nods again, like this, too, is acceptable. "And what about girls?"

"I play them." It's true. I do play them. Not in a completely jerky way. I just like to have fun. And something tells me this dude will appreciate that.

"I'm Marshall." I'm not sure if that's his first name or his last, but I reach out and shake the hand that he's offering. "You should stick with me," he says. "I'll show you around."

I think about it. He looks kind of like a jock meathead, but that's probably not the worst crowd to fall in with. Not to mention that he's the first person who's actually been nice to me.

Actually, no. That's not true. Melissa or whatever her name

is was nice to me. Which means that girl in the office was an exception to the rule.

Still. Beggars can't be choosers.

"Cool," I say to Marshall. And just like that, I might have my first friend.

Before

Kelsey

Okay, so the meeting with Mr. Lawler doesn't exactly go so well. You get kicked out of one school, and people think you're, like, some kind of criminal or something. Getting kicked out of a school isn't a *crime*. I haven't been sent to *prison* or anything.

I mean, you work your whole life for something, and then just like that, it's gone. Your previous record means nothing. Does Mr. Lawler even care that I've been an honor student my whole life? Or that I've been involved in tons of extracurricular activities? No. He only cares about one thing. That I got kicked out of Concordia Prep.

Which really shouldn't even be any of his business, when you think about it. This is a public school. Which means that it's open to the *public*. Any random person can just enroll here no questions asked. So why should they get to know all about *my* past history?

If it were up to me, I wouldn't have told them I got kicked out of my old school. Why not just pretend I transferred? But my parents were all about telling them the truth. Which is ridiculous. It's no one's business but my own.

Anyway, Mr. Lawler spent all this time telling me that I needed to really make sure I stayed focused here, and that it was the end of the line for me and blah, blah, blah. If you want to know the truth, I think he was kind of getting off on being some sort of disciplinarian. It was actually slightly disturbing.

I tried to tell him that he was preaching to the choir. No one wants to do better at this school than I do. I *need* to do well. Even better than before. Otherwise there's no way I'm going to get a scholarship to a good college. And if I don't get a scholarship, I won't be able to *go* to college, since my parents can't afford to send me.

I wish I was good at sports. Girls who are good at sports are so lucky. They don't even really have to worry about their grades. The academics standards for athletes are totally ridiculous—you have to have, like, a C average or something.

But I'm horrible at sports. I always preferred books to baseball. Or basketball. Or any kind of ball, actually.

Which is why it really sucks that I have gym first period. What kind of satanic person decided that someone should have gym first period? Actually, who decided to have gym in schools at all? I get the whole thing about physical activity, but really, does anyone get a workout during gym class? Sigh.

I'm usually not such a negative person, I swear. It's just that I'm really out of sorts this morning.

The good news is that since it's the first day, we don't have to get changed or anything.

We all just troop into the gym and up the bleachers, and sit there while the gym teacher, a young blond woman named Ms. Fitzpatrick, announces that we're going to get our height and weight measured.

I'm stunned to realize that there are *boys* sitting on the bleachers.

"Excuse me," I say to the girl sitting next to me. "Is this coed gym?"

She looks at me like it's the dumbest question ever, nods, and then turns back to her friend. Huh. I've never had coed gym before. At my old school we had girls' gym and boys' gym. Nice and separate.

At least our weight isn't going to be announced to the whole class. They're calling us up one by one and then recording our height and weight on a form. Not that I'm embarrassed by my weight. Ever since getting kicked out of Concordia Prep, I've hardly been able to eat due to all the stress.

I pull open my bag (Michael Kors, very chic, which I got at this consignment shop down the street—I almost didn't buy it because it cost two whole weeks' allowance, but now I'm glad I did, since my parents have taken my allowance away along with everything else, so it was good that I spent it when

I had the chance) and pull out the book I'm reading, this very exciting romance by Jennifer Crusie.

I used to get embarrassed that I read romance novels, especially when everyone at my old school was reading classics and literary fiction and then getting themselves all worked up about the real meaning of *Freedom* by Jonathan Franzen and if it counted as a real literary work when its sales numbers just screamed commercial.

But the minute I got kicked out of Concordia Prep, I decided to stop caring about stuff like that. I realized that it doesn't matter what the people around me think. The only thing that matters is what the admissions boards think.

I'm just getting into a really good part of the story (and yes, by "good part" I mean sex part—it's actually making me kind of embarrassed, if you want to know the truth. Not that I'm embarrassed by sex, but it's kind of weird to be reading a scene like that with tons of people around you) when someone sits down next to me.

Like, right next to me. Like, way too close for comfort next to me.

The person's leg is touching mine.

I slide down the bleachers a little bit, my eyes never leaving the page.

"What are you reading?" the person asks.

I look over, and lock eyes with the guy from this morning, Isaac Brandano. Up close he's even cuter than he is from far away, which you'd think would be impossible. His dirty-blond hair falls over his forehead, looking deliberately mussed. His jawline is perfectly chiseled and strong, and yet he has a tiny bit of stubble, like he didn't shave this morning. He's wearing a button-down shirt, but the top button is undone, and I can see a little bit of his chest. It looks hard. And tanned.

There's a tiny scar going through his eyebrow, saving him from looking like a total pretty boy. He's so hot that it kind of takes my breath away. Of course, I've probably been reading too many romance novels. Not to mention I'm sure that he's a total shit. And guys who are total shits do not turn out to be anything but total shits. At least, not outside the pages of books.

"None of your business," I say, and then scoot farther down on the bleachers.

He scoots after me. "Listen," he says, "I think we got off on the wrong foot. I'm Isaac." He puts his hand out. I ignore it. "And you are?" he tries.

"Not interested."

"Not interested in what?"

"Going out with you."

"I'm not . . . I wasn't . . . I'm not asking you out."

"Then why are you talking to me?" I shut my book, using my finger to hold my place, and look up at him. "Let me guess, because you can't stand thinking that there might be someone at your new school, or in the world, who doesn't like you?"

"Why don't you like me?" he asks. But he doesn't seem upset about it. In fact, he seems almost curious. And he's smiling.

And then I start to feel a little bit bad. Because even if he is a jerk, I *am* being pretty mean to him. Besides, I know this really has nothing to do with him. This is all about Rex, and what happened between us, and why I allowed myself to get so wrapped up in him that I got kicked out of school. So I'm about to tell Isaac that I'm sorry, that it's been a weird morning, and that I have nothing against him.

But before I can, he says, "Let me guess. I remind you of some guy who hurt you?"

I'm so shocked, it takes me a moment to respond. *"Excuse me?"* I ask finally.

"Some guy," he repeats, "who hurt you. I remind you of him, right? Maybe you dated him, or maybe you just admired him from afar, never being able to work up the courage to ask him out? And now I'm here, and so you've decided that I'm going to be the punching bag for whatever that dude did."

I swallow. Hard. And then I feel tears filling my eyes. I look away so he won't see, but it must not be quick enough.

"Hey," he says, "I'm sorry, I was just messing around with you. I didn't mean to make you upset."

"You didn't make me upset," I say. "But in the future, I'd really appreciate it if you just. Left. Me. Alone." And then I get up and move a couple of rows down the bleachers. The nerve! Who does he think he is, talking to me like that? I'm glad that I didn't apologize to him. I pretend to keep reading, but the words are getting all blurry because my eyes are still a little teary. Whatever. It doesn't matter. I'm not really in the mood to read anymore.

Before

Isaac

I shouldn't have done that. It's just . . . that girl *annoys* me for some reason. The way she seems all uppity and too good for people, and yet there she was, reading a fucking romance novel.

A romance novel! In gym class! Who does that? Only people who are trying to prove that they're way too cool, like they're making some kind of statement about how they don't care what people think. I mean, the cover alone. It has a picture of shoes on it. With cherries or hearts or some shit sprinkled all around.

I'm debating whether or not I care enough to follow her down the bleachers and try to apologize, or if I'm sick of her attitude, when a girl's voice yells, "Hey!"

I turn around. It's another girl. One with long dark hair and a tight blue sweater.

We had a dress code at all of my old schools. School uniforms, with ties for the boys and long skirts for the girls. The whole bit. The girls would get around it by hiking up their skirts as high as they could, but there was only so much you could do. Most of the time we had to wait until the weekends to be able to really see any skin.

But this chick, the one on the bleachers who's calling my name, is just begging to be checked out. Her sweater is so tight and low cut, her boobs are practically falling out of her push-up bra.

"You're new, right?" She's sitting at the top of the bleachers, and she gets up and leaves her group of friends, walking down toward me.

I see that romance novel girl glance over at us with a disgusted look on her face. She probably hates this girl just because she's in touch with her sexuality. Girls who are stuck-up and uppity hate chicks who are in touch with their sexuality. They think it's antifeminist or something.

"Yes," I say. "I'm new. Isaac Brandano." I take her hand and help her down the last few steps. "And who are you?"

She giggles and sits down next to me. The bottom of her sweater hikes up a little bit as she leans in toward me, and I can see a tiny strip of back. It's tan. And not that orange, fake tan shit that girls think is hot and makes them look like a *Jersey*

Shore wannabe. This is real tan. Suddenly I'm in love with this school. And this girl.

"I'm Marina," she says.

"Marina?"

"I was conceived on a boat."

"Really?"

"Yeah." She leans in even closer, and I get a whiff of her perfume. "I love the water."

Everything she says is sexy. I'm already thinking of her in a bikini, lying on the bow of my—well, my dad's—boat, sunning herself. I glance out of the corner of my eye, over to where that girl is still reading her stupid romance novel and pretending she's not listening to my conversation. She's so transparent. She's completely listening and wanting to know what's going on.

Well, if she wants a show, I'll give her a show.

"Me too," I say. "I love to water-ski. Have you ever been water-skiing?"

"Yeah," Marina says. "I have, like, the best water-skiing story. I mean, like, ever. For serious." She stops. Doesn't say anything else.

"What is it?" I try.

"My bikini top fell off," she says. "And everyone saw my boobs."

She smiles, proud of herself. Huh. You'd think this story would be hot—stories about good-looking girls' breasts usually are—but somehow, this one falls short. I think it's maybe the way she just blurted it out. Where was the buildup, the story line, the enticing details?

"That *is* a good story," I lie. Then I add, "I wish I'd been there." That part's true.

"Me and my friends are going to the beach this weekend," she says. "Kind of like a last hurrah before the weather gets cold. You should come." She wraps a lock of hair around her finger and gives me a flirty look.

"Aren't all the beaches around here closed already?" I ask.

She rolls her eyes like she can't even take how naive I am. "Yeah, but there are ways around that."

I like this girl. Of course, I'm supposed to be staying out of trouble. If my dad found out I had some kind of plan to sneak onto a closed beach, he'd really hate it. In fact, he'd probably start threatening me with boarding school again. Overseas boarding school. Which is bullshit.

There's no way I'm going to boarding school overseas. I'm all about the French and the German (accents on chicks are so hot), but I don't want to live in Europe. No. Fucking. Way.

"Cool." I reach into her bag, where I can see the top of her cell phone peeking out. I pull it out and tap in my number. "Text me."

"I will." She pushes her hair back from her face, and it seems like she's about to say something else.

But before she can, the gym teacher yells, "Marina Ruiz!"

She rolls her eyes, takes her cell from me, and puts it back into her bag. "God," she says, "like I need to get weighed.

Doesn't she know that I've been a hundred and fifteen ever since freshman year? What a waste of time. And unless they're going to really make sure some people lose weight, why do they even care? They need to make up their minds—weigh us once a week, like Weight Watchers, or not at all, you know?"

From a couple rows in front of us, that girl reading the romance novel snorts.

Marina turns her gaze on her and gives her a friendly smile. "I'm sorry," she says, her tone kind of tight, "but who are you?"

"I'm Kelsey," the girl says. She puts a big smile on her face and turns around to face us. "Sorry if I was eavesdropping. It's just that that story about your boobs falling out was reeeeeally compelling."

"Thanks," Marina says, not picking up on the sarcasm. "It might have sounded interesting, but it really was totally humiliating. My dad's friends were there. And they're, like, old." She shudders, probably imagining old dudes putting her in their spank banks.

"Marina Ruiz!" the gym teacher yells again. "I'm waiting!"

"Coming!" Marina yells back. But she rolls her eyes and makes no move to get up. "You're new too, right?" she asks Kelsey.

"Yup," Kelsey says. "It's my first day."

"It is?" I ask, surprised. So she *was* telling the truth when she said she didn't know where my room was.

"You should totally come to the beach with us," Marina

27

says. "Like, for real." What? Is she crazy? Why would she invite Kelsey to the beach with us? Kelsey's obviously not the relaxing-at-the-beach type. Marina waves her cell phone in the air. "What's your number?"

I see the look of panic that crosses Kelsey's face. She doesn't want to go to the beach. She doesn't want to be friends with this chick. In fact, she doesn't even want to be talking to her.

She starts to shake her head, but then she catches my eye. I give her a smirk like, *That's what you get for trying to spy on my conversation. Now you better figure out a way out of this.* But instead of making up an excuse, Kelsey narrows her eyes at me, and then she says to Marina, "Thanks, that's really sweet of you to invite me. My number's 555-0332. And the beach sounds amazing."

"Marina Ruiz!" The gym teacher sounds like she's about to have a coronary.

"I. Am. Coming." Marina rolls her eyes. "Check you guys later!" And she makes her way down the bleachers.

I turn back to Kelsey. Her face is bright red, and she has her eyes back on her book.

"The beach sounds amazing?" I ask her.

"Yeah," she says, and shrugs. "I love the beach."

"Really? That's great. Me too." I get up and start down the bleachers. "So I guess I'll see you there."

"Yup," she says, closing her book and putting it back in her bag. "See you there."

Before

Kelsey

Wow. How completely obvious was that? I mean, Isaac totally wanted me to see him flirting with that Marina girl. Like I even care! Was he trying to prove that some people think he's God's gift? Was he trying to *imply* that there's something wrong with me for not falling under his spell? Ridiculous!

Of course, now I have to go to the beach with him and Marina. Which is a horrible plan. I hate the beach. I always end up with sand in my shoes and a sunburn on my nose. Plus it's way too cold to go to the beach. It's only September, but the temperature has been in the low sixties all week.

Oh well. I'll just have to make up some kind of excuse. How hard can it be? I'll just happen to have something else planned.

Maybe I'll concoct a fake boyfriend from my old school. Kill two birds with one stone—that way Isaac won't think he got one over on me, since he's apparently decided I'm some kind of brokenhearted nut. Which I'm not. At least, not anymore.

The rest of the day, thank God, goes by without any more drama. No more Isaac spottings. No more crazy girls inviting me to hang out. Of course, it would have been nice to at least meet *someone* cool. I mean, I don't talk to anyone. Mostly because no one talks to me. I guess it's fine, because I do just want to fly under the radar, but flying under the radar with a friend or two wouldn't be the end of the world.

When I get home, my mom and dad are sitting at the table, leafing through a catalog. My mom's a teacher, and my dad's a computer programmer who works from home, so they're both around a lot in the afternoons. Which was fine when I was still at Concordia Prep. I'd get home, and we'd go out for an early dinner together, or watch whatever we'd DVR'd on TV the night before. But ever since I got kicked out of school, things have been . . . tense between me and my parents. Especially between me and my dad.

"Hey, guys," I say, slapping a smile on my face as I walk into the kitchen. "How were your days?"

I drop my bag on the counter and move toward the refrigerator to get an after-school snack. I haven't eaten all day. During lunch I hung out in the library so that I wouldn't have to deal with the whole "Where am I going to sit?" conundrum. At first it was a little depressing—no one else was in the library except for this weird-looking freshman who was eating an extremely smelly bologna sandwich.

But the time turned out to actually be really productive, because I made a list of things I could do to get my academic career back on track so that getting kicked out of Concordia Prep doesn't screw up all my college apps. Of course, the top three things on the list are fairly obvious: get amazing grades, figure out my class rank (apparently they do grade point averages at Concordia Public a little differently, so I'm going to have to work out where I stand—to be valedictorian or salutatorian would be amazing), and start some kind of club or group that becomes very popular but is also very important in a social or environmental capacity (not sure exactly what that could be, but I'm going to try to have a meeting with the principal to figure it out).

"My day was fine," my mom says. She flicks the page of the catalog they're looking through. My parents are redoing our kitchen soon. At least, that's what they claim. They've been saying for years they're going to remodel the kitchen. But the closest they've actually gotten to doing so is moving most of our food and dishes into the pantry in the dining room. That was a year ago.

But apparently, they've now gotten to the point where they're actually picking things out, like cabinets and countertops. Supposedly, a guy is coming over soon to take measurements and the contractors are starting next week. I'll believe it when I see it.

Everything about my parents is very methodical. They were math majors who met their junior year of college. They dated for two years, and then they mutually (well, according to them it was mutually, but in my limited experience, nothing about relationships is ever really mutual) decided that maybe they should see other people for a while after graduation. They'd read some statistic somewhere that showed that people who marry their college sweetheart without taking time to date other people had a higher divorce rate, so they thought it was a good move.

They kept in touch, though, and after a year they got back together. If you asked them, they would totally credit the success of their marriage to that year they took off to see other people. If you ask me, the whole thing sounds ridiculously unromantic. Then again, what do I know? My romantic relationships are a complete disaster. Well, my one romantic relationship.

"Did you pick out some cabinets?" I ask my mom politely. I open a bag of cookies and slide a couple onto a plate.

"Yes." She holds up the catalog. "Do you like the cherry?"

"They look really nice." Not that I can really tell the difference. A cabinet is a cabinet is a cabinet.

My dad doesn't say anything, just keeps his head down, poring over the pages of a brochure. This is how it is with me and my parents now. Polite conversation. Lots of tiptoeing around each other. No one mentioning the elephant in the room. Except for when my dad gets into one of his moods and refuses to talk to me. Which he's apparently in right now. Then there are just long silences. And except for when the two of them decide to sit me down and have big conversations about my future and how I'm screwing everything up. Then there's just yelling.

I pull a glass out of the cabinet and pour myself some juice. "I'm going to go upstairs and study."

"That's a good idea," my mom says, her eyes already back on the pages of cabinets.

I sigh, grab my cookies, and then make my way upstairs, where I spend the rest of the night studying and trying not to think about the fact that my parents consider me a total disappointment.

Before

Isaac

Okay, so that girl from yesterday morning, Marina? The one with the whole story about her boobs falling out? I think she might be stalking me. And when I say "I think," I mean I'm pretty fucking sure. I wouldn't say I'm *positive*, though, because if I'm being completely honest, I'm kind of sensitive about that kind of thing. Not to sound like a pompous asshole, but I've had girls stalking me before. And it's not pleasant.

I'm not talking about the kind of stalking where you have to get a restraining order or call the police or anything psychotic like that. I'm just talking about chicks being overzealous and getting all weird. Calling you all the time. Leaving tons of messages on your Facebook wall. Somehow getting your home phone number when you've deliberately only given them your cell. That kind of shit that's ultimately harmless, but still pretty annoying.

For example.

Since I gave Marina my number in gym yesterday, she's texted me eight times. In less than twenty-four hours. If you take out eight hours for sleeping, that's like a text every two hours.

The first time she said, *"Hey sexy."*

Which was actually fine. Because who doesn't like to be called sexy, especially by a hot girl, even if she does have the uncanny ability to make boob stories boring? I didn't reply, though, because I was in the middle of biology lab.

The second time, which came a couple hours later, said, *"y u don't reply? ☹ "* That's when I started getting a weird feeling. So I didn't write her back, hoping that maybe she'd get the hint and ease off. If she did, I was going to text her back.

She didn't ease off, though. She kept texting. And last night at around eleven, she wrote, *"That's it, I will meet you before school tmr."*

The "that's it" part definitely wasn't all that promising. It sounded like she was one second away from coming after me with a meat cleaver.

So this morning I'm trying to sneak into school without her seeing me.

Of course, it doesn't work. As soon as I step off the pavement of the student parking lot and onto the sidewalk, I see her. She's standing in front of the school waiting for me. She's wearing a pair of tight black pants and a black shirt. She looks extremely hot.

For a second I think maybe this could work out after all. I mean, to be fair, she didn't text me at all this morning, so maybe she's calming down a little. Maybe she realized she was coming on too strong. Maybe she wants to make it up to me, if you know what I mean. I could definitely use a little stress release.

"Hey, sexy," she says. Again with the sexy. So original, this girl. But I forgive her because she's hot. In fact, I kind of forgot how hot she was when she was texting me yesterday. Would have been better if she'd texted me a picture. If she'd done that, I probably would have gotten over the fact that she seems slightly stalkerish.

"Hey," I say. She wraps her arms around my waist and hugs me.

"Miss me?" she asks.

In the last nine hours when you weren't sending me text after text?

"Of course," I say, because I'm smart enough to know that this is one of those trick questions that girls are always asking. Of course you don't really miss them. They're usually being pains in the ass who want to talk all the time. But you can't tell them that; otherwise they get all pissy. It's easier just to lie. Not that I advocate lying. It's just that in certain situations, it's a lot easier.

"I missed you too." She bounces up and down. "Yay!"

"Yay!" I say back. Mostly because I don't know what else to say. She's bouncing so fast that I think maybe her boobs are going to spill out of her shirt.

"So what should we do after school today?" she wants to know. She reaches out and runs her finger up and down the front of my shirt. "Maybe we should go shopping. I know they probably had a different, um, sense of style at your old school."

"Did we have plans after school today?" I ask, confused. Also, did she just insult my wardrobe? What the hell is wrong with what I'm wearing? It's a button-down shirt with a pair of khakis. I look around. Huh. I guess everyone's wearing jeans. Well, whatever. It's not my fault they all want to look like slobs. This is a Burberry shirt, and my pants are from Ralph Lauren. I left my new sneakers at home, but that's as far as I'm willing to go.

"Well, not specific plans," she says, "but I was thinking that we could get together and hang out. We don't have to go shopping. We could grab something to eat or hang out at my friend Raya's house."

"I'd love to," I lie, "but I have plans." I don't know why I say it. I just know that I really do not want to hang out with her. In fact, suddenly I want to get far, far away from her. My crazy-girl radar is going off, big time. Going shopping together? Everyone knows that's, like, the first thing stalkers ask you to do.

"Plans?" She frowns like she can't possibly imagine I

would be doing something that didn't involve her. "With who?"

I rack my brain, trying to remember the name of the kid I met in homeroom yesterday. It was some kind of last name as a first name. Mitchell? Monroe? I look around for him, trying to see if maybe, by some miracle, I'll see him in the crowd. But of course I don't.

Whatever. I shouldn't be afraid of telling this girl that I don't want to hang out with her.

"I just have plans," I say firmly, deciding it's best not to offer any details.

"With. Who?" Her eyes are narrowing into two slits, and suddenly I'm a little bit . . . frightened. What if she really is dangerous? Isn't there always weird shit like this going on at public schools? This chick could be totally out of her tree. What if she really starts to stalk me, coming after me not just at school, but other places? My dad's not going to be happy if I have to get a restraining order. Definitely not good right before an election year.

"Well, it's not really . . ." And then I catch sight of that girl from yesterday, Kelsey. She's stepping off a big yellow bus (who the hell still rides the bus?) and starting to walk up the sidewalk toward school.

"Kelsey!" I yell like some kind of lunatic, waving my hands in the air. "Kelsey, hey!"

She looks around, a half smile on her face, trying to figure out who's calling her name. When she sees it's me, the smile disappears. Jesus. What the hell is up with this place? I'm already having issues with two girls. And I haven't even dated either one of them.

I wave her over.

She looks toward the school like maybe she's hoping that somehow she'll be able to pretend that she doesn't see me. But she must figure that she can't, because finally she starts to walk over.

"What?" she asks.

"What?" I say playfully, deciding to pretend that she's kidding. "That's not very friendly. Haha."

"Isaac was just telling me that you and him have plans after school," Marina says. "Is that true?" Her tone is challenging, and she crosses her arms over her chest.

Kelsey looks confused. "Um," she says, "I'm staying after school so that I can work on figuring out an extracurricular activity that I can get involved in."

"Yup," I say, nodding emphatically. "Me too."

Kelsey raises her eyebrows. "You? You're staying after school to figure out your extracurricular activities?"

"Yes." I nod. "I need to find out about lacrosse." This is perfect. And it's not even a lie. I do need to sign up for lacrosse.

"That's not what I meant," Kelsey says, then looks toward the school like we're keeping her from something super-important, not just homeroom. "I'm not signing up for a *sports team*." She says "sports team" like it's the same as joining a gang or something. "I'm having a meeting with the principal about what kind of group I can run."

"Well, yeah," I say, rolling my eyes. "That's what I meant. I'm going to do that too. After the lacrosse thing."

"You are?"

"Yeah," I say, "I'm very political. You know, because of my family. I love being in charge of groups."

Kelsey's not buying it.

But fortunately, Marina is. "You guys are such do-gooders," she says, grinning, I guess she's relieved I don't have a date. "Not me. I'm so not into all that stuff." She wrinkles up her nose. "All right, well, I'll see you later, Isaac. I'll text you. And you better text me back this time." She turns and walks into the school.

I let out the breath I didn't realize I've been holding. At least she let it go pretty quickly. That's the good thing about girls who are crazy. They have mood swings, and sometimes you get lucky enough to be on the right side of them.

"Thanks," I say to Kelsey, and then start walking toward the school. I go slow so that I don't catch up with Marina.

"Thanks?" Kelsey asks incredulously, falling into step behind me.

"Yeah," I say. "Thanks. You know, it's what people say when they're thankful?" Not my most witty retort, but enough for her to get the picture.

"You are unbelievable," Kelsey says. "Completely unbelievable, you know that?"

"Why?"

"Because! What were you just doing?"

"What do you mean?"

"I *mean* that you were obviously planning something. *Obviously*, you have some kind of plot going on, some kind of . . . of *scheme*. Something having to do with messing with that poor girl!"

"No, I don't. And trust me, she's not a poor girl."

She looks at me, her face doubtful. She knows I was doing something, planning something, plotting something. Which I was. But I'm not going to give her the satisfaction of knowing what it was.

"So you're going to be staying after to meet with the principal, then?" she asks.

"Yes."

"You?"

"Yes!"

She sighs. "And what time is your meeting?"

"What time is yours?"

"None of your business." She says it all bitchy, but she looks a little nervous, too. And then I get it. She's afraid I'm going to, like, steal her club or something.

"Are you afraid I'm going to get there before you and steal your idea or something? Because trust me, a romance novel book club is the last thing I'm interested in."

I'm completely joking—sort of—but she doesn't look like she thinks it's too funny.

"Ugh," she says, shaking head like she's disgusted with me. "It figures someone like you would say something like that."

"Someone like me?"

She steps away and starts walking toward the school now, I guess dismissing me. But I start following her. Her hair is swishing back and forth behind her, and for some weird reason, I have the inexplicable urge to reach out and run my fingers through it. "Someone like me?" I say again, because she's ignoring me.

"Yes." She keeps walking.

"What is someone like me?" Wait, that doesn't make any sense. I try again. "I mean, who is someone like me? What do you mean by that?" We're at the front door of the school now, and I reach out and open it for her.

"Thank you," she says, and slides inside. We're assaulted by the sounds of kids talking and lockers slamming, and for a second I think I've lost her in the crowd. But then I spot her again, her hair bouncing, and I push through a group of girls to get to her.

"So, are you going to tell me what you meant by that?" I ask. "Or do you make it a habit to insult people and then just walk away?"

"I didn't insult you," she says. The halls are a little bit clearer now, and we're able to walk next to each other.

"You said 'someone like you.'"

"Yes."

"So that sounds like something you'd say to someone you thought had something wrong with them."

"Look." She whirls around and looks at me. "All I meant was that you're the kind of guy who thinks it's okay to put other people down. You think you're better than everyone else."

I'm shocked. Seriously. "I don't put other people down! Just yesterday I became friends with a guy who probably has a steroid problem because I wanted to be nice!" I hope she doesn't ask what his name is. Because I still can't remember.

"How noble of you." She rolls her eyes.

"Whatever." I turn and start to walk away, because I don't have to take this. I don't even know this chick. I just met her yesterday, and now she's going to make all these judgments about me and make me feel like shit? No, thank you. But then I feel her hand grabbing at my shirt.

"Wait," she says.

I turn around. Because if I'm being completely truthful, I can't stand the idea of someone not liking me. It's one of my character defects.

She bites her lip. "I'm sorry." She really does look sorry too. "It's just that I'm trying really hard to do well at this school. And when someone like"—I raise my eyebrows, and she sighs and then starts over—"when someone who *seems* like the kind of person who's had everything handed to him walks in, it kind of makes me crazy."

I nod. That makes sense. I mean, I'm not stupid. I know I'm lucky. My dad's a state senator, for God's sake. And I *have* had a lot of things handed to me. My car, my trust fund. Well, not my trust fund yet. But I will when I turn twenty-one.

"I can understand that," I tell her. "But why is it so important that you do well here?"

"What do you mean?" she asks.

"Well, it's only public school. It doesn't really count, you know?"

Her eyes narrow, and her face pinches back up. "And that," she says, "just proves my point about the kind of person you are."

And then she turns around and stomps down the hall, leaving me standing there looking after her.

Before

Kelsey

Okay, so I know that I'm putting a lot of my own shit on that Isaac kid. I mean, *obviously* I have issues of my own that I need to work out regarding privilege and nepotism and the hierarchy of society.

Actually, I didn't even realize I had those kinds of issues until I went off on him in the hall. Not that what I did was that bad. I mean, I didn't throw a book at him or anything. But I *was* pretty mean.

It's just that guys like him really make me mad. He seemed so baffled by my preconceived notions of him, and then one second later he seemed like he was agreeing with me. Which actually only kind of made things worse, because someone who agrees that they've gotten everything handed to them and doesn't really care about it or appreciate it kind of sucks. And then that whole comment about it only being public school!

Sorry, mister, but some people actually *care* about how they do in public school. Some people actually *care* about getting good grades, because they don't have alumni parents or money or secret legacy keys or whatever else you have to have in order to get into an Ivy League school.

Still. Even though he deserved it, I do feel a little bad. Just because he's entitled and rude doesn't mean that I have to stoop to his level. Not that me feeling bad probably matters to a guy like him. He's so used to girls throwing themselves at him that I'm sure he doesn't even register it when someone's not. Just this morning that Marina girl was outside, trying to get him to hang out with her. And let's face it, that girl is hot. Perfect hair and perfect teeth and a perfect body that she squeezes into tight pants and shirts that she spills out of. She's like walking, screaming sex.

But the weirdest thing about my whole interaction with Isaac is that when I turned around to look back down the hall, he was standing there looking after me, and he had this kind of wounded look on his face, like I really *did* hurt his feelings.

I can't stop thinking about that look. Which is crazy. Since I hate him. And I should be *glad* that I hurt his feelings. Because *he* hurt *my* feelings with his comments about a romance book club. Seriously, who *says* things like that? Doesn't he know that there's been a whole slew of articles in the past few years about romance novels needing to be taken seriously? And how it's actually very feminist to read them, because feminism is about doing what you want, and if that's reading romance novels, then so be it? And furthermore—

"Ms. Romano?"

I look up. Oh. Right. I'm in math class. And judging from the look on Ms. Lee's face, I've just been called on.

"Um, could you repeat the question?" I ask.

"Number five on the homework."

I scan my paper. "X equals seventeen."

Luckily, it's the right answer. God! Fucking Isaac Brandano! Already messing with my day at school. I sit up and pay attention.

When the final bell rings, I stop off in the bathroom to reapply my lipstick and make sure that I look put together before I head into the principal's office for my meeting with Mr. Colangelo. I need to make sure that I look responsible, like the kind of girl who can handle being in charge of an after-school club.

I look over the list of activities that I'm thinking of proposing. (I spent my lunch period in the library again, although this time Bologna Sandwich Boy was gone. I wasn't sure how I felt about that—good that there was no meat smell, bad that he found friends before I did.)

Anyway, here's my list so far:

1. Newspaper. Apparently, the school doesn't have one. I know, isn't that insane? I mean, I know the printed word is on its way out, but still. From what I can tell, it got taken away when there was a round of budget cuts a few years ago. Then they got their budget back and just couldn't find anyone to run it. So I'll have to get a faculty adviser, which could be kind of hard since I don't really know any faculty yet. But what better way to meet them?

2. Debate Club. A little better than newspaper, but not by much. It's kind of boring, and not really special enough. Still, debate has a certain cache at the Ivies. It shows you have opinions, and that you can think on your feet.

3. LitFic Book Club. Soooo totally different from a romance novel book club! Not that there would be anything *wrong* with a romance novel book club, but I want to be accessible to the male students as well. Well, not me personally. Just the club. Although maybe there's a feminist bent to the romance novel thing that could be explored here. Hmmm . . .

4. Peer Counseling Hotline. This one's pretty amazing because it's so . . . I don't know, *helpful*. Plus let's face it—it's interesting. I love hearing about people's personal issues.

5. Parent/Student Communication Club. I don't really know what this would entail. Except for, like, bettering communication between parents and students. Kind of lame, but again, just the kind of thing the Ivies will love.

I'm putting my notebook back in my bag and am about to head out into the hallway when I hear it. Crying. Coming from one of the stalls.

I hesitate, not sure what to do. On one hand, I should probably at least ask whoever it is if they need help. I mean, what if something's really wrong? On the other hand, I don't want to be late for my meeting. So not the way to make a good impression on the principal, and getting Mr. Colangelo to think I'm capable and mature is an integral part of my plan.

I stand there for a second, debating. I'm about to walk out the door, but then I think about my karma. If I don't stop and help, my meeting probably won't go that well. Plus I'll be thinking about it the whole time and wondering if I left someone bleeding to death just so I could start a school newspaper.

So I sigh, then walk over to the stall door where the crying is coming from. On it someone's carved the words GO FUCK YOURSELF into the chipping light blue paint. Charming. That kind of shit would never fly at Concordia Prep. Every year the whole school got repainted. Not that we needed it. No one there would write that kind of thing on the walls. No one there was angry. And if they were, they knew how to deal with it—by stealing their mother's Klonopin prescription and/or shop-lifting Prada bags just for fun.

I knock. There's no answer from whoever's sobbing in the stall, so I knock again. There's a sniff, and then the crying stops.

"Hello?" I try.

Silence.

"Listen, I know you're in there. I just wanted to make sure you were okay, that you're not hurt."

Silence.

"Are you? Hurt, I mean?"

Silence.

Geez. This person is really being kind of rude. Here I am, taking time out of my important meeting schedule to make sure they're okay, and they're just ignoring me.

"Look," I say, "can you please just tell me that you're not beaten up or bleeding from your eyeballs or something simi-lar? I have a huge meeting with the principal, and if I'm late, it could seriously screw things up for me." I sound kind of harsh, which is probably why I get a response.

"I'm not beaten up or bleeding from the eyeballs," comes a small voice.

"Are you sure?"

"Yes."

"Okay. Well, um, I hope that whatever's bothering you gets better soon." Obviously, she doesn't want my help, and so my work here is done.

I'm starting to walk out of the bathroom when the door to the stall bangs open and a tiny blond girl appears. She's wearing tight skinny jeans tucked into soft-looking brown boots, and a black cashmere sweater that dips down over the shoulder, showing a candy-apple-red bra strap. Her hair is curly and hangs all the way down to her waist.

"It won't get better soon!" she says, and marches over to the sink. "It's three years of not getting better soon!" She turns the water on very forcefully, then pulls the lever on the soap dispenser, dispensing a bunch of soap into her hands. She starts rubbing them together under the running water.

"Oh," I say. Well. That sounds like something that's going to take a while to work out. I mean, three years of never getting better. That's serious. Definitely going to take a long time to figure out. A long time that I don't have. Probably some kind of major psychological problem. Girls that gorgeous always have a complete screw loose. More reason to start a counseling hotline at this school, for sure.

"I'm sick of it myself, even. I'm, like, *bored* with *myself*." She's looking at herself in the mirror now, and she reaches into her bag and pulls out a compact. She starts angrily applying foundation to her face.

"Wow," I say. "Well, I'm glad you're not hurt or anything." And I am. Glad she's not bleeding or beat up or otherwise incapacitated. I'm slowly moving away, toward the door. I have enough of my own drama going on without getting involved in someone else's, thank you very much.

"Not hurt?" the girl says. "Not *hurt*? Does this look like the kind of face you would have if you weren't hurt?" She points at her face. Which, while still beautiful, is streaked with tears and dripping eye makeup.

"Well, no. But, ah, I just meant that you're not *physically* hurt."

She turns from the mirror and stares at me. "What's your name?"

I swallow, not sure I want to tell her. "I'm Kelsey."

"Well, Kelsey, did you know that the pain of a broken heart causes the same activity in the brain as physical pain?"

"No," I say honestly. "I didn't know that."

"Well, it does. There was a scientific study on it and everything." She says it like all scientific studies are totally true, when everyone knows that scientific studies are totally dependent on the special interest groups that fund them. Not to mention that science is changing on, like, a daily basis. So whatever study came out even yesterday has almost instantly become irrelevant.

"I've been there," I say, "with the broken heart thing. And so, um, I'm really sorry you're having to go through that." I'm starting to shuffle my feet backward, toward the door, because like I said, I don't want to get involved in her drama. I'm searching my brain, trying to come up with something I can say to her, something that will be both poignant and helpful but also put an end to our conversation, when she slings her bag over her shoulder and pushes past me.

"Yeah," she says. "Me too."

"You're welcome for checking on you!" I yell after her. But she's already gone.

When I get to the office, the secretary has me wait, like, fifteen minutes before she lets me in to see Mr. Colangelo, which makes me a little bit annoyed, because I made sure to get here exactly on time.

And when she finally does usher me into his office, Mr. Colangelo's on the phone. He motions for me to sit down in one of the chairs in front of his desk while he finishes his phone call.

After a lot of "mmm-hmmms" he finally says goodbye to whoever it is and hangs up. Which is pretty disappointing. I mean, the first chance I get to eavesdrop on a conversation that the principal is having, and it's not even about anything good.

"Hello," he says, giving me an easy smile. He looks down at my file, which is sitting open on his desk. "So, Ms. Romano, what is it I can do for you today?"

I wonder if he had to look at my file to remember my name. If so, that's kind of rude. Especially since he didn't even want to take this meeting in the first place. I had to have a big conversation with the secretary this morning, where I begged and pleaded and practically promised her my firstborn. By the end she definitely hated me. I don't understand what it is with me and secretaries. Why do they all hate me? Maybe it's because

I'm focused and kind of pushy. But it's not my fault I know what I want.

"Well." I smooth my list out on the top of my binder and look at Mr. Colangelo across the desk, being sure to make meaningful and focused eye contact. "I'd like to start an extracurricular club here at Concordia Public."

He looks down at my file. Which makes me nervous. Why does he keep doing that? And why does he have to have my file in here, anyway? More importantly, what exactly does it say? I wonder if I could get a copy if I wanted it. There must be some kind of law, like the Freedom of Information Act or something.

"Hmm," Mr. Colangelo says. He takes a sip of this disgusting-looking cup of coffee that's probably been sitting there all day and is now totally stale. "I don't see anything in your file that would preclude you from doing so."

Yay! "Well, that's wonderful news," I say.

He's closing my file now, and his eyes flick to the clock over the wall. Does that mean that we're done here? Is it that easy? Is he going to dismiss me, basically letting me start whatever kind of club I want? "So I was thinking about maybe news-paper," I tell him. "I've always been interested in journalism."

"We don't have a newspaper here anymore," Mr. Colangelo says.

"Yes, that's why I was hoping I could start one."

"Start one?" He sounds shocked. "I don't think you need the kind of stress that comes from starting a school club when you've just enrolled here."

54

"But you just said . . ." Wait a minute. Did Mr. Colangelo think I said I wanted to join an *existing* club? And so he was giving me permission to do that? Way to listen. Not that there's anything *wrong* with joining an extracurricular activity, but let's face it: When you don't have an alumnus as a parent, or some kind of famous relative, you can't just *join* some clubs for your college applications. You have to do something big and meaningful. Especially if you've gotten kicked out of your last school.

There's a knock on Mr. Colangelo's door, and the secretary pokes her head in. "Sorry to interrupt," she says, "but Isaac Brandano is here. He said he was supposed to be joining you and Ms. Romano?"

"Is that true, Kelsey?" Mr. Colangelo asks.

"Um, well . . ."

But before I can tell him no, Isaac appears in the doorway of the office. He's now wearing jeans and a white T-shirt, with a blue zip-up on over it. Why did he change his clothes? And why is he here? Shouldn't he have scheduled his own meeting?

"Hey," he says when he sees me, like we're old friends and not two people who barely know each other and got into a fight in the hallway this morning.

"Hello," I say tightly. "It's nice to see you, Isaac, but Mr. Colangelo and I aren't done with our meeting. As soon as we are, you can talk to him about how you want to run an extracurricular too."

"Oh!" Isaac says. "I thought we'd talked about doing it together."

"You two?" Mr. Colangelo says. He looks interested, probably because anything Isaac does is going to get a lot of people signing up for it. Not to mention some kind of funding from his dad. Hell, maybe they'll even pass some kind of bill, like "Isaac's Law" or something, and his club will get a big grant from the state that won't ever be able to be taken away.

"Yeah," Isaac says. He's moving into the room now, I guess because he thinks he's been invited in, even though he so totally hasn't. He drops his book bag down at my feet and then slides into the chair next to me.

"Ow," I say, pretending that he dropped his bag on my foot. I move my feet away from him.

"We were talking about it this morning before school, remember?" Isaac asks, ignoring my fake injury.

He gives me a big grin, like he's challenging me to say we weren't.

"Well," I say, wondering how I'm going to get out of this one, "we *were* talking about it, that's true, but—"

"Well, Kelsey, why didn't you say so?" Mr. Colangelo bellows. "As long as you have another student helping you, I think starting a club is a great idea. Does either of you have any ideas about what it could be?"

"I do," Isaac says.

I cannot believe this. Not only is Isaac pretending that we had some kind of plan to do this together, but now Mr. Colangelo is giving me permission just because Isaac is involved. And now Isaac is even claiming he has some ideas about what kind of group we can start!

"Me too," I say, not wanting to be outdone. Maybe when Isaac starts giving his half-baked ideas for whatever stupid things he's come up with, I can jump in with mine. And then maybe Mr. Colangelo will see that I actually *can* do this on my own, and I don't need Isaac Brandano's name or influence to help me.

"That's so great," Isaac says. "Do you want to present your ideas first?" He's giving me this sort of smarmy smile, a smile that makes me think he just wants me to give my ideas first because he doesn't actually have any ideas of his own. So I'll give mine, and then we'll decide on one of them being perfect, and that will save him from the embarrassment of having to admit that he has no idea what he's even doing.

"No, that's okay," I say sweetly. "Why don't you go ahead?"

"You sure?"

"Positive."

Isaac shrugs, then reaches into his bag and pulls out a black leather notebook. Taped to the front is piece of computer paper with the words "Face It Down" printed in swirly script on the front. He opens up to the first page.

"Now," he says, "this is just an overview, of course. I was hoping we could get into the specifics later, if we do decide to move forward with the project."

"Of course," Mr. Colangelo says, like this makes perfect sense. He nods and leans back in his black swivel chair.

My mouth has dropped open.

Isaac turns his attention back to his notebook. "I was thinking that what we all need is some understanding."

I snort. Because honestly, what does he know about understanding? I mean, that sounds so political. He's acting just like a politician, someone who wants to get along with everyone, someone who wants to be one of the little people or whatever, while meanwhile, I'm sure he surrounds himself with people who are just like him. Not to mention that "what we all need is some understanding" are song lyrics. At least, I'm pretty sure they are.

"Something funny?" Isaac asks.

"No," I lie.

"So what I'm *proposing*," Isaac says, giving me an admonishing look out of the corner of his eye, like I'm a child who's interrupted the teacher during an important lesson, "is that we set up a group of students who are interested in advancing the idea of understanding and acceptance for everyone. We could work on spreading these things throughout the community. For example, I was thinking our first project could be setting up Face It Down Day, where students from Concordia Prep and Concordia Public join together and talk about how even though we come from different backgrounds and families, we're basically all alike, facing the same challenges and insecurities."

I'm speechless. The idea is so simple, and so brilliant, that I'm pissed I didn't come up with it myself. Mr. Colangelo is eating out of Isaac's hand. He's leaning forward over his desk, his eyes on Isaac's. Which makes me even more angry. I mean, it's not enough that Isaac has this kind of effect on girls, now he has it on guys, too, including the principal?

"That sounds absolutely amazing," Mr. Colangelo says, sounding like a smitten schoolgirl. He pauses, leaving the unspoken question hanging in the air. I resist the urge to roll my eyes.

"And I'm sure my dad would be happy to get involved," Isaac says, realizing what Mr. Colangelo is looking for. Which means that he's a lot smarter than I first gave him credit for. "You know, with money or whatever."

"Fabulous," Mr. Colangelo says. Seriously, he's about three seconds away from clapping his hands in glee. "So you two can get together and work on the club, and then report back to me about how it's going. You'll want to get it up and running as soon as possible, I'm assuming?"

"Don't you even want to hear my ideas?" I ask. Obviously, I'm not going to bring up the idea of a book club now, since Isaac's idea was so good, but you'd think Mr. Colangelo would at least *pretend* to want to know my ideas.

"Well, we're running out of time," Mr. Colangelo says. He's looking at the clock again and picking up his phone. Ugh, ugh, ugh.

"Sounds great," Isaac says. "Me and Kels will get to work on this right away."

Kels?

"Yeah," I echo weakly. "Sounds great."

The Aftermath

Kelsey

The superintendent's office is actually really nice, with a big huge oak desk in the middle and floor-to-ceiling windows that let in stripes of sunlight that fall against the soft cream-colored carpet. It's probably intended to foster a sense of security. Kind of like those newfangled dentists' offices where they hide all the equipment so you're blissfully unaware of the amount of torture you're about to be in for.

"Now," Dr. Ostrander says once we're sitting down. He's behind his desk, his hands crossed in front of him. "Which one of you wants to start?"

I look over at Isaac. He's slumped in his chair, the sleeves of his navy-blue shirt unbuttoned and rolled up. He's looking at the floor, a scowl on his face. Well. If he thinks that *I'm* going to be the one to start talking first, that *I'm* going to be the one to throw myself under the bus, then he's wrong. He can talk if he's so smart.

"Maybe it will help you two if I give you a recap of what happened at Face It Down Day," Dr. Ostrander says. He pulls a piece of yellow legal paper out and sets it down in front of him. "Isaac got into a fistfight with a student from Concordia Prep. The police were called. A boy had to be taken away in an ambulance. The NBC crew recorded the whole thing, and Marina Ruiz has filed a restraining order against Kelsey." He pulls his glasses off and sets them down on the desk. "Does either one of you want to tell me how all this happened?"

Isaac still shows no sign of moving, so I clear my throat. "Dr. Ostrander," I say, "first let me start by apologizing on behalf of both myself and Isaac for the things that went down last week. We truly had no idea that Face It Down Day would turn into such a, ah . . ." Mess? Disaster? ". . . situation, and if we did, we certainly wouldn't have held it."

Next to me, Isaac snorts.

"Do you have something to say, Mr. Brandano?" Dr. Ostrander asks.

Isaac starts to shake his head, but then he catches my eye. He sits up straight. "Yes," he says. "Actually, I do have something to say. Kelsey's lying."

I gasp.

"Oh?" Dr. Ostrander asks. "Do you care to elaborate on that?"

61

"She knew a lot about Face It Down Day that she kept secret." Isaac shrugs. "In fact, she keeps a lot of secrets from a lot of people."

I swallow. Because he's right. I do keep a lot of secrets from a lot of people. "Is that true, Ms. Romano?" Dr. Ostrander asks. And he's not saying it like he's curious. He's saying it like, *"If that's true, then maybe you're the one to blame for this whole mess."*

I think about lying, but honestly, at this point I've lied enough. It's over. They're probably going to kick me out of Concordia Public, too, and then I'll really never get into college. Forget the Ivy League, I'll be lucky to get into a state school.

"Yes," I say, looking down at my hands. "It's true."

Dr. Ostrander sighs and leans back in his chair. He looks toward the ceiling and rubs his eyes like he can't believe he's dealing with this. I kind of don't blame him. I mean, the man has a PhD in education, which probably means tons of horribly boring classes and hours and hours of studying, and where has it gotten him? Here, dealing with our teen drama.

"Okay," he says finally, looking at us. "Start at the beginning. And tell me how this happened."

Before

Isaac

So, the look on Kelsey's face when I pulled out that notebook? Yeah, that was pretty priceless. I don't even know how I come up with this shit. I just do. It's like some kind of underrated talent. I also don't know why it was so important to me that I show her there's more to me than she thinks. But it was.

And so what if there was really nothing in that notebook? She doesn't need to know that. The important part is that I did come up with the idea myself. For Face It Down Day. And I did design and print out the paper that said "Face It Down" on the printer in the library and then tape it on my notebook. It took forever to get the font size right. And then it took even longer to tape it down because I was trying to get the corners perfect.

I had the feeling that would be something Kelsey would really notice—perfectly taped corners.

To be fair, I didn't come up with the idea *completely* on my own. I was Googling around, and it turns out that a lot of schools have similar clubs. It seemed perfect since there's always been this weird competition between Concordia Prep and Concordia Public. Of course, I have no idea how to implement any of the things I was saying to Mr. Colangelo about facilitating communication and understanding and all that other bullshit. But I'll bet that Kelsey does.

Not that she seems like it right now.

At the moment she's stomping down the hall in front of me. The school's pretty empty since most people have gone home for the day, and the kids who haven't are over on the other side of the school near the gym.

She glances over her shoulder and glares at me.

"What's wrong?" I ask.

She ignores me. But then her desire to yell at me must take over, because she turns around and says, "What's wrong? *What's wrong?* You came into my meeting and crashed it, you're completely taking over, and you're asking me *what's wrong?*" She throws her arms up in the air in exasperation, and her face is getting all flushed. She looks pretty adorable, actually.

"Taking over? No, I'm not," I say, even though I kind of am. But doesn't she get that I want her to work with me?

"Then what would you call it?"

"Helping?" I try.

She throws me another glare, then turns around and starts to stomp down the hall again. She's wearing these very high, very uncomfortable-looking shoes. I don't get why girls wear those things. I get that they look good, but not enough to risk breaking your ankle or developing some kind of hip problem.

As she goes her heel twists, and she almost falls. And then I start to feel bad. This obviously means a lot to her, and I've gone and messed with it just because I wanted to prove a point. I don't want her getting so upset that she's stumbling all over the place.

"Hey," I say, running to catch up with her. She's walking faster now, facing straight ahead. "Wait a second." I step in front of her, and she tries to push past me.

"Move," she says, crossing her arms over her chest. Her eyes meet mine, challenging.

"I shouldn't have crashed your meeting," I say honestly. "I'm sorry."

She does a double take, like she can't believe I'm actually apologizing to her. She's not the only one. I don't usually apologize. To anyone. Ever. "You are?"

"Yes. I shouldn't have hijacked your meeting."

"Then why did you do it?"

I wonder if I can come up with a good excuse, something I can tell her that won't make her think I'm a complete loser. But then I think, ah, fuck it, and I just decide to go for the truth. And the truth is, it isn't all because of Kelsey. "Well," I say, sighing, "part of it is that I didn't like that you thought I

65

was the type of person who just got everything handed to him. And the other part of it has to do with my dad."

Her face softens. For the first time, I realize how pretty she is. Don't get me wrong. I always knew she was attractive, and she looked really cute when she was yelling at me. But Kelsey is, like, really, really pretty. Perfect skin. Light brown hair. Blue eyes. A few freckles that she doesn't try to cover up with a ton of makeup.

"What about him?" she asks.

"Well," I say, "he's always . . ."

A burst of noise comes from farther down the hall, and a couple of guys dressed in football jerseys come pushing their way toward us, jostling each other as they go.

I stop talking. And then, for some reason, before I even know what I'm doing, I'm leaning in close to Kelsey. I can smell her perfume, something that smells fruity and sweet, and her hair smells amazing too. "Do you want to get out of here?" I ask.

"With *you*?" She seems shocked.

"Yeah." I grin. "Let me buy you something to eat. You do eat, don't you?"

She rolls her eyes. "Of course I eat."

"Then come on. I'll buy you dinner. And then I can explain." She hesitates. I step back and lean down a little, looking into her eyes. "Please?"

She bites her lip, thinking about it. And then, finally, she nods.

Before

Kelsey

Isaac takes me to the bowling alley. The bowling alley! He asks to take me out to dinner, and then he takes me to a *bowling alley*. It's my own fault, really. Why did I agree to go out with him? He crashed my meeting, and he's obviously a total jerk. But he got to me for a second with that whole thing about his dad. I'm a bleeding heart when it comes to dysfunctional dad relationships.

"The bowling alley?" I ask as we pull in. I look at the Games 'n' Lanes sign doubtfully. The white paint is dirty, and the stick-on letters are starting to peel.

"Yup," he says, turning off the car. Seeing him here somehow doesn't compute. He's just so perfectly groomed and, well . . . *hot*. Not to mention his car is a supershiny black BMW. His whole vibe just seems out of place here.

"I thought you said we were going to get something to eat," I say. I look out the windshield as two guys with huge beer bellies and dirty T-shirts disappear through the front doors.

"We are," he says. "They have the best fries in town." He looks at me. "Don't tell me you're a food snob."

"I'm not a food snob," I say haughtily. "*You're* the one who . . ." I'm about to tell him he's the one who's a snob, but he's out of the car now. I sit there for a minute, debating whether or not I should just tell him to take me home. I don't even know why I'm here.

But then he's at my side of the car, and he's opening my door for me. Which, let's face it, is kind of cute. Besides, I'm already here. And if I tell him to take me home, who knows what kind of stunt he'll try to pull with this whole Face It Down Day thing. I have to stay on his good side now that we're going to be working together.

So I step out of the car and head into the bowling alley.

The restaurant in the bowling alley is called Strikes, and it's actually surprisingly cozy, with big oak tables and comfy, oversize brown chairs. A flat-screen TV is mounted on the wall, and it's tuned to ESPN, where they're showing a Red Sox game.

"I always sit here," Isaac says, leading me over to a table in the corner with a view of the lanes. The two guys I saw come in a couple of minutes ago are plugging their names into a console on lane eleven, and their names flash on the scoreboard. One's named Butch. The other's named Harry. It's very fitting.

A few seconds after we sit down, a waitress comes over to take our order. She's older, probably in her fifties, with close-cropped ash-blond hair and bright pink lipstick.

"Isaac!" she says, grabbing him by the face and kissing him on both cheeks. She leaves a lipstick mark, which Isaac, surprisingly, doesn't seem to mind.

"Hey, Irene," Isaac says, grinning while Irene wipes the lipstick off his face with her thumb. "How's it going?"

"Don't 'how's it going' me, mister," she says, and wags one acrylic-nailed finger at him. "I haven't seen you in here for ages."

"Yeah." Isaac shifts on his seat and kind of looks uncomfortable. "I've been busy."

"I heard," she says, clucking her tongue at him. "Had to start a new school, did you?"

"Yeah." They exchange a look, and I wonder why she cares that Isaac's starting a new school. Everyone knows it's because his dad wanted to prove some big point about how the public schools are just as good as the private, don't they? Unless there's something else going on. Something more scandalous. Does Isaac have a secret? A potential secret and/or nefarious past definitely makes him a little more interesting. But not much. Being a pompous jerk totally trumps any hidden scandals.

"Who's this?" Irene asks. She looks at me suspiciously, her eyes traveling up and down my whole body. I feel like I'm under a microscope, and I smooth my hair self-consciously.

"This is Kelsey," Isaac says. "My friend from school."

"Your *friend* from school? From Concordia Public?" She's looking at me skeptically, and she puts emphasis on the word "friend" like she can't believe anyone would ever be just friends with Isaac. Which makes me wonder how many other girls he's brought here. Probably lots. Probably they all looked like Marina. Although the thought of Marina in a bowling alley is pretty hilarious.

"Nice to meet you," I say, giving Irene a smile.

"Mmm-hmm." She disappears without saying it back or taking our order.

"She didn't take our order," I say. So far? Not so impressed with this place. Yes, it's cozy. But the service leaves something to be desired, for sure. Talk about impolite.

"She doesn't have to take our order," Isaac says. He reaches for the bowl of popcorn Irene placed on our table before she disappeared and pops a handful into his mouth.

I look around, pretending to take in the surroundings. "But isn't this a restaurant?"

"Yes," Isaac says, "but she already knows what we want." He glances at the television. "Hmm," he says, "I wonder if they'll switch it to the lacrosse game."

"You ordered for us?" I ask.

"No," Isaac says, "Irene just knows what we want. You'll see. Trust me."

"Trust you? Ha!" I laugh at the absurdity of it. And yet, for some reason, I'm here, sitting in the bowling alley, munching

70

on popcorn, and watching while a guy named Butch bowls a strike and then shakes his butt in the middle of the lane.

"You don't think I'm trustworthy?"

"Are you seriously asking me that?"

"No." He grins. "It was rhetorical. I'm not trustworthy. Like, at all."

"That's good," I say, nodding mock seriously, "that you're able to admit your problem. It's the first step on the road to recovery."

"Who says I want to recover?" he asks. "And besides, shouldn't that make me more trustworthy? That I'm at least able to admit it?"

"No," I say, "because you're only doing it to make me think you're trustworthy. It's like manipulation." He smiles at me and shakes his head like I'm just too much. Something about the way he's looking at me makes me a little uncomfortable. Almost like he's amused by me, but also . . . I don't know, like he *likes* me. Not likes me, *likes me*, but just that he's . . . I don't know, enjoying being here with me. It's making me feel weird, joking around with him like this, and not in a bad way.

Now I understand why all those women went so crazy over Bill Clinton. It has to be a politician thing. Not that Isaac's a politician. But his dad is, and so it's probably in the genes. They have this way of getting one over on you. How else do you explain how Bill could cheat on his wife with Monica Lewinsky and still come out as one of our most-loved presidents?

Before I can analyze this any further, Irene returns to the table and sets down two steaming plates. On each one is a mound of crispy-looking French fries and a grilled cheese sandwich with bacon and tomato peeking out from under golden-brown crusts. Then she plunks down two vanilla milk shakes and disappears again before we can even say thank you.

Suddenly I'm starving. I usually try to stay away from high-fat stuff like cheese and meat, but this meal looks delicious. There's nothing I want more than that sandwich.

"This does look really good," I admit, picking up the sandwich and taking a bite. It's perfect. Buttery, with crisp bacon, juicy tomatoes, and the exact right amount of gooey melted cheese.

"See?" Isaac says. "I told you you'd get what you want."

He's looking right into my eyes as he says it, and giving me this really sexy smile, and I feel a little bit of an excited shiver go up my spine. Because even though he's talking about food, I can't help but think he's also talking about something else.

We make small talk while we eat, mostly about our new school. He tells me a funny story about some guy named Marshall who he's kind of sort of becoming friends with, and how they had to be partners in biology today until Marshall dropped a microscope and shattered it, and then freaked out and tried to put it back on the shelf because he thought he was going to have to pay for it. And then he tells me a little bit about how he thinks Marina is stalking him.

"She seems harmless," I say.

He raises his eyebrows at me and drains the rest of his milk shake. "Trust me," he says, "she's not."

"Oh, please," I say, popping the last bite of my sandwich into my mouth. "She's just a little overeager. Don't guys like you like that?"

"Guys like me? Are we doing that again?"

I roll my eyes. "Calm down," I say. "I'm not stereotyping you. I'm talking about guys in general."

"Then why did you say 'guys like you'?"

"I don't know." I take a fry and drag it through some ketchup. "Force of habit."

He grins. "Well, I'm not interested in her."

"Not enough of a challenge?"

He shrugs. "Sometimes you just know when you like someone."

He's looking right at me again, and that same shiver of excitement rushes through my body.

When we're done eating, we bowl. I'm kind of horrible at it. And when I say "kind of," I mean, you know, completely. Isaac is really good, and he does his best to give me some pointers, but I'm sort of a lost cause.

At one point he's trying to show me how to stand. "Like this," he says, putting his hands on my hips and moving them slowly into the right position. I feel a flush of heat fill my body, and when I turn my head toward his, he's so close I can see the scar through his eyebrow, the curve of his mouth, and the small scratch he has on the side of his neck.

By the time we leave, I realize that we never talked about the stuff with his dad. And I'm also starting to think that I might be starting to like him.

Before

Isaac

"That was fun, right?" I ask Kelsey as I open the door to my car and wait for her to climb in. I don't know why, but suddenly I want her to say that it *was* fun, that she had the best time, that she wants to do it again. Maybe it's because I like her. And maybe it's because *I* had the most fun I've had in a really long time.

I know, it makes no sense. That I like her, I mean. She's completely controlling. And she's constantly giving me shit. But she's also pretty. And smart. And funny. Not always-making-jokes funny (although her jokes are really hilarious), but just funny in the sense that her reactions to things make me laugh. Like how she got all flustered when she realized I was taking her to a bowling alley. And how she freaked out when Irene didn't take our order. It's like she can't let go for one second, or surrender control to anything. I want to be the one who makes her let her guard down.

"It was okay," she says, and shrugs, trying to be all cool.

I roll my eyes, then walk over to the other side of the car. "Come on," I say as I climb in and buckle my seat belt. "You had fun, just admit it."

"Why?"

"Why what?"

"Why is it so important to you that I admit it?" she asks, turning slightly in her seat so that she's looking at me.

"Why is it so important to you that you don't?"

"Anyway," she says, obviously ready to change the subject because she doesn't like the fact that I have her on the ropes. "We should probably talk a little bit about this Face It Down Day thing. I mean, if we're going to be working on it together."

Oh. Right. Face It Down Day. I'd kind of forgotten about that. That's the thing about me. I never think ahead when I get myself embroiled in these crazy schemes. Earlier today when I brought that notebook into Mr. Colangelo's office, it was mostly about showing Kelsey that I could. I never stopped to think about the fact that now I'm actually going to have to do some work on this thing.

Oh well. It will keep my dad happy, at least. And I'll get to hang out with Kelsey.

"Sure," I say. "Well, I'd love to hear your ideas." It's a trick, of course. It's something that my dad does when he wants to get ideas from other people.

"Oh no," Kelsey says, and shakes her head, obviously too smart for that. "You came up with the idea. Why don't you let me know *your* thoughts?"

"Of course I will." As soon as I have any. "Do you want to come over to my house and work on it?" I don't know why I ask her that. The words just come out of my mouth. Partly I think it's because I'm stalling for time. And partly it's because I don't want to stop hanging out with her.

"Right now?" she asks.

"Sure. I can show you my ideas, and we can go over how we're going to advertise." I pull onto the highway and start heading back toward my house, even though she hasn't agreed to come over yet.

"Advertise?"

"Yeah, you know, how we're going to get people to join? Of course, once they find out I'm involved, it should be easy. But we don't want to take any chances." I give her a grin.

"You think we need to *advertise* for our club?"

"Of course."

"What are we, Coca-Cola? You've obviously never done this before."

"And you have?"

"Of course." She smooths her skirt, and I sneak a look at her legs. She has great legs. Long and tan. I think about how it felt to have my hands on her hips back at the bowling alley. I wonder what it would feel like to run my hands over her legs. She catches me looking and raises her eyebrows at me, and I look away quickly.

"When?" I ask her, trying to keep my focus on the road and resist the urge to keep looking at her.

"When what?"

"When have you done this before?"

"Are we still talking about starting a school club?"

I look over at her, shocked. Is she flirting with me? Is she trying to make me feel like a perv for looking at her legs? I'm a red-blooded American teenager! Of course I'm going to look at her legs. Especially when she goes around wearing skirts like that.

"Of course we're still talking about starting a club," I say, feigning confusion. "Aren't we?"

"Yes," she says, "we're still talking about starting a club."

I'm a little disappointed. Half of me was hoping she'd be like, *"We're talking about how you're looking at my legs,"* and then slide across the seat and kiss me. Which is ridiculous. Because she doesn't like me like that. In fact, she thinks we're enemies.

"And you advertised?" I ask her.

"No," she says, "that's what I'm trying to tell you. Are you even paying attention to me?" She starts to rummage through her bag and then pulls out a lip gloss. She lines her lips, making them shiny. And kissable. "You don't advertise. Do you know what kind of crazies will show up if you do that? No." She shakes her head and drops her lip gloss back in her bag.

"We'll just ask a couple of people we know to join. We won't need many. Maybe, like, two each?"

"Do you even know two people at our school?"

"Um . . ." She thinks about it. "I know this one girl. Who I met in the bathroom."

"Who you met in the *bathroom*?"

"Yeah, but she could definitely be crazy, so I'm not sure if I should invite her." I give her a look. "What?" she asks, sounding defensive. "What's wrong with meeting her in the bathroom? Girls talk in the bathroom. Besides, who are you going to invite?"

"I'll invite Marshall."

"Marshall who might be on steroids and dropped a microscope and then tried to cover it up?"

"Yeah."

She closes her eyes and leans her head back against the headrest.

"Fine," I say, "you don't like Marshall? We'll advertise. I'll make some really nice posters with—"

"No, no," she says, "the devils we know are better than the ones we don't, right? And besides, it worked really well at my old school."

When she mentions her old school, she sits up and looks out the window, and her tone kind of changes.

"Did you like your old school?" I ask, trying to keep my tone light.

She shrugs, still turned away from me. "It was okay. It was a school, you know?" But something about the way she says it

79

makes me think that she really does miss it. Which is a foreign concept to me. Yeah, I can understand maybe missing your friends or whatever. But a school? They're all the same. School sucks, no matter where it is or what goes on there.

"Why'd you transfer?"

She doesn't say anything for a moment, and then finally she says, "My parents couldn't afford the tuition anymore." She turns away from the window. She's smiling, but something about it seems forced. "What about you?" she asks. "Why did you leave your old school?"

"Got kicked out," I say happily.

Her mouth drops. "You got kicked out? For what?"

"A bunch of shit," I say. "The thing that finally got me kicked out was that I pulled a prank on the headmaster and stole his wig during an assembly. But that was just the last straw. I'd been getting in trouble for months."

"Were you upset?"

"That I got kicked out? Not really." I shrug. "I'm used to it."

"But you had to leave your friends."

"Most of my real friends are all over the place," I tell her. "They've been kicked out of tons of schools too, so it doesn't really matter."

"Must be nice," she mumbles.

"What?"

"Just that you can get kicked out of school and not really have to worry about if it goes on your record or not. You'll get into college because of who your dad is."

I think about it and realize that she's right. But the thing is, I'm not sure I even want to go to college. College, to me, seems like a complete waste of time. If you're talking about college like what most people think of as college, it seems fun. A state school, maybe, with lots of frat parties and kids going to class in their pajamas. But the kind of college I'm expected to go to? An Ivy League, where I'll have to take some specialized curriculum and write some kind of thesis on environmental policy or whatever the new issue of the moment is? That sounds horrible.

We're pulling into my driveway now, and I cut the engine.

My dad's car is in the driveway, which is a surprise. My dad spends a lot of time in the capitol, obviously, and he wasn't supposed to be home today. The last thing I want is for him to meet Kelsey, (a) because he might scare her away, and (b) because he's going to judge her. Not to her face, of course. Oh no, he's way too smart for that. But later he'll call me into his study and start asking me all kinds of questions about who she is, who her family is, what she's into, etc. My dad's a real dick like that.

It's not that he doesn't have reasons to question my choice in girls—at pretty much every school I've gone to, I've picked out the one or two hot girls who are there just to party. And you'd actually be surprised by who they are. In fact, they're usually the students who have the most high-profile parents. But they're definitely not the kinds of girls you'd marry. Or even bring home.

"Hello?" Kelsey's asking. "Are we going inside, or . . . ?"

But before I can answer, the front door of my house opens, and my dad comes walking down the cobblestone steps toward the driveway. I can tell from his face that he's pissed.

I sigh and step out of the car.

"Hey, Dad," I say cheerfully, "what's going on?"

"Where have you been?" he asks. He steps close to me and looks deep into my eyes. He's checking for redness. My dad is always concerned that I'm going to start taking drugs. Which is crazy. Despite all the trouble I've gotten into, I've smoked pot maybe three times in my life. Drugs just don't really interest me.

"Just been hanging out with my new friend Kelsey." I turn toward the car, where Kelsey's still just sitting there in the passenger seat. She's looking through the window at my dad, and she's all starry-eyed. Which is how pretty much everyone gets when they see my dad. Even people who don't like him or don't agree with his politics. Something about him is just so . . . I would say fake, but it's really more . . . I don't know, *shiny*. Like he stepped out of the pages of a magazine or something. It's like my dad has airbrushed himself into real life. The thought makes me want to laugh, and I bite my lip to keep from doing it out loud.

My dad looks over at Kelsey, and his expression instantly softens, back to being Mr. Politician.

He waves. "Hello, there!" he says loudly, like she's eight or something.

"Hi!" Kelsey yells back, acting like she is.

"I'll be right back," I yell to her. "I'm going to grab some of the stuff that we need, and then we'll go somewhere and work, all right?"

She nods. If she's surprised that we're not going to be working at my house, she doesn't show it. But there's no way I could bring her inside. Not with my dad around.

I start walking up the path toward the front door. My dad follows me. "Kelsey and I are working on a school project together," I tell him.

I don't wait for a response, just push the door open and start making my way down the hall toward my room. Everything in our house is totally immaculate, and that includes my bedroom. My bed is perfectly made with a navy blue and gray comforter. There's an oak desk in the corner with a bunch of my schoolbooks stacked on one of the shelves (they're totally for show, since those books are from my old school—don't need those anymore, haha), along with a wireless printer and my laptop.

The truth is, I'm a slob. And actually, so are my parents. The neatness is all for show because you never know when someone's going to be stopping by the house. Reporters, sure, but also just random people. A sports team that's done well and been invited to our house for dinner. A single mom who won a contest and is going to have a meeting with my dad about social policy. Other members of the senate who would love to find something out of place so they could use it against my dad later.

So if anyone were to end up wandering into my room, you definitely wouldn't want them to find a stack of porn DVDs. Or even a candy bar wrapper—God no. Which is why we have a housekeeper who takes care of everything.

I go over to my desk and start rummaging around, trying to figure out what I can grab that's going to make Kelsey think I have some idea about what the hell I'm doing.

Finally I just pick up my laptop case and shove my laptop into it. Maybe I can Google some stuff when we get to wherever we're going (a coffee shop, maybe?). I'm good at coming up with things on the fly—in fact, I work best under pressure.

"What kind of project are you working on?" my dad asks. He's followed me to my room and is now standing in the doorway, leaning against the door frame. My dad has no respect for anyone else's privacy. I think it's because no one's ever had any respect for his—everything in his life is fair game for his opponents and the press. And that attitude makes him think no one else deserves any either.

"We're starting a school club." I'm deliberately vague, mostly because this is the only kind of power I have over my dad. I can mess with him all I want when it comes to school because he's terrified that people will find out what a fuckup I am.

"What kind of club?" His voice is even, but it has a slight edge to it, and I know he's worried.

"An after-school club." I'm wrapping up my power cord now, twisting it around my hand. I shove it into my bag.

"What kind of after-school club?" He's imagining the worst now. Some kind of gambling ring, maybe. Or some activist club that's trying to get marijuana legalized.

"Don't worry," I say, starting to push past him. "It's only a go if enough people want to join."

He puts his arm out, blocking my exit from the room.

"It's called Face It Down," I say finally, after waiting a beat just to be an asshole. "It's going to help foster a sense of community between our school and Concordia Prep, and other bullshit stuff like that."

He relaxes a little bit but doesn't remove his arm. He looks surprised, and a little suspicious. "And you're organizing it?"

"No," I say, "I lied. I'm actually just going to have sex with the girl who's organizing it. You know, sleep my way in. Maybe I'll even get her pregnant. That oughta really give us some notoriety. Try the whole Bristol Palin route." I pat him on the shoulder.

He sighs like he can't even take dealing with me. "Don't be a smartass, please, Isaac," he says.

"Don't patronize me, Dad."

"I'm not patronizing you," he says. "Given your track record, you can't blame me if I'm a little suspicious of anything that sounds too good to be true."

"Don't worry, Dad," I say, rolling my eyes. "This isn't going to tarnish your pristine reputation." I push through his arm, and he lets me. He won't ever get physical with me. That's where he draws the line. I'm not sure if it's because of some deal he has with himself, that even he knows that would be going too far, or if it's because hitting me would leave marks, real evidence of something that he's done.

I stalk back out to the car, and suddenly I'm really not in the mood to be playing around with some kind of after-school club. Face It Down? How fucking ridiculous. I don't want to mend fences with any little prep school snobs or get to know my new public school classmates.

"Change of plans," I say when I get in the car. I slam the door angrily, and the sound reverberates through the car.

"What?" Kelsey asks. She looks nervous, like she's worried about me. I don't even think it has to do with her liking me, although I definitely have the sense that she's gotten to be more fond of me over the time we've spent together. It's more just a sense of empathy, like I could be anyone and she'd be worried about my well-being.

It's such a nice thing, that she seems concerned, such a sweet thing, that for a second I almost feel like I can push past the anger at my dad. That I can just drive to a coffee shop, that I can just sit and talk with her, plan with her, drink a smoothie or some shit and forget about everything else.

But then, in a flash, it's back. White-hot anger that pulses through my veins. Why the hell should I work on some club that's going to make my dad happy? That's the last fucking thing I want to do.

"I'm taking you home," I say.

Before

Kelsey

Wow. I mean, talk about a mood changer. One minute we're just sitting there, having fun, bowling and eating grilled cheese, and the next everything's all dark and broody. I hate that about guys. At least girls have the decency to be fake and pretend everything's okay when shit gets weird. Whenever guys get upset, they get all angry and scary.

It was so obvious that something happened with his dad, too. You could feel the tension radiating off of them both as soon as his dad came outside. Probably they were yelling at each other in there. Over something stupid, too. Like something that wasn't even important in the moment, but somehow brought up some issue they've had for years. I know all about tension with dads, and trust me, there was definitely some going on there.

Anyway, I'm willing to cut Isaac some slack on the dad thing. But still. He doesn't have to shut down and be all dicky. I mean, I didn't even want to go to the stupid bowling alley with him. And when we were done, I wanted to go home. He's the one who wanted to keep hanging out. So then why do I feel like I'm annoying him, like I'm some kind of hanger-onner, like that Marina girl who he's convinced is stalking him?

"Thanks for a great time," I say sarcastically as he pulls into my driveway. We haven't been talking, even a little bit, except for me giving him directions to my house. He's just been staring straight ahead, his jaw set, his gaze never moving from the road. I get out of the car and slam the door. I'm not sure if it's my imagination or not, but I think I hear him call my name. But I don't care. I don't look back. I just keep walking.

When I get into the house, I can hear voices coming from the kitchen. My mom. My dad. And another guy. I stop at the foot of the stairs, listening, trying to see if I can figure out who it is. Loud, bellowing voice. Annoying Boston accent. Sounds kind of like a used car salesman. Jim Marsh, my dad's boss. Great. I'm wondering if anyone heard me come in, if there's any way I can sneak upstairs and get away with it, when my mom calls, "Kelsey? Is that you?"

Shit, shit, shit.

She comes bustling down the hall. "Honey! Jim is here!

And he brought Rielle." I sigh and take my right foot off the first stair. So close. "She's outside," my mom says. "Maybe you could go and see what she's doing?"

"I know what she's doing," I grumble. "She's on her cell phone." Rielle's always on her cell phone. And not just texting like a normal person. Talking, too. When we were in eighth grade, she ran up over two thousand dollars in cell phone bills. In one month. That was before they had those unlimited minutes and text plans. Her parents had a shit fit. She'd been on the phone for over four thousand minutes that month. Most of them with me.

"Kelsey," my mom says, "just because you two don't go to the same school anymore doesn't mean that you and Rielle can't be friends."

I resist the urge to roll my eyes. Rielle and I have hardly talked since I left Concordia Prep, and when we have, it's been fake and strained. Parents don't get that, though. They don't understand about the fragility of teen friendships. They don't understand how easy it is for things to break apart, how someone you thought would be by your side forever can just disappear, or turn on you, or decide she likes someone more than she likes you. Parents always talk about romantic relationships being so ephemeral and fleeting in high school. What they don't get is that friendships can be the same way.

"It's not that easy, Mom," I try.

"Well, she's in the backyard," my mom says, like Rielle being out there is a situation that has to be dealt with. I start to shake my head, but then she says, "Please. It would mean a lot to your father."

"Like I care," I say before I can stop myself. My dad is always trying to kiss up to Jim. And he's always thought the fact that me and Rielle were so close gave him a leg up with his boss. I think it's another one of the reasons my dad hates that I got kicked out of Concordia Prep.

"Kelsey—" my mom starts.

But I don't want to hear it. Talking to Rielle is better than getting a lecture. Only slightly, but still. So I turn away from my mom and walk through the house and onto the back porch. I can see Rielle through the screened-in windows. She's standing over by my mom's rosebush, and as I suspected, she's on her phone. I watch as she chatters away, then absentmindedly swats at a bug with her free hand. She's wearing a pair of low-rise khaki shorts and a butter-yellow sweater, and her light brown hair is pulled back into a low braid.

My heart catches at the sight of her because I miss her so much it hurts. I've been doing my best not to think about everything that's gone on between us, but now that she's here, standing in my backyard, and I'm confronted with the sight of her, it's hard not to.

When she sees me watching her, she waves me over. She looks happy to see me. It's an act, of course. She's not *really* happy to see me. And if she is, it's only so she can assuage her own guilt for hardly calling or talking to me after I got kicked out of school.

Rielle pulls her phone from her ear and ends her call. I walk over to her, and she envelops me in a hug. My mouth gets pressed against her hair, and I can smell her shampoo. Once a completely familiar smell, now it feels almost weird, like we're not close enough for me to be having this kind of moment with her.

"You look great," I tell her honestly.

"Thanks, so do you." She flips her braid over her shoulder and points to the patio chairs. "Wanna sit?"

"Sure."

I follow her over to the chairs, and once we're seated, she reaches into her bag and pulls out two bottles of Snapple lemonade.

"I brought you a drink," she says, holding it out to me with a grin. Lemonade is our tradition. Ever since junior high, we've always drunk Snapple, even in the winter, while spending countless hours gossiping about our crushes, watching TV, and flipping through magazines. The fact that she brought me one is a gesture of apology. At least a little.

"So how's public school?" she asks, the same way she'd ask about the weather or something. She opens her Snapple bottle and turns the cap over, reading the interesting fact that's printed on the underside.

"Fine," I say, wondering if we're really going to do this, if we're really going to just sit here and make small talk. Not that it would be that bad. It's better than getting into a big screaming fight.

"How are the guys?" She takes a sip of lemonade and then

looks at me, her eyes filled with panic. "Oh my God," she says, "I shouldn't have asked you that. I mean, I know you're probably not ready to date or anything, and I totally shouldn't have even brought it—"

"No guys," I say firmly. "And not because I'm not ready to date." The truth is, I'm *not* ready to date, but Rielle doesn't need to know that. I get the feeling she thinks I'm a little damaged and crazy, which is why she's been so distant. And I don't want to do or say anything that reinforces that opinion. "I mean, they're *public school* boys." I roll my eyes. There was a time that Rielle and I would make fun of public school boys, talk about how there was no way in hell we'd ever date them. Of course, that was when we thought there was no way in hell that we'd ever actually be going to public school either, so, you know, times have changed.

For a second I consider mentioning Isaac, just so she'll think I'm over Rex and everything that happened with him. But after the way Isaac was all dicky to me on the ride home, I've decided not to think about him ever again, much less say his name.

"So listen," Rielle says. She sets her Snapple down on the patio table and turns toward me. "I'm sooo sorry I haven't called. It's just that school's been crazy." She rolls her eyes up toward her perfectly plucked eyebrows. "The SAT prep class alone is, like, three hours of homework a night."

"I hear ya," I say. "School is totally crazy for me, too." If you count the fact that a girl was having a breakdown in the bathroom and my meeting with the principal was crashed by John Brandano's son.

Rielle looks shocked. "Really?"

"Yeah," I say. "Why?"

"I don't know," she says. "I guess I just thought that public school wouldn't be as demanding. You know, academically."

I'm not even insulted, because I've always thought this too. And the truth is, public school *is* easier than private school. But there's no way I'm going to admit this to Rielle.

"It is," I say. "Sooo much work. Plus I'm starting up this club, Face It Down. I'm working with Senator Brandano's son on it. Isaac." Whoops. So much for not saying his name.

This earns even more of an eyebrow raise from Rielle, and I can tell she's impressed, which makes me happy. I know it's silly, especially because she is (was?) my best friend. But this is how it's always been with us. Rielle has money. She has a powerful father. She has everything that's the latest—clothes, purses, makeup, cars.

It's always been me trying to keep up with her.

"So why haven't you called?" I ask her now.

She looks uncomfortable. "I told you," she says, twirling the end of her braid around her finger. "School stuff."

"Bullshit."

She looks at me and opens her mouth, probably to lie again. But then she changes her mind. "I didn't know what to say." Her voice catches, so I know she's telling the truth. "And besides, you didn't call me, either."

"Because you didn't call me!" Doesn't she know that the person who got kicked out of school (me) doesn't have to call the one who didn't (her)? She should have called to check up on me, to see how I was doing. She should have come over with lemonades and ice cream, keeping me company, helping me nurse my broken heart. That's what best friends do. It's so common it's cliché.

"It's just weird," she says, "not seeing you every day. I miss you sooo much. I've had to hang out with Michelle and Anna, and it's just . . . I don't know, it's different. Do you think you'd ever . . ."

The door to the porch opens and closes, and both of our dads come walking outside. My dad is laughing hard at something Rielle's dad is saying. This is how it always is with the two of them. My dad, a step behind, laughing and trying to impress Mr. Marsh. It's kind of funny how his relationship with Rielle's dad mirrors the one that I have with Rielle. I wonder what my dad would think if he ever met Isaac's dad. Probably he would freak out.

"Rielle," her dad calls, and Rielle squeezes my hand and then gets up and moves across the lawn. I follow her.

"Jim was just telling me about how you're going to be a Connor Mitchelle Scholar," my dad says to Rielle. "That's amazing."

Rielle blushes.

"You are?" I ask. "Why didn't you tell me?"

"I just found out today."

She looks at me, her eyes apologizing for not telling me sooner. And if she just found out today, it really shouldn't be that big of a deal. But it is. Because there was a time when she would have told me immediately, would have texted me as soon as she found out. But either she didn't think of it, or worse, she didn't want to brag. The Connor Mitchelle Scholar is a designation given to any junior enrolled in an accredited prep school who has an overall average of ninety percent or higher. If I was still at Concordia Prep, I would have been a Connor Mitchelle Scholar too. In fact, we probably would have celebrated together. I know Rielle's GPA, so it's not like it's a surprise or anything. But still. I wish she would have told me.

"That's really amazing," I say, pulling her toward me for a hug, which feels just as awkward as the last one.

I hate this new dynamic that we have. And the worst part is, I have no one to blame for it but myself.

I get to school early the next morning because I need to get going on this whole Face It Down Day, and there's no way I'm going to count on Isaac Brandano to get the ball rolling. He's obviously completely and totally unreliable. I mean, honestly, the guy is so hot and cold he could be a thermometer.

The cafeteria is pretty much deserted, so I snag a table by the window and pull out a notebook. I'm just about to open it up and start brainstorming some ideas and making a list of deadlines when someone sits down next to me.

"Hello," the someone says.

I look up. Isaac.

"Hi." I keep my voice deliberately short, hoping he'll get the point. The point being, you know, to go away. Why is he always showing up wherever I am? The other day in the gym. Yesterday in the principal's office. Seriously, forget about Marina being the stalker. Isaac's the real stalker. In fact, he's probably trying to deflect the suspicion onto her, when *he's* the one who's dangerous.

"Are you working on our club?" He sits down next to me. His hair looks rumpled, like maybe he forgot to brush it after he showered. He's wearing a pair of dark jeans, a black sweater, and a backward baseball hat. He looks hot. But since I'm off boys, and especially off him, I try not to notice.

"Oh, now it's *our* club?" I pull my notebook closer to me so that he can't steal my ideas. Not that I have any written down yet. But he doesn't know that.

"Wasn't it always?"

"No," I say, "first it was mine. Until you crashed my meeting. And then it was ours. Until you got in some kind of big snit yesterday and left me. And now it's mine again."

"I didn't *leave* you," he says. "Something came up."

"And you couldn't have told me that?" I ask. "That would have been the polite thing to do. Actually, never mind polite, it would have been the *normal* thing to do." I'm kind of mad now. Mostly at myself, for believing even for a second that he could be cool. Or that we could be friends. Or that when he made my stomach get all flippy, it could mean something other than that my hormones are obviously completely and totally out of control.

"Well—" he starts.

But at that moment someone else comes over and slams their books down on the table. Hard. So hard that the whole table shakes.

"Wow," Isaac says. "Watch it." He picks up his coffee and pulls it toward his chest protectively.

I look up. It's a girl. She looks kind of familiar, but I can't exactly— Oh. Right. The girl from yesterday, the one who was in the bathroom. The one that was crying. The one who I said was going to join our club.

"*You,*" she says, pointing.

Yikes. She must have been crying over Isaac. Wow. I mean, he's only been here, like, one day, and he's already got one girl, Marina, stalking him, and this other girl crying over him. And now Curly-Haired Blond Girl must be here to confront him, to give him a talking-to, to yell at him for hurting her. Good for her.

I sit back in my chair and cross my arms over my chest. It's going to be nice to watch the show. I only wish there were more people here to witness it. Isaac's looking at Curly-Haired Blond Girl like he doesn't even know who she is. Which isn't very nice. Either he's going to try to play it off like she's crazy, or he was probably so drunk when they hooked up that he—

"Don't look so smug," the girl says. Which is weird, because

Isaac doesn't really look that smug. Just confused. But he *is* a smug bastard, so I'm all for her calling him smug.

I wait for him to contradict her, but instead, he's looking at me. In fact, they're both looking at me. Why are they . . . ?

"Are you talking to me?" I ask. I almost look behind me like they do in movies when they can't believe the person in question is talking to them. But I realize that would be going a little too far since all that's behind us is a wall.

"Yes," she says. She plops down in a chair across from us. "I've been looking for you."

"You have?"

"Wow," Isaac says, "and I thought lesbian experimentation was supposed to happen more with private school girls." He reaches into his bag and pulls out a package of animal crackers, then pops one in his mouth.

I give him a mean look, but Blond Girl just ignores him. It makes me like her a little bit. Anyone who can treat Isaac like he's an inconsequential annoyance is okay in my book.

"Yesterday in the bathroom," she says, "you said that you have experience with broken hearts."

"I did?" I bite my lip. I don't really remember what I said in the bathroom yesterday. I was in too much of a rush to get to my meeting.

"You did?" Isaac asks. He sounds interested. "Who broke your heart?"

"I didn't say that," I try.

"Yes, you did," the girl says.

And then I remember. When she came out of the stall and told me she had a broken heart, I told her that I'd had experience with that kind of thing. She really shouldn't be asking me for my opinion, though. I mean, my broken heart got me kicked out of school, made my parents think I'm some kind of hopeless fuckup, and ruined my relationship with my best friend.

"Oh," I say. "Well, um—"

"Who broke your heart?" Isaac asks again. He's looking at me like he's actually concerned.

"No one," I say.

"So you *lied*?" Blond Girl asks. She narrows her eyes at me, and suddenly I'm nervous. If she's in a slightly crazy place like I was when I got my heart broken, who knows what she's going to do. I took my rage out on Rex, but this girl might decide to turn on someone she doesn't know. Someone like me. Someone who she's marked as the person she could commiserate with and who then took it all away. It's like those crazy psychos who go back and kill the boss who fired them six years ago, because they blame them for being the one who set their life on a bad course.

"I didn't lie," I say.

"Then who broke your heart?" Isaac asks for the third time.

"Yeah." Blond Girl pulls out a chair and sits down. "Who broke your heart?" She reaches into Isaac's bag of animal crackers and pulls one out. She puts it in her mouth and starts to munch away. Isaac doesn't seem to mind. He pushes the bag closer to her in case she wants another one, then pulls one out for himself. They both sit there, eating animal crackers and looking at me like they're waiting for me to provide them with their entertainment for the morning.

"No one," I say. "I mean, yes, I had a broken heart. It was this guy at my old school."

"What happened?" Blond Girl asks.

"Shouldn't I, like, know your name first?" I ask her. "Seeing as how you seem to be all interested in the intimate details of my life?"

She swallows the rest of her animal cracker. "Sorry," she says. "I'm Chloe Schwimmer." She looks like a Chloe Schwimmer, with her long, curly blond hair and small features. "And you are?"

"Kelsey Romano."

"And I'm Isaac Brandano."

"Oh, right," Chloe says. "The senator's kid. Far out."

Does anyone say "far out" anymore? I don't have time to think about it because Chloe's attention is already back on me. "So what happened between you and this kid? What was his name?"

"Rex." My mouth goes dry just when I say it. Suddenly I'm back there, in the lab, the day I found out. The day I went crazy. I inhale the scent of the chemicals and the paint and the glass. I push the image out of my mind. "And there was nothing scandalous about it," I lie. "So you guys can stop looking at me like that. I just really liked him and then he broke up with me."

"Why?" Isaac wants to know.

"Why did I really like him?"

"No." He rolls his eyes. "Why did he break up with you?"

"He just wasn't into it anymore," I say. "He wanted to date other people." It's not exactly the truth. Rex did want to date other people. But he started doing that before he broke up with me. Hence my meltdown.

"So how'd you get over it?" Chloe asks.

"Normal stuff." I shrug. "Time. Ice cream. Cheesy romance movies." Lie, lie, lie.

Chloe looks disappointed. I would be too, if I were her. Obviously, the only reason she sought me out and asked me all these questions is because she was hoping I'd have some kind of secret, miracle heartbreak cure. She should have realized that if I did, I certainly wouldn't be sitting in school. I'd be off writing a book about it and getting rich.

The bell rings then, signaling the beginning of homeroom. I breathe a sigh of relief, glad my time in the hot seat is over. I start to gather up my stuff.

"So do you want to have our first meeting next Wednesday?" Isaac asks. "I could make posters. I mean, if you've rethought that whole advertising thing?" He grins.

"Wednesday?"

"Yeah."

"And you're going to make posters?"

"Yeah."

I think about it. I'm sick of him, but I also still need him.

If he can somehow get his father involved, or even if we can get some kind of media attention because of his involvement, it could be great for me. Just the kind of thing that a good college would think balances out the fact that I got kicked out of my old high school and that I'm not going to a great prep school anymore.

He can help run things, like, in name only. He'll be a silent partner. I mean, let's face it, once things get up and running, once we actually have to *do* something, he's going to disappear. And then I won't even have to be around him that much.

"You guys are starting a club?" Chloe asks.

"Yeah," I say. "It's called Face It Down. You should come." She nods, but she still looks let down, like she came to me hoping for boy help and all she got was an invitation to an after-school activity. I turn to Isaac. "Wednesday sounds good. And knock yourself out with the posters."

It might be a little crazy, but I spend all night working on posters myself. I know I put Isaac in charge, but there's no way I'm going to allow myself to expect that much from him. So I make twenty posters, which is so not easy to do when you're working with the cheapest markers they had at the drugstore.

But when I walk into the front foyer of school the next morning, struggling to keep the rolled-up posters from spilling out of my bag, there are already posters. Tons of them, flanking all the hallways. Professional-looking. Blue and white.

Crisp, clean. Talking about Face It Down, using words like "community" and "all in this together," and making it look like the kind of club you'd want to join.

"Awesome, aren't they?" Isaac asks when he catches me staring at one between second and third period. "I went down to a printing shop and spent a long time going over exactly what we wanted."

"That's great," I say. "Um, how much were they? I should pay half—"

"Don't worry about it." He waves me off. "I put it on my dad's tab. He was thrilled."

He squeezes my shoulder before turning around and heading down the hall. I feel my stomach fill with butterflies and my heart start to race at his touch. Stop, I tell myself, you are *not* going to start liking Isaac Brandano. So what if he made amazing posters? That doesn't erase the fact that he's completely self-centered. And besides, let's see if anyone's even going to come. Feeling determined, I head to my locker, forcing Isaac out of my mind.

On Wednesday, twenty kids show up to our meeting. Including Chloe.

The Aftermath

Isaac

"It sounds like everything was off to a great start," Dr. Ostrander is saying. He's leaning back in his chair, looking like he really is interested in the story.

I don't blame him. Kelsey's a great storyteller. That's one of the things I always loved about her. Most chicks cannot tell a good story. They either start blabbing away, adding all kinds of details that you don't need, or they tell some story that no one gives a shit about, usually involving some other girl stealing their thunder.

Marina's a perfect example of this. So is my mom. I love my mom, but her stories are very long, very involved, and very boring. I think that might be why her and my dad don't have the greatest relationship. He can't stand to listen to her. I always vowed that the girl I ended up with would have to be able to tell a great story. And Kelsey can.

But now I'm thinking that wanting to end up with a great storyteller might have been a bad idea. Because girls who can tell great stories are also great liars.

"It *was* off to a great start," I pipe up. Until this point I've been silent, deciding I was going to do the brooding, unhappy thing and hopefully show that I don't give a shit about Kelsey or this ridiculous meeting. But she's doing so well that I'm afraid she's going to talk her way out of the whole thing. "The problem is, everything was built on a lie."

"A lie?" Dr. Ostrander looks confused, and Kelsey looks panicked.

"Yeah," I say. "A lie about Rex Gray."

Dr. Ostrander looks down at the police report in front of him. "Rex Gray," he says. "He was the student from Concordia Prep? The one who was taken away in an ambulance?"

I roll my eyes. "He wasn't taken away in an ambulance," I say.

"It says here he was seen by the medical team and taken away in an ambulance."

"He was looked at by the EMTs, who said he was fine," I tell him. "But he insisted he get taken to the hospital. They didn't even put on the sirens." Rex wanted to cause some big scene; he wanted to be able to tell the press that he was taken away by an ambulance, and it was all Isaac Brandano's fault. Well, boo hoo. Seriously, what a little bitch.

"Anyway," Dr. Ostrander says, "it seems that things were going well with the club. So how did everything fall apart?"

"Because of Kelsey," I say simply.

She looks down at her hands, and for a second I feel my heart break. I hate seeing her upset. But then I remember how she lied to me, and anger flows through my veins. So much anger that I almost can't take it. It's so hard and so strong that it comes close to overtaking my whole body.

"Because of Kelsey?" Dr. Ostrander asks.

"Yes," I say, "because of her lies."

Before

Isaac

"Hey, can everyone quiet down?" I ask. I'm standing at the front of the room with twenty kids sitting in front of me, trying to get everyone to come to attention. They do. They all quiet down in, like, five seconds, which is pretty surprising. I thought I'd have to stand here for at least a minute or two trying to get everyone to shut up. But everyone's quiet. And now that they are, I don't even know what I'm supposed to be saying.

I don't even know why I'm here, honestly. That day when I dropped Kelsey off? I could have just let it be. I could have gotten out of this whole Face It Down Day thing. But that night, in an effort to cool down after what went on with my dad, I found myself driving around by myself. And I couldn't stop thinking about her. Not just that night, either. The day after, too. And before I knew it, I was at that ridiculous printing shop, getting a bunch of posters printed up for Face It Down Day. And I was so excited for her to see them the next morning.

The problem is, I'm more excited to make Kelsey happy than I actually am about Face It Down in general. And so when everyone quiets down, I don't really know what to say.

"Thanks, everyone," I try. They're all staring at me, and I'm about to turn the floor over to Kelsey when I spot Marina sitting in the crowd. She gives me a little wave, and it makes me lose my train of thought.

That chick is certifiably out of her fucking tree. It's to be expected, really, because she's so hot. All hot chicks are crazy. It's almost like they've been able to get away with being insane because they're so good-looking. No one cares that they're completely crazy, because they're nice to look at.

"Hi," Kelsey says to the group. She's wearing a really tight sweater. I have not been able to stop staring at her chest all day. That dude from my homeroom and science class, Marshall Durbin, is here too. And he's staring at Kelsey's chest too. Douche. The only reason he's even here is because Marina is. I'm pretty sure he wants to get into her pants.

Also at the meeting is Chloe, that girl from the cafeteria the other day. The rest are a bunch of kids I don't know, but they look like the types you'd expect to show up at a meeting like this. Do-gooders.

"I'm Kelsey Romano," Kelsey says. "And we're here to talk about Face It Down Day, a day where we can get together with Concordia Prep and try to work on our differences."

"Aw, man, I hate Concordia Prep," Marshall says. "They're all a bunch of stuck-up jerks." He holds his fist up to the guy next to him and waits for a pound.

"I used to go there," Kelsey says.

"Oh," Marshall says. "I didn't mean you." He's talking to her chest. "But their football team really is a bunch of shits."

"It's okay," Kelsey says, "but that's kind of the point. I mean, you can't tell just from looking at someone where they go to school or whether or not you should be friends with them."

I like the way she says it. It's not corny, the way it could be. I see a lot of the kids nodding, and then we all start throwing out ideas for a letter we can send to the president of the student council at Concordia Prep, so that we can invite a bunch of them to our school and see what happens.

On our way out of the meeting, I tell Kelsey she did great. She really did, too. Totally in control, never letting things get cheesy, and never putting up with shit from anyone while at the same time not being a total control-freak ball buster.

"Thanks," she says. She looks happy and excited, her cheeks flushed from her success. She shifts her bag on her shoulder. "So I'll see you tomorrow?"

"Yeah," I say, "see you tomorrow." I feel like we should go out and get some food, a burger, *something*, because I feel like we accomplished a lot in there. Even if the only thing I did was lend my name and make some posters. But the moment to invite her has passed, and she's already walking away. And then I notice that she's walking toward the row of late buses.

"Hey," I say, jogging up to her. "You need a ride home?" I'm trying to sound nonchalant, even though I really want her to say yes.

"No thanks," she says, "I have a ride."

"The bus?"

"Yes, the bus. What's wrong with the bus?" Then she nods. "Oh, I get it," she says. "You're a bus snob."

"A bus snob?"

"Yeah, one of those people who's had a car since, like, forever, and so you can't imagine taking the bus. Or any other kind of public transportation."

"Not true," I say. "I am not a snob about buses. I love buses. Especially late buses." I've never ridden the late bus, and I'm pretty sure I wouldn't be a fan, but whatever.

"Really?" We're in front of the bus now and she turns around and looks at me. "How old were you when you got your car?"

I think about lying, but she's not stupid. "I got it on my sixteenth birthday," I admit. "Well, technically, I got it the night before. There had been this mix-up on the lot, and so the guy dropped it off at eight at night instead of eight in the morning. My mom was not pleased, she had this whole surprise planned with eggs Benedict and . . ." I stop talking because she's staring at me, her eyebrows raised incredulously.

"Goodbye, Isaac," she says, and starts to get on the bus.

"Wait." I grab her arm. "If you won't let me drive you home, then I'm going to take the bus with you."

"*What?* Why?"

"Because I can't have you going around thinking I'm some kind of transportation snob. It's not good for our friendship."

"So we're friends now?"

Do friends kiss? "Aren't we?"

She thinks about it. Like, really thinks about it. She looks really cute when she concentrates. "I guess so," she says. "Except for the fact that you were kind of rude to me the other day."

"Let me make it up to you," I tell her.

"How?"

"By riding the bus home with you?"

"You don't really want to do that."

"No. I don't really want to. But I will. As penance." I start to hop up the stairs. "Hello," I say to the driver. He's actually getting kind of annoyed because he wants to get on his way, and he can't with us just standing there.

"On or off," he says. And he's pretty grouchy about it too. Which makes a lot of sense, since he's a bus driver. They're always in a perpetual state of being pissed off. The dude probably needs to get laid.

"On or off?" I ask Kelsey, holding my hand out to her.

"Off," she says emphatically, and my heart sinks. "Because you're driving me home."

I smile.

• • •

"You want to drive?" I ask as we make our way over to the student parking lot.

"You'd let me drive your car?"

"Sure," I say. "Why not?" Normally, I wouldn't let anyone touch my car. It's a black BMW, and I love it. I used to call it "baby" when I first got it, but that's pretty corny. So I stopped. Plus chicks used to get really pissed off because I never called *them* "baby." And then they'd be all, "Why do you love your car more than me?" and blah, blah, blah.

"Because you love this car," Kelsey says.

"How do you know I love it?"

"It's obvious," she says. "You're always staring at it adoringly."

"I am?" Huh. "Well, whatever. Do you want to drive or not?"

"Sure." She holds her hand out for the keys, and as soon as they're in her palm, I'm kind of regretting it. But I push my trepidation down and head over to the passenger side. It's weird, opening the door on the passenger side of my own car.

"You were really going to let me drive?" she asks, looking at me over the top of the car.

"Yeah. What, you don't want to anymore?" I'm kind of relieved. In fact, if she says she doesn't, I'm not even going to try to convince her to do it. I'm just going to take the keys back.

"No, I do," she says. "It's just . . . I can't."

"Why not? I already said you could." So much for not trying to convince her. It's just that she looks so forlorn, like she really wants to drive and is really going to be upset if she can't.

"I know," she says. She walks around to the passenger side of the car so that she's standing right in front of me. It's all I can do not to reach out and pull her close to me. That's how freakin' cute she looks. Which is a very new feeling for me. Usually when I have the urge to pull girls close, it's because I want to have sex with them. I want to pull them close and get them naked. Not pull them close just to have them close, the way I want to do with Kelsey. God, I must really be losing it.

She's holding the keys out to me and I almost don't trust myself to take them. But finally I do. Her fingers brush against my palm, and it's like a burst of flames rushes up my hands and through my arms.

"I don't have a license," she says.

"You don't have a license?" I cannot comprehend this. Everyone has a license. It's, like, a rule that you get a license when you turn sixteen. "Everyone has a license," I tell her.

"Not me. I failed my test twice."

"You don't know how to drive?"

She shakes her head.

"Why not?"

"Dunno." She shrugs. "I guess I never really had anyone to teach me."

"Your parents?"

She shakes her head again and then stares down at the pavement, which makes me think it might not be the best idea to delve into that. Shit with parents is the last thing I want to talk about, anyway.

"Well, we need to fix that," I say. The words are out of my mouth before I even realize what I'm saying, and I kind of want to take them back, but mostly I don't. I hand the keys back to her. "I'll teach you."

"You'll teach me how to drive?"

"Yup." I'm opening the passenger door now, and I drop down into the seat. Definitely better buckle up for this one. Girls are horrible drivers. I know that probably sounds sexist, but it's true. I've been in two accidents, both of them in the parking lots of my old schools, both of them with girls who weren't paying attention and/or just didn't understand anything about spatial relations.

Kelsey leans down so that she's looking at me through the open window. Her hair brushes against the bottom of the window frame, and she's so close it would be easy to just pull her toward me and kiss her.

"I can't drive!" she says, and opens my door.

"Yes, you can." I shut it.

"What if I crash your car?"

"You won't."

"But what if I do? This car looks superexpensive."

"It's actually not as expensive as you would think," I lie.

"Still." She looks doubtful. "What if I crash it? I can't pay for it."

"That's what insurance is for."

"But I'm not on your insurance."

"No," I say, "but I am. And if you crash it, then I'll just say I did it. Now, are you going to get in or not?"

She starts to shake her head, but then she catches my eye. And I want her to go for it. I want her to drive my car. And not just because I want to spend more time with her. I mean, yeah, I do want to spend more time with her, and I have to admit that suddenly something about the thought of her behind the wheel of my car is pretty sexy.

But more than that, I just have this weird feeling that it would be good for her, that if she can drive and be good at it, she might get a little of her confidence back. I don't know how I know her confidence is down, or how I know it would be good for her to get it back, but I do.

"Okay," she says finally, nodding.

And the next thing I know, she's in the driver's seat next to me.

Before

Kelsey

This is not good. This is a horrible disaster just waiting to happen. I can't drive Isaac's car! I've hardly ever even driven. Like, ever in my life. I have my permit, but that's only because all you have to do to get your permit is study this little booklet and then go down to the DMV and take a written test. A multiple-choice written test, where they basically ask you things like what color light means caution. Seriously, you pretty much have to be an idiot to fail.

But being behind the actual wheel of an actual car? I've only done that a few times, when my dad took me out to try to teach me how to drive. Which was definitely not the best time

I've ever had, mostly because I'm a really bad driver. My dad was nice about it (this was before I got kicked out of school, and before he thought I was a total failure), but I would still get really frustrated. And then I would come home and cry. I tried to take my road test anyway, mostly because by the time I realized I was a horrible driver, it was already scheduled. I failed it. So I took it again. And failed it again.

I've always really wanted to be able to drive, though. I mean, who doesn't? Driving equals freedom. Of course, even if I got my license, it's not like I have the money for a car. But if I'd still had my after-school job, who knows if I could have saved up enough to get one? At least some kind of junker. It would have been amazing.

Even though I'm supernervous, I have to admit that driving Isaac's car is kind of a rush. At first we just circle the student parking lot. A couple of times he reaches out and grabs the steering wheel while I'm driving, which you'd think would be annoying, like he's trying to take over, but it's not. It's more like he's just looking out for me. Plus every time his fingers brush against mine, my stomach explodes with butterflies.

We're going around the traffic circle in front of the school when it happens. I kind of, um, crash against the curb. There's a scratching sound, and I slam on the brakes. "Ohmigod," I say, feeling the blood drain out of my face. "Oh my God, oh my God, oh my God."

"It's okay," Isaac says, but he looks nervous, and even though he's *saying* that it's okay, he sounds scared.

I get out of the car and rush around to the other side so I can check the damage. Isaac's out too, standing there and looking down.

"Is it bad?" I ask, not waiting for him to answer before I look myself. There's a small scratch on the bottom of his car, on the passenger side near the tire. It's not tiny, but it's not big, either, and it's just a scratch. No big dent. No smashed-in metal. I breathe out a huge sigh of relief.

"See?" he says. "No big deal."

I don't know why, but I'm holding my breath again, and I'm so, so happy that it's nothing, that there's nothing wrong with the car, that I start to cry.

I know. Lame. I don't even know why I'm doing it. Maybe it's because I'm so thankful that I won't have to figure out how to pay for something superexpensive on top of everything else I'm dealing with. Maybe it's because Isaac is being really nice to me, and I didn't want to do anything to screw that up. Maybe it's because my dad has been so hard on me lately that anytime I think I might be in trouble, it's a huge relief when I'm not. Or maybe it's just because for the past hour, while I've been driving around with Isaac, I haven't thought about getting kicked out of school, or what happened with Rex, or me and Rielle, or anything else. I've just been having fun.

"Hey," Isaac says. "Are you crying?"

"No." I wipe at my eyes with the back of my hand. "I'm just relieved."

"Come here." He pulls me close to him, and I press my cheek against his chest. I can feel how hard his muscles are. Damn. The boys at Concordia Prep never had chests like that. At least, I don't think they did. I wonder if Isaac works out a lot. He must. No one's that muscular naturally. I bet he looks amazing with his shirt off. The thought of Isaac shirtless makes me catch my breath and makes my heart beat fast, and before I know what's happening, I'm looking up at him.

"I'm sorry," I say, "I'm usually not so crazy."

"I don't think you're crazy," he says.

"You don't?"

"No." He pushes a strand of hair off my face.

"Well, I am."

"You don't give yourself enough credit," he says. And now his lips are right there, like, two inches away from mine and ohmigod I want to kiss him. The moment is perfect, with us pushed up against his car, and the late-afternoon sun streaming through the trees around the parking lot. There's a light breeze that's ruffling his hair, and it smells like summer even though it's fall.

I shiver again, and he pulls me closer, and now his lips really are right there, and I'm just about to go crazy from wanting him to kiss me when he finally does.

He brushes his lips against mine, keeping them there for a long beat and then pulling away. He looks into my eyes, asking me if it's okay without saying anything, and I keep my gaze on his, letting him know, until he kisses me again.

This time the kiss is longer, but still sweet. His lips are perfect. He tastes like mint gum and strawberries, and I lose myself in the moment.

When he finally pulls away, he rests his forehead against mine. "I think I should drive home," he says, and grins. "You know, just in case."

"Fine," I say. "But I get shotgun."

Before

Isaac

After I drop Kelsey off, I can't stop thinking about her. I didn't want to drop her off. I wanted to hang out with her more, but I'm supposed to be home tonight for some dipshit dinner that my dad has planned. My dad's always scheduling dipshit dinners at the worst possible time, like when I've just kissed a girl I really like. He has some kind of ability to know exactly when I'm having fun.

Anyway, these dinners are usually with people who are big campaign contributors, or people who are in charge of some big cause that my dad is about to fuck over, and so he has them over to make them think that he's taking what they have to say into consideration before he votes for some measure that's going to cut their funding.

Technically, I don't really have to be at these dinners since they have nothing to do with me. But my dad likes to have me there because it makes it seem like we're one big happy family.

"Isaac," he says, all smiles when I walk in the door. Our guest is there already. Some douche bag wearing a suit and tie. They're both holding glasses of scotch, which my dad thinks is really impressive. Seriously, the dude loves to pull out his expensive scotch and be all, *"Would you like some of this expensive scotch that's meant to make you think I'm cultured and refined?"*

"I'd like you to meet George Donahue," my dad says.

I reach out and shake George Donahue's hand, giving him a smile. It's not his fault my dad's a shit. "Nice to meet you, sir."

"Nice to meet you, too," he says. "You might know my son, Kevin Donahue? He's at Taft."

"Yeah, I know Kevin," I say. "He's a good dude."

My dad gives me a sharp look, I guess because I used the word "dude." But honestly, if this guy is Kevin Donahue's dad, he's not going to care. Kevin Donahue and I were never close while I was at Taft (I got kicked out after a couple of weeks because of a fight—they have a zero-tolerance policy for fighting there, which is ridiculous, especially when most of the guys there are assholes who deserve a good beat down), but he was always really friendly to me and seemed like a really chill, laid-back guy.

"Your father tells me you just started at Concordia Public," George says. "Good for you. I always wondered if Kevin would be better off at public school." He shakes his head. "But his mother was insistent."

I give him a sympathetic smile, and the three of us stand there for a while making small talk until my mom pokes her head into the family room.

"Dinner's ready," she says. She's wearing a black dress and her hair is up in a bun. "Hi, Isaac," she says, "I'm glad you're home."

"The food smells wonderful," George says, carrying his scotch with him as he walks toward the dining room.

"Chicken cordon bleu," my mom says.

We all start following George, and on the way I hear my dad whisper angrily to my mom, "I thought you were making filet mignon."

"I was," she says, "but by the time I left work, there wasn't enough time to stop at the butcher. I had a big client meeting and—"

"You couldn't have sent Mia?"

This is why my dad is a dick. He always wants us to seem like we're this completely down-to-earth family who does things for themselves. Then he gets on my mom for not sending the housekeeper out to get the filet mignon he wanted her to pick up. I'm starting to feel angry, which doesn't bode well for this dinner.

"Leave it alone," I say, a little louder than I intended.

"Everything okay?" George Donahue asks, looking over his shoulder at us with concern.

"Everything's great," my dad says cheerfully.

I roll my eyes behind his back. We sit down at the table.

It's set with a flower centerpiece, and there's already a pear-and-walnut salad at each place.

"This looks amazing, Mom," I say honestly.

"Yes, Ellen," George Donahue says, "it looks delicious."

We make it through dinner without any mishaps. We talk and laugh, and I think George and my dad both get a little tipsy on scotch. Which probably helps to set the scene for what happens next.

When dinner's over, my dad walks George to the door while my mom starts to work on the dishes.

"Well, I guess that went well," my dad says as he comes back into the kitchen. "Do you think George had a nice time?"

"Dad," I say, heading to the sink and grabbing a sponge so that I can start helping my mom, "it was a great night. Everyone had fun."

"Hopefully, he'll be able to overlook the off-color jokes and overcooked chicken," my dad says.

"What off-color jokes?" my mom asks.

"Stop," I say.

"Excuse me?" my dad asks. He leans back against the counter and crosses his arms over his cranberry-colored sweater.

"Knock it off," I tell him. "You're acting like an asshole. Mom made an amazing dinner for us, no one told any off-color jokes, and you're making it out like the whole night was a disaster."

"Isaac," my mom says, "it's fine, don't—"

"It's not fine," I say. "Dad's being a prick."

"Don't talk to me like that, Isaac," he says, and takes a step toward me. "You show me respect in this house."

"You have to give respect to get respect," I mutter under my breath. But my dad must hear me because the next thing I know, he's right there next to me, breathing scotch into my face.

"What did you say?" he growls.

"You heard me."

"Go to your room."

"Please." I throw the sponge down in the sink. "I'm not twelve."

I walk out of the house without looking back.

I end up at the Sportstar Arcade, mostly because they have batting cages. Baseball's never really been my thing, but I need to blow off some steam, and swinging the bat will be good for me.

I feed a twenty into the change machine, collect my quarters, then pump them into the batting machine. Sportstar's more like a sports complex than an arcade, with not only games, but laser tag, a food court, and even a few rides. It's usually packed, but the batting cages are dead tonight.

I put on a helmet and step into the middle cage. I whale away at the ball, not caring if I swing and miss, not even aiming for anything, just trying to hit hard. After half an hour I've worked up a sweat, and I'm starting to feel a little better.

I'm also starting to think that maybe boarding school overseas might not be that bad an idea. At least it would get me away from my dad.

I'm just about to start up another round when I·hear someone clapping behind me. I turn around. Marina.

"Hey," she says, giving me a smile. "Wicked swing."

I don't answer, just sort of nod.

"What are you doing here?" she tries.

"What does it look like I'm doing?" I ask. I sound like an asshole, because even though I'm feeling better, I'm still in a horrible fucking mood. And to be asked what I'm doing when I'm obviously using the batting cages doesn't exactly brighten up my night. It just annoys me.

"It looks like you're whaling away on some balls," she says, giggling. She walks right into the batting cage, even though you're not supposed to be in here without a helmet. "So either you're really frustrated, or you're angry." She gets really close to me then, and I can feel her boobs pushed against my chest. "Or maybe both."

"Probably both." I take a step back. She's hot, I won't deny it. But I was just kissing Kelsey a few hours ago. And I like Kelsey. A lot. She's cool and fun and smart, and she makes me feel like I'm cool and fun and smart. And Marina's crazy. She stopped texting me when it became obvious I wasn't going to reply, and she stopped bothering me at school when it became obvious I was avoiding her. But she still makes me nervous.

"So, what are you doing after this?" she asks.

"I'm busy." I put money into the machine, and it whirs to life.

"That's too bad," Marina says. She's on her way out of the batting cage, and she glances over her shoulder. "We're all going down to the beach. You were supposed to come, remember?"

"That's tonight?"

She nods. "We couldn't go last week. Rain." She puffs out her bottom lip. "There's going to be beer."

The baseball comes flying out of the cannon, and I pull the bat back and slam it into the ball. It goes flying against the backstop. Beer sounds good. Really good. I think about how I have nothing to do after this except go home. How my dad's probably waiting up for me, hoping for some kind of confrontation.

"Fine," I say, slamming the next ball as hard as I can. I turn around to look at Marina. "But can I invite Kelsey?"

Her smile falters for a second, but then she recovers. "Of course."

She waits while I finish my round of balls, then brings me over to the snack bar, where a couple of other girls are sitting at the counter sipping fountain sodas and eating nachos. "This is Raya and Nicole."

"Hey," they say. The spin around on their stools and size me up. I'm not in the mood to meet new people.

"Hi." I give them a nod.

"He's the strong, silent type," Marina says, giggling. She leans into me, and I think I can smell alcohol on her. Has she been drinking already? Who the fuck drinks and then comes to the arcade?

"Whatever," I say. "Are we going to go?"

"Geez, impatient much?" Marina asks. Her friends laugh.

"Do you want to leave your car here? Raya's the designated driver."

"Fine." I hate the thought of leaving my car, but I'm too amped up to drive. So I follow them out to the parking lot, pulling out my phone so that I can call Kelsey on the way.

The Aftermath

Kelsey

"So, it seems like things were on the right track," Dr. Ostrander says. "You had a meeting. You were getting ready to send a letter to Concordia Prep."

"Yes." I nod. "We did, and we were—"

Next to me, Isaac laughs.

"Is there something you'd like to add to the discussion, Mr. Brandano?"

"No," Isaac says, shrugging. "If you want to know the truth, I don't really give a shit about this whole thing."

Dr. Ostrander has been pretty cool this whole time, considering the PR nightmare that the school is having. But Isaac's remark seems to make him mad. Justifiably so. I mean, Isaac, as usual, is acting like an asshole.

"Mr. Brandano, that kind of language won't be tolerated in here."

I look down at my hands and feel my eyes start to fill with tears. Isaac pulling an attitude is definitely not going to help my cause. Whether I like it or not, we're in this together. What he does affects me. And vice versa. The worst part is that I know some of the reason he's acting like this is because he wants to see me get in trouble. Not that I can blame him. But it still sucks.

"Sorry," Isaac mumbles. But he's back to slouching down in his chair, and he doesn't sound like he means it.

"I'm going to step out for a minute," Dr. Ostrander says. "And when I come back, I trust that you'll both be ready to discuss this like adults." He keeps his eyes on us for a moment, looking back and forth between us like he's trying to convey just how serious this is. Then he stands up and walks out of the room, leaving me and Isaac alone.

"Isaac—" I start.

"Save it," he says, looking away from me and down at the floor. "Just save it."

"I know you're mad," I say quietly. "And I don't blame you. But—"

"You know I'm *mad*?" he spits. He sits up in his chair and turns toward me. "Are you *kidding me*? Kelsey, I told you I was *falling in love with you*. Do you know how many girls I've said that to?"

I don't say anything because there's a huge lump in my throat that's making it impossible to talk.

"None," he says. "You're the only one. The very first one I ever said that to. So when I found out you lied to me about Rex, do you know how that made me feel?"

"Terrible," I whisper. I think about it. How Isaac looked at Face It Down Day, how he looked when Rex told him the truth about everything. I can't stand that I disappointed him like that, that I let him down that way, that I hurt him so much.

"Terrible's an understatement," he says bitterly. "So, sorry if I'm not psyched to sit here and try to convince the superintendent that we shouldn't be punished."

"Isaac," I say, "I'm so sorry. I am. I'm embarrassed and humiliated, and if you just . . ." I'm crying now, big sloppy tears that are making it hard to talk. I wipe them away with the back of my hand.

Isaac's looking right at me, and for a second his face softens. For one wonderful and perfect moment I think that maybe he's going to forgive me, that maybe he's going to take me in his arms and tell me that it's all okay, that he forgives me, that we're going to be together, that we'll work it out.

But then his face gets hard again, and he shakes his head and looks away.

And then Dr. Ostrander is back, a cup of coffee in his hand, a serious look on his face.

"So," he says, "now that we've had a break, I'm going to

assume that you've both had sufficient time to get your anger under control."

And then, suddenly, it's like a switch flips inside me. It pisses me off that Dr. Ostrander's acting like just because *Isaac* freaked out and swore at him, that means *I'm* the one who has to get my anger under control. And that's when I feel my fire come back. I sit up straight. If Isaac's determined to bring me down, then I'm going to have to fight like hell to prove this thing isn't my fault, that it was just a bunch of bad circumstances and coincidences that led to everything going wrong.

"Yes," I say. "We're ready."

Isaac's head snaps up, and he looks at me. I guess because my tone is completely different than it was just a second ago. I wipe my eyes carefully with a tissue from my bag, making sure not to smudge my mascara.

"Now, where were we?" Dr. Ostrander asks.

"We were just about to talk," I say, "about how Isaac kissed Marina Ruiz."

Before

Kelsey

"So, you kissed him?" Rielle's asking. We're in her room later that night, drinking lemonade, sharing a bowl of popcorn mixed with M&M's, listening to music, and trying on her sister's clothes. Rielle's sister, Nadia, is away at Harvard, and so we regularly raid her closet. Nadia doesn't mind, as long as we wash the stuff and put it back when we're finished. Not that I've been over here much lately, raiding closets or doing anything else.

Like I said, me and Rielle have hardly talked. So when she called me earlier tonight and invited me over, I was shocked. I had a nagging feeling that maybe she had other plans that got canceled and was just calling me because she was bored. But I decided to give her the benefit of the doubt, because (a) I miss her a lot, and (b) I was dying to tell someone about what happened with me and Isaac.

"Well, *he* kissed *me*," I say, pulling out this really adorable off-the-shoulder ruffly top in a paisley print. It still has the price tag on it. "Do you think your sister would mind if I wore this?" I ask. "It's brand-new."

Rielle waves her hand. "She probably won't even know it's gone." She drops the slinky blue dress she's holding into a heap on the floor. "So, how was the kiss?" she asks.

"Perfect," I say. "Amazing." I'm pulling off my T-shirt and trying on the ruffly top.

"So then what?"

"What do you mean, 'then what'?" I yank the top down. I'm going to need a strapless bra with this one, for sure. I'm not the kind of girl who can get away with not wearing a bra. My boobs are a little too big. Plus I'm always paranoid that I'm going to have some kind of wardrobe malfunction and everyone will be staring at my nipples without me even knowing it.

"Then what happened after you kissed?"

"He drove me home."

"He drove you *home*?" Rielle frowns, and I feel a little bit of panic start to rise up in me. So far I haven't really let myself think too much about the kiss. Yes, I was dying to tell Rielle about it, but other than that, I've been working really hard not to get too worked up. I mean, the last thing I need is a boyfriend. Or even a crush.

"Yeah," I say. I shrug and throw the shirt onto the growing pile of stuff that I'm borrowing. "It's not like it's a big thing or anything."

"Okay," Rielle says, not sounding convinced. "Are you sure?"

"Yeah," I say, "I'm totally sure." Suddenly I want to change the subject, to stop talking about Isaac. "Hey," I say, "you want to go for pedicures? There's this new place in the mall I've been dying to try."

Rielle looks at me like she wants to say something else. But then she just shrugs. "Yeah," she says, "sure."

An hour later we're at the pedicure place, our feet in those little paper flip-flops and drying under the dryer.

"So are you upset?" Rielle asks. She turns the page of the magazine she's reading, an old *Us Weekly* that has the best and worst bikini bodies on the front.

"No," I say, looking down at my crimson toes. "I love this color. The only thing that sucks is that I'm not sure it's going to be warm enough to wear sandals and show them off." They really should figure out a way around that. I mean, you spend all this money to make your feet look cute, and then after summer there's no way to really show them off.

"No," she says, "I mean because that guy Isaac hasn't called you?"

"No." I shrug. "Why would I be upset about that?"

"Um, because you guys kissed?"

When I think about kissing him, my heart starts to beat fast. But then I see the way Rielle's looking at me. With a mixture of concern and worry. I know it's because she thinks that if I get involved with another guy, I might go crazy again, the way I did with Rex. And I'm about to open my mouth to tell her that I'm fine, but then I shut it. Because the truth is, I'm not sure if I'm fine.

I mean, how do I know for certain that if I get close to another guy, I'm not going to go crazy again? I don't. And so letting myself start to even think that anything could happen between me and Isaac is probably a really bad idea.

And besides, even if I *were* ready to get involved with someone, the last person it would be is Isaac Brandano. I mean, the guy's like a big red flag. A red flag with arms and legs and killer abs. In fact, they should call him Red Flag Guy.

"I'm not upset at all," I say to Rielle. "He's like Red Flag Guy. Fun to kiss, but now that that's been accomplished, I'm totally going to stay away from him."

She grins, showing off her professionally whitened smile. "God, Kels, I am sooo glad you just said that. Honestly, after what happened with Rex, I was really worried about you."

"Why? Were you afraid I was going to get all crazy again?"

"No," she says, "just that, I don't know, you might be scarred for life or something." She holds her hand out in front of her face and frowns down at her nails. "I knew I should have gotten a manicure, too."

"Scarred for life?"

"Yeah." She pulls her feet away from the dryer and wiggles her toes. Rielle has very cute feet. Perfect size six, which means that we can never share shoes. I'm an eight and a half, a nine if I'm being completely honest. "You know how you always hear about things like that? Like, how people had a bad relationship in high school, and now all their relationships are a big mess?"

"Who?" I ask, and frown. "Who have you heard about that happening to?"

"I don't know." She shrugs. "All those people on those shows about thirtysomethings, like *Sex and the City* or whatever. They're all, like, damaged."

"I think that's because they all have daddy issues," I say, "not because they had broken hearts in high school."

"Well, you have daddy issues too," she says, grinning. "We all do."

Ain't that the truth. Still. I'm not sure I buy into her whole theory. It seems crazy that a high school relationship could mess you up for life. But something about the conversation must strike a chord with me, because when my phone rings a few minutes later and it's Isaac, I don't know if I should answer it or not.

"It's him," I say, staring down at the caller ID. "He's calling me."

My heart is bouncing around happily in my chest. It almost doesn't seem real, his name flashing on the screen. I feel like I need to peer at it closely, to look at each letter, to make sure it's really him. Weird, right? Even weirder is that even after that whole semilecture from Rielle, I really, really want to talk to him.

"Are you going to answer it?" Rielle asks. And maybe it's the way Rielle's looking at me. Or maybe it's just because I want to prove to myself that I don't need Isaac Brandano. But before I know it, my hand is over the reject button. And then I decline the call and send it to voicemail.

Before

Isaac

I'm drunk. At least, I think I am. It's hard to tell. Probably because I'm so drunk. All I know is that this was the right choice. Definitely a good idea to come out here and have fun at the beach. I love the beach! There's water! And sand! Everyone thinks it's cold, but it's really not.

We have a fire. All my classmates are around the fire. I love the fire.

The only thing I don't love is Kelsey. She didn't answer when I called her earlier, and even though I'm drunk drunk drunk, it's bothering me. I want to call her again, but Marina will not leave me the fuck alone.

At first I kind of liked it. It was fun. I even danced with

her after I had my third beer. But now she's just annoying. She won't stay away from me. I think maybe my good-time drunk is starting to fade.

When I get drunk, there are always two phases. Happy Drunk Isaac comes first. This is when I'm the life of the party, dancing and having fun. I love everyone. Then Mean Drunk Isaac comes. Actually, I wouldn't call it mean, exactly. More like Ornery and Slightly Irritable Isaac.

"Don't you want to dance some more?" Marina asks. She might be even drunker than I am. But she's still very much in happy mode. She's sitting next to me on the sand, and she leans in close, slurring her words against my neck.

"No." All I want to do is call Kelsey. "I'll be right back. I have to make a phone call."

I walk a little ways down the beach and pull out my phone. I can't believe I'm calling a girl for the second time in one night. I never, ever do that. Usually I have a list of girls I call, and if one doesn't answer, I just move on to the next. Okay, that sounds horrible. It's not, like, *literally* a list. I just like to have options.

I dial Kelsey's number. It takes me two tries. I keep messing up, hitting Ken in my contacts list instead. I don't even know a Ken, hahaha.

Oh! It's ringing! Ring . . . ring . . . ring . . .

This time she answers!

"Hello?" She sounds hesitant.

"Well, hello there," I say, trying to sound suave.

"Are you drunk?" she asks immediately.

"Why would you ask that?" God, what is it with this girl? Every time I talk to her, she's always thinking the worst of me. I decide it's time to turn on the charm.

"Because it's eleven o'clock at night and you're calling me saying things like 'hello there.'"

"I tried to call you earlier," I point out. "But you didn't answer." I plop myself down in the sand and almost fall over. On the other end of the line, Kelsey's silent. "Did you say something?" I ask. "If you did, I missed it."

From down the beach, around the fire, I hear the sound of laughter.

"Where are you?" Kelsey asks.

"At the beach," I say. Then I remember something. Something very important. "Hey!" I say. "You were supposed to come here with me! Remember? We were both invited!" I realize I'm talking kind of loud. So I decide to lower the volume. "You were invited," I whisper. "You should come down here." I don't know how to get here. But maybe she has a GPS. Wait. She doesn't drive. "Maybe your parents can drop you off," I try.

"I can't believe you're calling me when you're drunk," she says. "I have to go."

"You have to *go*?"

"Yes."

"Why? What are you doing? Where were you before? I wanted to talk. It was important." Suddenly I feel really upset. I'm thinking about what happened with my dad earlier. And I want to tell Kelsey about it for some reason.

"I was at the mall with my friend," she says.

"And you didn't have your phone?"

"I had my phone," she says. Then she sighs. "Isaac, you're drunk. Do you have a way home?"

"Yes," I tell her. "There's a designated driver." I forget her name, though. Ray? No, that's a boy's name. Actually, it could be a girl's name too. But it's not Ray. Rochelle? Rachel? Raymond? Raymond is definitely a boy's name. I laugh.

"Good." She pauses. "I'll talk to you later, okay?" That's it. That's all she says. Not *"Call me tomorrow"* or *"Hey, that was really nice when we kissed"* or *"I'm going to come down and meet you at the beach so I can make sure that Marina girl doesn't steal you away from me."*

"I'll talk to you *later*?" I ask incredulously.

"Isaac," she says. "You. Are. Drunk."

"Yeah? And what do you have against drunk people? Ooof." I fall over into the sand. It gets in my mouth and I try to spit it out.

"Nothing," she says, "but I don't want to talk to you when you're drunk."

"I fell into the sand," I say.

"Goodbye, Isaac." The line goes dead.

Well. I guess that's that. I stare at the phone, kind of unable to believe it. How could she just hang up on me like that? Especially since I haven't been able to think about anything but her. Well, that's not exactly true. There was that whole thing with my dad. But still. The point is, I've been thinking about her, missing her, wanting to talk to her. And she was just . . . I forget what she said. At the *mall*. With her *friend*. Probably a *boy*friend.

"What are you doing down here?" Marina asks. She's somehow lost her shirt and is now wearing just a bikini top. All of a sudden I'm very warm. Probably because I've had so much to drink.

"I was making a phone call," I say, holding up my phone. "But now I'm done."

"Good." She leans into me. She smells very good. Like flowers mixed with baby powder and something else that only girls can smell like. A slight breeze blows her hair into my face, and she reaches up and pushes it back behind her ear.

"Hi," she says, smiling at me. And the next thing I know, she's kissing me. I pull back.

"What's wrong?" she breathes into my ear. "Don't you want to kiss me?"

I think about it. I don't want to kiss Marina. I want to kiss Kelsey. Don't I? My head is all cloudy now. Kelsey doesn't want to kiss me. Kelsey is trying to blow me off. She's not even answering her phone when she's out, she's . . . she's rejecting me. I can't even believe it. I never get rejected.

My drunk brain cannot wrap my mind around this. Or, I mean, my brain can't wrap its . . . Fuck, I don't know. All I know is that Marina is here and I'm drunk and I want more beer and she wants to kiss me.

But before I can figure out if I want to kiss her, or answer her, she's moving her lips back toward mine. And then she's kissing me. And there's nothing to do but kiss her back.

Before

Kelsey

I can't sleep. I'm just lying here in bed thinking about Isaac. I was hoping he'd call me back. I hate the idea of him being at the beach with Marina. I hate the idea that he called to invite me, and that I didn't answer just because of some stupid thing that happened at my old school with Rex. I hate that I'm awake thinking about it, that the exact thing I'd wanted to avoid— obsessing over Isaac—is happening.

At around two in the morning I give up and turn my light on, deciding to try to read. But I can't find any books I'm interested in. The crazy thing about it is that my to-be-read pile is so high it's about to fall over. But there's nothing I want to read. The thing about me and books is that whichever one

I'm reading always reminds me of whatever's happening in my life during that time.

And since I like to reread really good books, I'm afraid to start reading something new. What if it's a really good book that I want to read again sometime? And I can't because it will always remind me of the night I spent lying awake thinking about Isaac. That's what happened with this book by Susan Mallery that I was reading when that whole thing happened with Rex.

The book was so good, and it had the best romance ever. But I couldn't finish it. It's still sitting there on my shelf. I can't read it. It'll bring up too many memories.

At around five the sun starts to peek up over the horizon. I wish I was the kind of girl who was always going out for runs. Runs are supposedly really good for your mental state. The girls in the books I'm reading are always going out for runs really late at night or early in the morning to work out all their sexual frustration or get some guy off their minds. It always works, and they get superfit in the process, causing whatever guy they were all brokenhearted about to want them back. Of course, by then they've moved on to someone better.

I've always hated running. Too boring. And hard. I've tried listening to music, but even then it sucks. You can't even turn the music up too loud, because if you do, you won't be able to hear, and then you might get accosted by some kind of crazy attacker.

Still. As long as I'm awake and it's technically morning, I might as well get up and do something. Maybe some homework.

I throw on a pair of yoga pants and a hoodie, then tiptoe downstairs. I brew a pot of extrastrong coffee, then grab my bag and set it down on the table. I pull out my notebook and start to make a checklist of all the work I have to do. I like to have checklists. That way, I can make a check next to each thing as I do it. It's very satisfying.

I'm done with my list and just deciding that I should probably start with my math, since it won't take too long, and that way I can earn a check right off the bat, when I hear the sound of footsteps on the stairs. Someone's coming down, and I can tell right away that it's my dad. My mom's usually not awake this early, but my dad sometimes is. He'll get up early so that he can work in his office on some of his web design projects.

"Good morning," he says to me, nodding as he walks into the kitchen. He looks at all the books spread out in front of me. "Doing some work?"

"Yes."

He nods. He just stands there, and I just sit there, neither of us knowing what to say. Awwwk-ward.

"How's your new club going?" he asks finally.

"Fine," I say. I've been deliberately vague about Face It Down, telling my parents only that I'm working on something with the senator's son. I just don't want them getting all involved in it, asking me all kinds of questions, putting me on the spot. Especially because it might not work out.

"So what's going to happen?" my dad asks. "What's the objective?"

the thing about the truth

"Um," I say, "well, we're going to be inviting some students from Concordia Prep to get together and do some community building."

He nods, then crosses the kitchen and pulls a mug down from the cabinet. He walks over to the coffee pot and then pauses. "Do you mind if I have some coffee?" he asks.

"No," I say, "there's a whole pot."

He pours himself a full cup, adds milk and sugar, and then sits down at the kitchen table across from me. "And how has it been, working with Isaac Brandano?"

I think about it, trying to keep the fact that we kissed and that I've been up all night out of my mind. "It's been okay," I say. "At first I thought that maybe he wasn't going to take anything seriously, but it seems like he's really on board."

"That's great." My dad takes a sip of coffee. "This is good," he says.

"Thanks."

There's another awkward silence. "So, I heard that you hung out with Rielle last night," he says. "That's nice."

"Yup." I nod.

"Well," my dad says, standing up, "I guess I should get to work."

"Yeah, I should get back to work too," I say, for some reason not wanting him to think he's the one who's cutting our conversation short.

But once he's gone to his office and the kitchen is quiet, I can't concentrate. I decide to pack it up and head to the university library. It's the perfect place to study—it's within walking distance, it's open twenty-four hours, and they never ID. They have comfy chairs, and the place is always deserted on Saturday mornings.

I used to go all the time when I was at Concordia Prep. It was like my secret little place—I never told anyone about it, even Rielle. I didn't want any distractions, and I didn't want anyone else going there. I was competitive like that. I used to think that everyone else was going to keep me from getting what I wanted. Kind of ironic that the one person who kept me from getting what I wanted was myself.

I pack a bag with a few Rice Krispies Treats, my schoolbooks, my laptop, and some extra pens. I grab a thermos out of the cupboard and fill it with coffee, adding extra sugar, figuring if I keep a steady stream of caffeine pumping through my veins, it'll combat the inevitable sugar crash.

It's a really nice day out already, and the fresh air and the walk to the library help lift my mood. Once I'm there, I give the girl working the front desk a friendly smile. I always smile at the student workers to avoid any kind of suspicion. I mean, why would I be so smiley if I was sneaking in?

I head to my favorite table, all the way in the back of the second floor, in front of the huge picture windows that look out over Lake Swanscott. It's peaceful and picturesque, and my favorite place to study.

But when I get to the table, someone's already sitting there. A girl.

"Hey," she says, looking at me like she knows me. It takes me a second to place her. That happens to me sometimes when people show up places where they shouldn't be.

But then I figure it out. It's Chloe. That girl from the bathroom at school. The one who kept asking me about my broken heart.

"Hi," I say. "What are you doing here?"

"What are you doing here?"

"I come here to study." I sit down across from her. She doesn't have any books or anything, so I'm assuming that maybe she pulled an all-nighter and now she's packed up her stuff and is ready to leave. In which case, I'm happy to have my table back.

"You came here to study?" she asks. "At six o'clock on a Saturday morning?"

"Yeah. Didn't you?"

"Didn't I what?"

"Come here to study."

"No." She shrugs. "I was at a party near here last night." And that's when I notice that she's definitely not dressed for a study session. She's wearing a short black skirt and a tight black shirt, her hair looks kind of wild, and her eyeliner is all smudged.

"So if you were at a party," I ask, "then why are you at the library?"

"Because," she says, "this is where I wait."

She's eyeing my coffee, and so I pull the top off the thermos, pour some into the cup that doubles as the top, and slide it across the table toward her. She accepts it and drains it in a few long swallows. I refill the cup. But that's all she's getting. I mean, I haven't slept all night. I need the caffeine.

"This is where you wait for what?" I ask her. Whatever it is, I hope it's not going to take too long. She's definitely cutting into my studying time. Although, when I think about it, she's also providing a distraction from thinking about Isaac. Not that I'm having to work really hard not to think about him, la la la.

She bites her lip, and I can tell she doesn't want to tell me.

"Is it"—I lean over the table and lower my voice to a whisper—"your drug dealer?" It's supposed to be a joke, but I say it like I'm totally serious in an effort to get her to smile. It works.

"No," she says, "it's not my drug dealer." She thinks for a second. "Although, in a way, I guess it is."

She pulls her bag up onto the table and takes out a tiny little mirror. "Oh my God," she says, studying her reflection. "I look horrible."

"No, you don't," I say. It's kind of true. She looks a little disheveled, yeah, and like she's been out partying all night, but she also looks kind of sexy. Kind of . . . dangerous. If I was a guy, I'd be all over it.

"Yes, I do." She sighs, then wipes some stray eyeliner from under her eye. She puts the mirror back in her bag, then leans back in her chair and crosses her arms over her chest, her blue eyes boring into mine. She tilts her head to the side like she's sizing me up, giving me some kind of test, trying to see if I'm worthy of what she's about to tell me.

"Did you mean what you said before?" she asks.

"About what?"

"You know, the broken heart stuff."

I nod. I thought we already went over this.

"What does that mean, exactly?"

"I told you," I say. "It means—"

She holds up her hand, silencing me. "Please," she says. "That's so not the whole story, and you know it. You just didn't want to get into it because that Isaac kid was there."

"Whatever." I shrug, deciding not to deny it but not to admit it either. I mean, I don't owe this girl anything.

"So what happened?" she asks. "I know it's something scandalous."

"What happened with your broken heart?" I counter. "I know it's something scandalous." I try to mimic her tone of voice.

"You first," she says, "and then I'll tell you mine."

It's the oldest trick in the book, obviously. She wants to know my secrets and gossip while reserving the right to keep hers quiet. But I think about telling her anyway. No one knows exactly what went on with me and Rex except for Rielle. And my parents. And some choice administrators and teachers at school. Even the students at Concordia Prep who think they know don't *really* know for sure. They just speculate, start rumors, etc. Rex knows. At least, I'm pretty sure he does. I haven't talked to him since it happened.

I wonder if keeping it a secret is what's giving it so much power. I mean, what happened at my old school has been the reason everything in my life is going the way it is. The reason I'm starting Face It Down. The reason things with my parents are so weird. The reason things are different with Rielle. The reason I didn't answer my phone last night when Isaac called, which probably ended up forcing him into Marina's arms. Not that that last one is a big deal. Isaac and I obviously weren't going to be anything. We're way too different. But still. Even if it was just going to be a fling, what happened with me and Rex is what's keeping that from happening.

"Fine," Chloe says, getting up from the table and slinging her bag over her shoulder. "You don't have to tell me. You don't even know me. I get it." She's acting like she's fine with it, but her tone says she thinks I'm being a big baby. And I kind of agree with her. I mean, the stuff with Rex *happened*. Maybe the first step to getting over it is really owning it.

"Fine," I say. "I used to go to Concordia Prep."

"I hate that school," she says.

"You do?"

"Yes. Bunch of stuck-up preps." She reaches into her bag and pulls out a cigarette, then plops back down in the seat across from me.

"Are you allowed to smoke that in here?" I ask. It's rhetorical, of course. Obviously, you're not allowed to smoke in a library.

"It's an electric," she says. "You know, it just blows water vapor? They can't ban you from using them anywhere. It's, like, the law."

"Oh." I'm not sure if this is true, but whatever.

"Anyway," she says, "so you used to go to that superpreppy school. Is that why you're starting Face It Down? You want us all to realize that those jerks aren't as jerky as we think they are?"

"Sort of. I mean, I am starting Face It Down because I used to go there. But also because I need to figure something out that's going to look really good on my applications." I take a deep breath. And then I say it out loud. "I got kicked out of Concordia Prep."

She nods. "Makes sense."

"It does?"

"Yeah," she says. She takes a drag of her cigarette and then blows water vapor into the air. At least, I hope it's water vapor. The last thing I need is to go home with my clothes smelling like smoke. My dad would definitely not be thrilled.

"You could tell I got kicked out?"

"Well, obviously *something* scandalous happened. You came in to school all, like, I don't know . . . determined to make your mark. And I could tell you weren't interested in making friends."

I'm not sure if it's an insult or not, and so I can't figure out if I should be offended. "Anyway," I say, "don't you want to know *why* I got kicked out?"

"Duh." She rolls her eyes and blows more water vapor toward the ceiling.

"I smashed my ex-boyfriend's car."

She sits up straight, her eyes getting wide. "No fucking way," she says. "Like, with a bat?"

"A crowbar," I say. "And don't get all excited, it wasn't his real car." She looks disappointed, and for some reason, I don't want her to be disappointed. I want her to be impressed with my scandalousness. So I rush on. "It was a car that he'd been working on, this electric hybrid car he was building."

"You got kicked out of school for smashing his model car?" She shakes her head. "That's kind of lame. I mean, couldn't he just buy another one?"

"It wasn't a model car," I say. "It was full-sized, and it was going to be entered into this national science competition. And there were a bunch of other people working on it too. They'd been written up in the *Boston Globe* for it and everything. If they finished, and it was successful, they were going to be the first group of high school students to do anything like it."

"So why'd you smash it?"

I shrug. "I got mad. We'd been going out for about five months, and I loved him. I found out he was cheating on me with this totally skanky girl named Gwyneth. And I just . . . I don't know. I guess I just snapped."

I remember now, how I felt in that moment. How dark the school was. How empty the halls were. How I'd looked at that car, the car that Rex was so proud of. He was always bringing it up in conversation, the same way he'd bring up his football stats or how many points he'd scored in a basketball game. Everyone at Concordia Prep was athletic, and all the guys were expected to play sports, so triumphs on the athletic field weren't all that special or impressive—everyone had them.

But when it came to academics, everyone tried to outdo each other. And this car thing was a major score. Rex got a ton of attention for being the head of the team that was putting it together. Not like he needed any more attention. Rex was one of the most popular guys at Concordia Prep. And I was one of the most popular girls.

The day I found out Rex was cheating on me, I'd gone into his locker to grab his cell phone. I needed to call home to let my mom know I was staying after for a math review, and since Rex and I had been texting each other all day, my phone was dead. Concordia Prep had a very lax policy when it came to things like cell phones. They figured that treating us like adults would make us act like adults (haha).

Anyway, since I knew Rex left his phone in his locker while he was at football practice, I figured I'd use his. When I pulled the phone out, it was beeping with a text.

"I had an amazing time last night, xx, G."

I knew who it was from immediately. Gwyneth Adelman. I'd suspected that they'd been messing around, since Gwyneth was constantly shooting daggers at me with her eyes, and I'd caught Rex not-so-discreetly ogling her ass on game days, when she wore her cheerleading uniform to school.

I stood there for a full minute or two, just staring down at the text. Rex had tried to be smart about it, and he'd saved Gwyneth's number under the name Adam. He didn't have any friends named Adam. But I guess he figured if I ever saw it, he could just make something up.

I felt like I was in a dream. Everything felt blurry around the edges, including my emotions. I could tell I was upset, but I couldn't quite access it. I put the phone back into Rex's locker and shut the door. I stood there for another moment. And then I walked down to the technology lab.

When I got there, like I said, it was dark, and it felt wrong to be in there, in the dark, with no one around. But then I flipped the light switch, and the lab flooded with brightness, and there it was. The car. Rex and I used to joke that he loved that car more than anything, except for me. But now, since it had become apparent that he was cheating on me, it seemed like the car was the thing he loved the most. And it was the only way I knew how to hurt him.

There was a wooden dowel sitting against the wall, and I picked it up and gave the car a few whacks. At first nothing happened. Yeah, maybe there was a little bit of a dent, or a few scratches in the paint, but really, it was just bodywork. If I had left then, if I'd stopped, it could have been fixed easily enough.

And for a second I did think about stopping. But then I spotted something else. A crowbar. Hanging from a hook on the wall over a workbench. And I know it sounds stupid, but suddenly I remembered that Carrie Underwood song "Before He Cheats," and I remembered watching the video for that song and watching Carrie wreck her cheating boyfriend's car, and thinking I'd never do something like that, no matter how much I'd gotten hurt.

I remembered thinking about how you could get in a lot of trouble for doing shit like that. I'd spent my whole life staying out of trouble, not doing anything that would cause me to shatter the perfect image I'd worked so hard to create. But in that moment, standing there in the lab by myself, wrecking Rex's car seemed like a really good idea. The kind of thing that just had to be done.

The crowbar felt light in my hand. At first I thought maybe it wasn't a real crowbar, that it was some kind of special crowbar they used for high school students because they couldn't trust us with the real thing. But now I think I was in such a daze of anger that I just didn't realize how heavy it was.

When I brought the crowbar down on the car the first time, it shattered one of the windows right away. There was no warning, no time to wrap my head around what I was doing. No crack in the window. No shaking of glass. Just complete shattering. It was scary. But it was also freeing. I could feel my anger pouring out of my body as I destroyed that car. The smashing, the grinding, the breaking. Every sound, every pound, every hit made me feel better. While I was doing it, I wasn't thinking about anything. It was purely physical.

When I was finished, and the car was in pieces, I dropped

the crowbar and looked at the mess I'd made. Then I went home.

When I got there, I plugged my phone in and then calmly texted Rex and told him what I'd done. I didn't want to get away with it. I wanted him to know that I'd caught him, and that I'd made sure there would be some kind of punishment for what he'd done.

I knew there would be repercussions for wrecking the car, although I definitely didn't think that I would get kicked out of school. I thought maybe I'd get suspended and have to pay for the car or help put it back together. But the principal was pissed. And they didn't even give me a chance to plead my case. The next day I was gone. I could have fought it, I guess, but what would have been the point? I'd told Rex what I'd done; he had the text and the proof.

"Wow," Chloe says. She's looking at me with a mixture of awe and admiration. "That takes balls. I wish I had the balls to do something like that."

"Trust me," I say, "having balls is overrated."

She shrugs. "Yeah, well, it's better than what I've been doing."

"So, what's your story?" I ask. "Who broke your heart?" I take a sip of coffee from the thermos.

"This guy," she says, "Dave Cash?"

She says his name like I should have heard of him, but I haven't, and so I shrug.

"He graduated last year," she says. "He was really popular,

all the girls wanted him, blah, blah, blah. But he's really nice, you know? The kind of kid who's nice to everyone, no matter who they are."

"And you're in love with him?"

She nods miserably. "He's my best friend. He has been since, like, the eighth grade. Which is how long I've been in love with him."

"Does he know?"

She shakes her head emphatically, her blond curls bouncing from side to side. "No! I would never tell him. Which is why *this* always happens." She looks around the library, then leans back in her chair with a sigh.

"Why what always happens?"

"Why I always end up here."

"You always end up in the university library because you won't tell Dave Cash you're in love with him?" I knew this girl had a screw loose.

"Yes," she says. "See, this is how it works: Dave invites me to come and hang out with him at school. We go out to a frat party or something, and while we're there, he picks up some *girl*"—she wrinkles her nose up in distaste—"to bring home with him. So then I wait at the library for him to finish with her. And then he calls me and we go out to breakfast."

My mouth drops. "You just wait for him at the library? All night? While he's off hooking up with another girl?"

She nods.

"And he just *lets you*?" I ask. Seriously, what is wrong with boys these days? I thought the human race was supposed to be evolving.

"No," she says, looking horrified. "Dave would never agree to that. I just make him think I'm going home with some guy."

I stop with my thermos halfway to my lips. "Wait," I say. "You tell him that you're going home with a guy?"

"Of course," she says, sounding like she can't believe how clueless I am. "It's all part of the facade. It would be super-awkward if he knew it bothered me that he was bringing girls home."

"So it's better that he thinks you pick up random guys at parties?"

She nods. "Yeah," she says, "otherwise I'm the lame girl who's secretly pining away for him, all the while pretending to be okay with just a friendship."

"Ooo-kay." I know I should probably say something to deter her from doing this, but she seems like the kind of girl who has her mind made up. Plus who am I to say that her plan is bad? My plan got me kicked out of school.

"Guys are such dicks," she says. "Complete assholes."

She's talking kind of loud, and so I glance around to make sure no one's heard. I kind of like the fact that she's swearing and putting it all out there. Not to mention that it felt good to finally tell someone what happened with me and Rex, someone who seems like they understand.

Rielle tried, but she never really got it. She couldn't under-stand why I'd be so angry that I would do something like wreck a car. She didn't think Rex was worth it. She didn't think anyone was worth it. Rielle's always been the type to go through guys like they're tissues, throwing them away like she can just pick up another one whenever she wants.

"Total fuckups," I say, agreeing with Chloe.

"It's like, why can't they just be *normal*?" she says. "And why do they only like the skanky girls? Like Marina Ruiz. She's not even that pretty."

Of course, this is a lie and we both know it. Marina's gorgeous. She looks like J. Lo. But saying she's not that pretty is one of those things girls tell each other to make themselves feel better.

"Definitely not that pretty," I say, taking another sip of coffee. I try to think of something specific I can say about Marina's looks. But I can't come up with one bad thing. Her boobs are too big, maybe?

"It's like, last night," Chloe says, "she was totally making out with that new kid. You know, the senator's son? Isaac?"

I spit my coffee all over the table. A couple of kids in the study carrels turn around and give us dirty looks.

"Isaac was making out with Marina?" I whisper. I pull a napkin out of my bag and start wiping up the coffee.

"Yeah," she says, "at the beach."

I feel my heart squeeze. "I thought you were here last night," I say, hoping that maybe she's made a mistake.

"I was at the beach first. College parties don't start until, like, after eleven, so I stopped at the bonfire for a little while."

161

She sighs. "Total waste of time, though. I'm so over everyone at our school." She sighs again and then looks at her watch. "I guess I'll start heading back to Dave's dorm. He should be finished by now." She peers closely at my face. "Are you okay?"

"Yeah," I say, "I'm fine."

She looks at me skeptically, and then I see a wave of understanding come over her. She opens her mouth, like maybe she's going to ask me if I like Isaac. But she must realize that I don't want to talk about it, because instead she grabs a pen and jots her phone number down on my folder. "Call me later," she says. "You know, if you want to hang out or something."

She squeezes my shoulder as she goes by, and I just sit there, looking out the window for a few minutes after she's gone. And then I shake my head and tell myself to forget about him. I have a very bad track record when it comes to love. There's no reason to think that's going to stop now.

Before

Isaac

Head. Hurts. There's light coming in through my bedroom windows, and it's making it feel like a jackhammer is pounding against the inside of my forehead. Fuck, fuck, fuck. That's the way it works with me, though—I can get completely drunk and be fine the next day, and then other times I'll have a few drinks and wake up feeling like someone's taking a sledgehammer to my skull.

I sit up in bed and take a sip of water from the bottle on my nightstand. I can hear the sounds of pots and pans in the kitchen. My dad. Probably making eggs or some shit. On weekends my dad likes to have the house to himself, meaning no housekeepers or cooks, even if that means he has to make his own breakfast.

He's the last person I want to see, so even though I feel groggy and my head's still pounding, I pull on a pair of track pants and a sweatshirt and head out to my car. I have nowhere to go, so I just pull out of the driveway and start to drive.

I turn on the radio and start to think about last night. Making out with Marina. That was a huge, huge mistake. One, because she's kind of crazy. (I'm not sure, because it's a little fuzzy, but I could have sworn that at around midnight she started naming our children. Like, the children we would have someday. From what I remember, she was saying that she wanted to name the girl Harmony and the boy G-Money. That can't be right, can it? Maybe it was Giovanni? Either way, those names are not going to cut it. Not that we're really going to have kids. But come on. Who the fuck does that? Starts naming your children after one kiss? Okay, so it was more than one kiss. It was a few kisses. But still.)

Anyway, obvious mental issues aside, the other reason it was a mistake to make out with Marina is because I like Kelsey. A lot. I know it sounds weird, but kissing Marina just cemented it further in my mind. Kelsey is the one I want to hang out with, to be with. I can't stop thinking about her. And I know that I have to tell her that I kissed Marina. And I know she's going to be pissed.

I think about calling her, but she didn't seem too excited to talk to me on the phone last night. Plus she'll probably just hang up once she hears what I have to say. So before I know it, I'm driving over to her house. Which is crazy. That's, like,

movie shit or something, driving over to a girl's house to confess your love. Not that I'm going to be confessing my love.
Maybe just my like.

When I pull into her driveway, there are two cars parked
there already, a gray sedan and a minivan. I'm assuming they
belong to her mom and dad, since Kelsey doesn't drive. There's
no way to tell if she's home, so I get out of the car and head up
to the porch.

I ring the doorbell.

After a few seconds a man opens the door. He's tall and
kind of grumpy-looking, and when he sees me, he frowns.

"Hello, sir," I say, deciding to play the politeness card
because parents love that shit. "I'm Isaac Brandano." I empha-
size the Brandano part because parents love that shit too. "Is
Kelsey home?"

Usually, when parents meet me, they love me right off the
bat. Partly because I can be very charming when I want to be,
and partly because they know my dad. They get totally caught
up in thinking that their daughter might marry a politician's
son, and that maybe *I'll* become a politician and that maybe I'll
run for president or something, and that maybe their daughter will be first lady. Sometimes I want to let them know that
the reality of the whole thing is very different from whatever
crazy fantasy they've come up with, and that they should ask
my grandparents on my mom's side what they think about
marrying a politician. But I don't. Because then they wouldn't
be too happy to see me.

Anyway, I don't have to worry about that with this dude. He's looking at me like I'm a maggot or bug that needs to be squashed.

"Yeah?" he asks, like he didn't hear what I just said.

I decide to start over. "Hello, sir," I say, pasting on my best smile. "Is Kelsey home?" This time I decide to leave out my name since maybe he's on the other side of the political divide.

"No," he says, "she's not. Why?"

"I'm her friend," I say. "I was just coming over to, ah"— probably shouldn't say I'm here to confess that I kissed someone else after I kissed his daughter—"talk about the school group we're starting, Face It Down." He's still giving me that look, so I quickly add, "It promotes cultural and community solidarity." And then, for good measure, "And abstinence." Just in case he thinks I want to get into Kelsey's pants.

"Kelsey's not here," he says again.

"Oh. Okay." Why doesn't he tell me where she is? And where could she be on a Saturday morning, anyway? He's probably lying. This dude is very shady. I glance behind him, half expecting to see Kelsey standing there. But she's not. Just some pictures of her on the wall. One of her at a picnic or something, with her mom and dad, which is actually very cute.

"Anything else?" The guy's looking at me now, his arms crossed over his chest like he's daring me to ask him another question.

"No, sir," I say. "Um, it was nice meeting you."

He shuts the door without saying goodbye. Wow. I get back

in my car, then drive around the corner and pull out my phone. I dial Kelsey's number. She sends the call to voicemail. I can tell because it only rings, like, half a ring. I try again. Same thing. One more time, I think, because third time's the charm.

She picks up.

"Yes?" Wow. She sounds very . . . cold. It kind of makes me nervous.

"Hi," I say brightly. "What's up? What are you doing?"

"Nothing."

"Where are you?"

"Home."

"Liar."

She snorts. "You should talk."

"What's that supposed to mean?"

"How do you know I'm not home?"

"Because I went to your house."

"You didn't!"

"I did."

"What did you do there?"

I roll my eyes. Through the windshield, I see a guy wearing pink slippers and what appears to be a blond wig crossing the street to get his mail. "Did you know that one of your neighbors is a cross-dresser?"

"What?" she screeches.

"No, I mean, I'm not judging or anything, it's just funny."

She pauses. "Is she wearing pink slippers?"

"Yes, and she has a gray beard."

"That's not a cross-dresser. That's our neighbor Mrs. Sullivan."

I squint at her. I guess she does have kind of a feminine walk. "Huh," I say, "she really should get that mustache taken care of."

"Goodbye," Kelsey says.

"How come every single time I talk to you, you're trying to hang up on me?"

"Because I don't have anything to say to you."

"That's not what it seemed like yesterday afternoon," I say, grinning. "Not that you had a lot to say, but you weren't complaining about kissing me."

"Yeah," she says, "well, it seems like you have a thing for kissing unsuspecting girls."

"You weren't unsuspecting," I say. "And what's that supposed to mean?"

She doesn't say anything. And I know she knows. About last night. About Marina. Fuck. I've blown my chance with her before it's even started.

"Listen," I say, "I need to talk to you."

"No."

"Then hang up," I say, calling her bluff. But she doesn't. "Can you meet me?" I ask. "At the mall or something?"

"The *mall*?"

"Yes."

"You want to have a big talk at the mall?"

"Why not? I'll even buy you something."

"Like what?"

"A coffee? Some fries? That chicken teriyaki they have at the Japanese place?"

"That stuff is food poisoning waiting to happen," she says.

"Please?" I ask. She doesn't say anything. "Just for ten minutes," I say. "And then if you want to leave, you can leave."

She sighs. "Be there in fifteen." And then the line goes dead.

Before

Kelsey

This is a really stupid idea. Meeting Isaac at the mall? Why, why, why am I doing it? What's that definition of insanity that people always say? "Doing the same thing over and over again, hoping to get different results?"

The mall's about a fifteen-minute walk from the library, but there was no way I was going to ask Isaac to pick me up. I don't need any favors from him, thank you very much. I call Rielle on the walk over, hoping maybe she'll somehow talk me out of going to meet him.

"Rielle," I say, "I am about to do something really stupid."

"Really?" She sounds interested. "Like what?"

"I'm going to meet Isaac at the mall."

"You're not!"

"I am," I say.

"Why?"

"Well," I say, "last night he—"

"Hold on." She covers the phone and I hear her talking to someone in the background. "Listen," she says when she comes back, "I can't talk right now. I'm at my grandma's, and my parents are bothering me about being on my phone."

"Okay," I say, "but are you going to be around later? Maybe we could go to dinner or something. I could tell you all about my drama."

"I wish I could," she says, "but we're going to be here all weekend."

Rielle's grandma lives in New Hampshire, and she's the one who controls the purse strings in Rielle's family. Every so often Rielle and her parents have to troop up there and stay for a weekend to keep her happy.

"Call me later, though, okay?" She lowers her voice. "I gotta go, Gran needs me to help her open her arthritis medicine."

I laugh. "Okay," I say, "I'll talk to you later."

I hang up. I think about maybe calling Chloe, but we're not the kind of friends who can just call each other up out of the blue, especially not right after we just left each other. I look down at my phone, wondering if there's anyone else I can call who might talk me out of this. But there isn't. And besides, I'm not sure if I want to be talked out of it. So I just keep walking.

• • •

Isaac's sitting at a table in the food court, and in front of him are five or six different drinks.

"I didn't know what you like," he says, "so I got you milk shakes, chocolate and vanilla—because, really, who likes strawberry?—an orange juice, a soda, an iced tea, and a lemonade."

"Hmm," I say, sitting down across from him. "Trying to be cute, huh?"

"Cute?" he says, putting an innocent look on his face. "Who's trying to be cute?"

The thing is, trying or not, it *is* cute. Very cute. I mean, who does that? Orders six different drinks because he doesn't know what I'd like? Adorable. I pick up the lemonade and take a sip.

He looks hot, too. Not the way he does at school, in his khaki pants and button-down shirts and expensive-looking sweaters. Now he's wearing a rumpled-looking sweatshirt, and his hair is all messy, and he has on dirty, comfortable-looking sneakers and a pair of navy track pants.

Then I remind myself that I should not be swayed by his rumpled cuteness, because his rumpledness is most likely caused by the fact that he's been out all night hooking up with Marina and getting into various other kinds of debauchery.

I put the lemonade back down on the table. "I'm not thirsty," I say.

He shrugs and reaches for one of the milk shakes.

"You wanted to talk," I say. "So talk."

"What'd you do last night?" he asks conversationally.

"The better question," I say, "is what did *you* do last night?" Suddenly I'm superaware of the fact that I'm looking just as rumpled as he is. At first I wish I'd gone home to change. At least then I'd have the upper hand in the appearance department. But then I realize that the fact that I look so rumpled could mean that maybe I've been out partying too. He doesn't know.

But before I can come up with some great story about how I was at a fabulous college party with tons of hot, eligible college men, he decides to get serious and answer my question. He leans back in his chair, puts the milk shake down, and says, "I was at the beach, like I told you."

"And?"

"And I called you because I really wanted to see you. But then . . . well, you seemed like you wanted nothing to do with me. And I'd had a really bad night, something to do with my dad, and I just . . . I started drinking. And I ended up kissing Marina." I start to open my mouth to yell at him, but he goes on. "And it's not an excuse, I know that. But I want you to know that it won't happen again. I don't want to kiss anyone else but you."

He's looking at me really intensely then, and I feel my heart melt just a tiny little bit. Because at least he's being honest.

But I still want to yell at him. I mean, just because he's telling me the truth doesn't mean he's not a shit. The only reason he's probably even telling me what happened is because he knows that I already know.

So I open my mouth to give him a little bit of shit. But before I can, I hear something coming from the other side of the food court. A laugh. A laugh that I know really, really well.

A laugh that belongs to Rielle.

Before

Isaac

I really thought that Kelsey was going to go batshit crazy on me. I realized after I'd bought all those fucking drinks that it was going to make it really easy for her to throw a bunch of liquid at me. For a second I thought about maybe getting rid of at least a few of them since I wasn't in the mood to get wet. But it was too late; she was there. And besides, if she *had* thrown a drink at me, I would have deserved it.

But then, right before she's about to freak out on me, her whole face changes. She's staring at something over my shoulder, and I turn around to see what she's looking at. It's a bunch of girls. A bunch of stuck-up girls. I know it sounds fucked up, but I can tell just by looking at them.

"You know those girls?" I ask. I'm trying to sound non-chalant and uninterested, because if there's one thing I've learned about girls, it's that you need to stay out of their drama. If you don't, you'll end up regretting it. No one can understand teen girl drama. One minute they love each other, the next minute they hate each other. You just need to not get involved, and agree with whatever they're saying. (But not *too* much, just in case they're saying something horrible and then they end up making up with whoever it is they're saying horrible things about.)

"Yes," she says. Then she stands up and starts to walk out of the food court and toward the mall's main entrance.

I chase after her, taking the lemonade with me. "Where are you going?" I ask.

"Home," she says. She's almost running now, and the mall is kind of crowded, so I'm pushing through people in an effort to keep up with her.

"Home?" I say. "But we haven't talked."

She's still walking. I follow her all the way out to the parking lot. I don't say anything. She keeps walking and walking, weaving through the rows of cars.

"How did you get here, anyway?" I ask. "Since you don't drive?"

She doesn't say anything. There's an island in the middle of the parking lot with a tree on it. She kicks the curb.

"Wow," I say, "anger issues?"

She whirls around and looks at me. "Isaac," she says, "you have no idea."

I nod. "I can respect that." She starts pacing up and down the parking lot, through a bunch of empty spaces, making sure her feet stay between the yellow lines. I sit down on the curb and watch her, waiting.

"That," she says, "was my best friend in there. Or, at least, she *was* my best friend. And she lied to me about where she was." She raises her eyebrows and looks right at me. "I hate being lied to," she says. "I hate, hate, *hate* it."

I nod. "That makes sense."

"I lied to you," she says, "when I told you I stopped going to private school because my parents couldn't afford it. The truth is, I got kicked out. Just like you."

"Wow." I'm kind of shocked. I never would have guessed. She seems so in control and, like . . . I don't know, into rules.

"Are you mad?" she wants to know. "Because I lied?"

I think about it. "No," I say honestly, "I'm not."

"Why not?"

"Because I'm sure you had your reasons," I say.

She nods. "I did," she says. "I was embarrassed." She's still pacing. "But I'm sick of all the lying. No more lying. I'm not doing it anymore."

"Good idea," I say.

"So why did she do it?" she asks. "Why did Rielle lie to me?"

"I don't know," I say. "What kind of person is she?"

"She's . . ." She sighs. "I'm not sure. I mean, I thought I did, but . . ." She sits down next to me, and I hand her the lemonade that I'm holding. She takes a sip.

"I didn't lie to you," I point out, just in case she's forgotten and is getting any ideas about throwing her drink at me.

"Not technically," she says, "but you sort of did."

"How?"

"You kissed me. And then you kissed someone else."

"So?"

"So a kiss is like a promise."

"It is?" I move a little closer to her now. "What kind of promise?"

"A promise that you won't kiss anyone else." She looks away then, thinking about it. "At least for that same day."

"What about if the person you really wanted to kiss wouldn't come and meet you?"

"It doesn't matter," she says, shaking her head. "You still shouldn't kiss someone else on the same day you kissed the first person."

"What if I didn't know it was a promise?" I say. I inch even closer to her, so that our legs are touching. "And what if I promise that this time, I won't kiss anyone else?"

"For how long?" she asks.

I tilt my head and look at her. I remember what she said about how she really hates when people lie to her. But what I'm about to say won't be a lie. I really, really mean it. So I say, "As long as you want me to."

And then I kiss her again.

The Aftermath

Isaac

"Kissing Marina Ruiz has nothing to do with it," I say, because this is such bullshit. Kelsey's the one who lied to me, *she's* the one who fucked everything up, and for her to bring up Marina Ruiz is insane. It's old news. And if Kelsey didn't think—no, if she didn't *know*—that this whole thing was her fault, she wouldn't have even brought it up.

Dr. Ostrander is looking down at the paper in front of him. I wonder if it's the police report. "It says here that Marina fainted and was also taken away. It says that some girls from Concordia Prep assaulted her."

"Those girls were Kelsey's friends," I say, giving her a look. "You should ask her why they went ballistic on Marina."

"They're not my friends," Kelsey says. "Things between me and Rielle are weird. You know that, Isaac."

I don't like the way she says it. Like I'm supposed to know things about her life. I don't want to know things about her life. At least, not the same way I did before.

"All I know is that they got into a fight because of you." I shrug and look at the superintendent, like, *"What can you do? This whack job obviously set up some kind of community-building day and then invited all her enemies."*

"Who assaulted her?" Dr. Ostrander asks. "Because Marina claims that you hit her, Ms. Romano."

"You hit her?" I gasp.

"No," she says, "I didn't hit her. I was trying to get those girls to stop, and she freaked out and started screaming, yelling at me to get off of her."

"I don't know," I say, giving Dr. Ostrander a pointed look. "Kelsey does have a history of violence, so maybe we should look into this more."

"You're an asshole," Kelsey says.

"Ms. Romano!" Dr. Ostrander says. "I thought I told you that kind of language would not be tolerated."

"Sorry," she says. Her cheeks turn pink, and my heart starts to ache. I want to pull her close, to hold her against me and tell her it's going to be okay. I know how anxious she must be about this whole thing, how badly she wanted to make sure she did well at this school. I know she must be stressed out about what's happening, that it's probably been keeping her up at night.

"Look—" I start to say to Dr. Ostrander, because this whole thing's gotten out of control, and I'm sick of being here. What good is rehashing all this stuff going to do? I want to know my punishment, and then I'm out of here.

But before I can voice any of this, there's a knock on the door. "Dr. Ostrander?" the secretary asks, poking her head in. "There's someone here to see you."

"I'm in the middle of an important meeting," Dr. Ostrander says. He sounds really exasperated, and then he looks at me and Kelsey and kind of rolls his eyes like, *Can you believe how stupid this woman is?*

"Yes, I understand that," the secretary says. Her name is Ellie Winters. I know because I saw her nameplate when I got here. She looks like an Ellie Winters too, with gray hair piled up into a tight bun. "But it's Mr. Brandano."

"Mr. Brandano is right here, Mrs. Winters," the superintendent says. He points at me, then takes his glasses off and puts them on his desk. He still has one of those old-fashioned calendars, where you write things down on a grid. Doesn't he have an iPad or a BlackBerry or something? Is he that out of it? Obviously, he must be, since he's calling his secretary Mrs. Winters. No one calls women "Mrs." anymore. Everyone is "Ms." This dude is completely behind the times.

"No, I mean the sen—" Ms. Winters starts to say, but before she can finish, I hear my dad's voice out in the lobby.

"Is he in there?" he's asking, trying to sound like he's a

personal friend of Dr. Ostrander or something. He's acting like he's at a party, not like he's trying to worm his way into his son's disciplinary meeting.

I look over at Kelsey and try to apologize to her with my eyes. I know how this is going to go now—my dad will come in here, and Dr. Ostrander will fall all over himself trying to make sure that everything gets smoothed over, and poor Kelsey will be left out in the cold.

But she's not looking at me. She's just staring down at the floor. "Senator Brandano," Dr. Ostrander says as my dad comes pushing his way into the room.

"Hello, Dr. Ostrander," my dad says, and smiles. He adjusts the buttons on the cuffs of his suit and gives the super-intendent a big smile. To my knowledge, the two of them have never even met. But that's how my dad is. He's built his career on getting people he's never met to instantly like him.

"Senator Brandano, this is highly inappropriate," Dr. Ostrander says. Which actually makes me kind of like the dude. Because behind the times or not, he's right—this *is* pretty inappropriate. "Parents were not invited to this meeting. If you'd like to speak with me, you'll have to make an appointment with my secretary."

Poor Ms. Winters. She's standing by the door looking nervous. Probably because she's afraid my dad and/or Dr. Ostrander is going to flip out on her.

"That won't be necessary," my dad says. "I'm just here to pick up Isaac." He comes and stands behind me, resting his hand on my shoulder. "I'm sure by now you've realized that he had nothing to do with this."

His tone is careful and calculated—it's friendly, but there's also a hidden meaning behind it. The meaning being that even if I *did* have something to do with it, it better be overlooked because if it's not, the school is going to incur my dad's wrath. He's tried similar things at the other schools I've been to, and it works, for a while. But then inevitably some other richer, more important parent starts to complain about me, or the school gets worried about its reputation, and then I have to go. But since this is the first time I've been in trouble here, my dad probably figures his little dog-and-pony show is going to save the day.

"We're still figuring everything out," Dr. Ostrander says, "so if you don't mind, I'm sure Isaac will call you when he's done."

My dad's grip on my shoulder tightens. He looks like maybe he's about to say something else. But instead, he just keeps that fake smile pasted on his face and says, "Fair enough. Isaac, call me when you're done. And I'll talk to Ms. Winters about setting up a meeting with you, Dr. Ostrander."

"You do that," Dr. Ostrander says, not sounding too pleased at the prospect of a meeting with my dad.

"So," Dr. Ostrander says once my dad's gone, "where were we?"

I don't say anything. I just stare at the floor. I'm sick of this whole thing. I don't want Kelsey to suffer anymore. I don't feel like getting revenge. I'm not even angry. I'm just tired. And I want to go home.

"We were talking about my violent past," Kelsey says.

"That's right," Dr. Ostrander says. "Mr. Brandano, it's your belief that this past led to what happened? Even though you're the one who was violent?"

"I was only violent," I say quietly, "because I was the last one to *know* about Kelsey's past." And then I turn and look right into her eyes. "And I hate being lied to."

Before

Kelsey

Okay, so the thing is? Isaac and I are kind of together. And when I say "kind of," I mean, like, completely. At least, I think we are. We've spent, like, every day together for the past two weeks. We hold hands in the hallway. We sit by ourselves at lunch. We spend the day texting and making plans to meet up after school. We've gone to, like, five different movies where we spent the whole time making out.

And the most surprising part? Isaac is *nice*. He's always asking me how I'm doing, if I'm okay with things. He's always looking out for me.

Like right now, for example.

We're having a Face It Down meeting to draft a letter to

send to the head of the student council at Concordia Prep. It's a small meeting, a committee we put together just to work on the letter—me, Isaac, Isaac's friend Marshall, Chloe, and Marina. If it were up to me, Marina wouldn't have even been on this committee, but she insisted, and I couldn't exactly tell her no just because she and Isaac kissed. I mean, hello, jealous girlfriend. So she's here and she's being a little bit . . . I guess you could say, um, annoying. Like, she keeps muttering things under her breath and questioning me on *everything*.

"I don't understand why we have to send it to the head of the student council," she says. "Wouldn't it be better to just send it to the principal?"

"Well, we'll definitely send a copy to the principal, too," I say. I'm sitting at my laptop, reading over the draft we've put together, checking it for any typos or inconsistencies. "But the point of Face It Down Day is really to connect with the students. We want the *students* to be the ones who come together."

The fact that we're sending this letter to the student council is definitely a carefully constructed plan on my part. First of all, because I really don't think the principal of Concordia Prep is going to be too excited to see anything with my name on it come across her desk. And second, because the fewer adults involved, the better. That way I can make it out to colleges like I'm the one who put this whole thing together.

"Great," Marina says. "And I guess the rest of us don't have a say in it?"

Isaac and I glance at each other nervously.

"Not really," Isaac says.

"You do have a say," I tell her, mostly because I'm afraid she might get all psycho. "We can take a vote if you want." I already know I have the votes to do it my way; otherwise I wouldn't have offered. And Marina knows it too.

"So you and Isaac can gang up on everyone and get them to vote with you? No, thank you." She picks up her books and then flounces out of the room, her dark hair bouncing as she goes.

"What's wrong with her?" I ask.

"She's mad because Isaac kissed her and then dumped her for you," Marshall says. Marshall's one of those people who has no filter. Seriously, he just says whatever crazy thing pops into his brain. He and Isaac have actually become sort of close, which is funny. They don't seem like two people who would be friends.

"How do you know?" I ask, glancing at Isaac. He's suddenly superbusy writing something down in his notebook. I hit print on my laptop, and the wireless printer in the corner whirs to life.

"Because she told me." He shrugs. "Besides, everyone knows it."

"They do?" I'm shocked by this. I didn't know I was the subject of school rumors. Not that it's really anything new. I was the subject of a few school rumors at Concordia Prep. Hell, I'm probably the subject of a few rumors over there right now. I can't even imagine what crazy stuff they're saying about me. I suppose if I really wanted to, I could ask Rielle about it, but I don't care to know.

Rielle. I still haven't talked to her about seeing her at the mall a couple of weeks ago when she told me she was at her grandma's. She's called me a few times and sent me a couple of texts, but for the most part, I've been avoiding her.

"Yeah," Marshall says. "Marina is very pissed off."

"Apparently," I say.

"She'll get over it," Isaac says.

"Maybe you should talk to her," I say to him. I don't really like Marina all that much, for obvious reasons. But maybe Isaac should try to smooth things over. I mean, even though I don't like her, the last thing I want is to have enemies.

"Talk to her?" Isaac looks aghast, like I've just suggested he go talk to the Taliban or something.

"God no," Chloe pipes up, looking equally horrified. "That's just going to make it worse."

"How can it make it worse?" I'm creating a mailing label now, typing in the address of Concordia Prep so that I can print it out and put it on the envelope. It's addressed to Kristin Smith, the president of the student council. She's this sort of type A control freak, but she's going to love something like this. I just know it.

"Because if Isaac goes and talks to her like she's some kind of pathetic loser, she's just going to think you're patronizing her," Chloe says.

"He wouldn't treat her like a pathetic loser," I say. "And

besides, isn't it better to just get everything out in the open?" I type in the zip code on the mailing label and then hit print again. "Then we can all move on."

"I'm with Chloe," Isaac says. "It will just make things worse."

"You're saying that because you don't want to talk to her," I say.

"True." He wraps his arms around my waist and pulls me toward him. "I don't want to have to talk to anyone but you," he whispers so that I'm the only one who can hear. "Are we done here?"

I grin, and he kisses me on the lips.

"God, you guys are so cute it's gross," Chloe says. She's sitting cross-legged on a desk, and she jumps down, then flips her head over and gathers her hair up into a ponytail.

"Seriously," Marshall says. "Get a room."

"La la la," I say, pretending to ignore them. "Hey, we should all go out and do something to celebrate getting our letter sent out."

"Celebrate writing a letter?" Chloe asks. "Isn't that the easy part?"

"Yeah," I say, "which is why we should celebrate it. It's going to be weird having these kids at our school, and who knows what's going to happen? Plus it doesn't have to be all play. We can make it a working dinner, try to come up with a good list of ways to facilitate communication between the two schools."

"Oooh, can we go to Chili's?" Marshall asks. "I'm really in the mood for Mexican."

"Chili's isn't Mexican," Chloe says, rolling her eyes.

"They have chips and salsa," Marshall points out. "And queso. If you're good, I'll even buy you some."

Chloe's cheeks flush. Huh. Are they flirting? I don't really see her and Marshall as a couple, but I didn't see me and Isaac as a couple either, so . . . who knows?

Two hours later Isaac pulls up in front of my house to drop me off.

"That," he says, shifting his car into park, "might have been the most boring thing I've ever been involved in." We spent the past hour and a half at Chili's coming up with lists of questions and prompts to facilitate communication between our school and Concordia Prep. It was really productive, but he's right—it was also really boring.

"Really?" I ask. "That's shocking."

"How come?"

"Because I would have thought that as the son of a senator, you'd have been involved in way more boring stuff—state dinners, inaugurations, that kind of thing."

"Nope," he says, and unhooks his seat belt. "My dad likes to keep me hidden away when the important shit comes up." He gets out of the car, then circles around and opens my door for me. I step out and into his arms.

"So I'll call you later?" he asks, and kisses my neck.

"Yes," I breathe.

Suddenly the front door opens, and my dad's standing there, his face stormy. Shit, shit, shit. There's nothing worse than having your dad catch you in the middle of making out with a guy.

"Dad!" I say.

Isaac jumps back from me like I'm on fire. "Mr. Romano," he calls, recovering quickly and pasting a smile on his face. He gives my dad a friendly wave. "It's nice to see you again."

I haven't brought Isaac around my family. One, because it's way too early for that. And two, because my family is crazy. My dad is definitely not going to be excited that I have a boy-friend. If Isaac even is my boyfriend. I mean, I'm assuming he is, but we haven't exactly had the talk about us being official or anything. But we're spending every second together, so that has to mean something, right?

"Nice to see you, too," my dad says. But it's all sarcastic, like, *"Nice to see you, too, even though I've hardly ever seen you before."*

"Well, I should get going," Isaac says. He pauses for a second, waiting for my dad to say something like, *"Why don't you stay for dinner?"* or *"You don't have to leave on account of me"* or *"Where are you headed off to so fast? Stick around for a bit."*

But my dad, apparently, is not a fan of fake politeness or pleasantries. So Isaac squeezes my hand, kisses me on the cheek, and then climbs back into his car and pulls out of the driveway.

"So," I say brightly to my dad as I push by him and into the house, "how was your day?" I take my shoes off and then head over to the pantry, where I pull out a Rice Krispies Treat. I wanted to get dessert at Chili's, but I could tell Isaac really wanted to get out of there.

"So that's your boyfriend?" my dad asks, folding his arms across his chest as if it's more of a challenge than a question.

I think about it. "Yes," I say finally, deciding not to get into the whole I-don't-know thing. But then I think, Fuck it, why shouldn't I just tell the truth? "Actually, I'm not sure. I guess we're just seeing each other."

"Do you think that's such a good idea?" my dad asks. "Given what you just went through because of a boy?"

"Um, I don't know," I say honestly. "But I know that I like him, and so I'm going with it." I open the Rice Krispies Treat and take a bite.

My dad shuts down. I can literally see his face shutting down.

"Don't get too full," he says. "We're going to dinner at the Marshes'."

My stomach does a flip. "Dad," I say, "I really don't—I mean, I already ate, and I have a lot of homework." I don't want to see Rielle.

"I wasn't asking if you wanted to go," he says. "I was telling you that we're going. All of us."

An hour later I'm standing on Rielle's front porch with my mom and dad, holding a Bundt cake. The awful thing about the Bundt cake (besides the fact that it's a Bundt cake, and honestly, who the hell wants a cake with a big hole in the middle?) is that it's store-bought. Apparently, my mom had forgotten that she'd agreed to bring dessert, and so she didn't have time to make anything.

My dad, surprisingly, didn't really seem to care and said we could just pick something up on the way. But my mom freaked out, and was all, "Sharon Marsh would never show up with something store-bought," because Rielle's mom is kind of like Martha Stewart. (Of course, Rielle's mom doesn't have a job, and she took, like, private cooking lessons last year in France after reading that book about Julia Child, *Julie & Julia*. Actually, I'm not sure she even read the book. She might have just watched the movie.)

So then my mom had this great idea that she was going to go to this fancy bakery downtown to buy something because she'd had this warm fruit compote tartlet there once, and apparently it was very elegant and wonderful, the exact kind of thing you should bring to dinner at the Marshes'. But when we got there, the bakery was closed, so we had to go to the normal grocery store.

Which is how we ended up with this Bundt cake. Which is actually very plain-looking. It doesn't have fruit or chocolate on it or anything. It was slim pickings at the store since most of the stuff looked like it had been sitting out all day.

Anyway, so my mom picked out this Bundt cake, and then she ran next door to Target and bought this very fancy-looking cake stand, and she put the Bundt cake on it. She did this in the car, which caused one side of the cake to get sort of smushed, but in the end I think it helped because now it at least looks more homemade.

"How's it going?" Isaac texts to me while we're getting out of the car.

"Mom bought a Bundt cake and is trying to pass it off like it's homemade," I text back.

"LOL."

Yeah. Real funny. Not if you're here.

Rielle answers the door.

"Yay!" she squeals, jumping up and down. She's wearing a black boatneck sweater and white capri pants. Her hair is pulled back in a messy bun, and she has a single string of pearls around her neck. She looks effortlessly put together, exactly like the kind of girl my dad would want as a daughter. "I'm so glad you're here!"

She grabs me in a hug. It feels forced. And weird.

"We brought dessert!" my mom declares. "A Bundt cake!" She thrusts it into Rielle's hands.

If Rielle's surprised by my mom's enthusiasm, she doesn't show it. "Great," she says. "Let's go put it in the kitchen."

When we get there, Rielle's mom is pulling appetizers out of the oven, some kind of meat wrapped in a pastry crust.

"Here's the dessert," Rielle exclaims, and then plops it down on the counter.

"Great," Mrs. Marsh says. She doesn't even look at it twice. Yikes.

"Let's go upstairs," Rielle says, and grabs my hand. Whenever my family comes over here for dinner, Rielle and I go upstairs and leave the adults downstairs. Sometimes we'll snag some of the appetizers her mom makes and munch on them while we hang out and gossip about boys. Rielle hates these dinners as much as I do, mostly because it keeps her from doing the two things she loves the most—talking on her phone and listening to music.

As soon as we get upstairs, Rielle heads to her computer.

"I have the best song for you to listen to," she says. "I met the drummer the other night at The Stage." Rielle is a bit of a groupie. And not just for one particular band or group. She finds these little local bands and stalks them down at different shows. Then she finagles her way backstage to meet the singers or drummers and dates them for a few weeks until she gets bored. Never the guitar players, though—Rielle thinks guitar players are too full of themselves.

The first bars of an alternative rock song start to filter through Rielle's superexpensive speakers, the kind of speakers that can make almost any song sound good. Maybe that's why she's always falling in love with these guys.

"Good song," I say honestly. I'm sprawled out on her bed, trying not to think about the fact that she lied to me about being at her grandma's house for the weekend. I wonder what Isaac is doing right now. I want to pull my phone out and send him another text, but I'm afraid Rielle will ask me who I'm texting. And then I'll have to tell her, and then she'll be all up in my business.

I guess that's one of the good things about not having many close friends right now. I don't have to listen to anyone else's opinion of what I'm doing with my life. Although, my dad obviously felt free to make it perfectly clear what he thinks about me and Isaac.

"I haven't hooked up with him yet," Rielle says. She pulls up the band's website and shows me a picture. The guy in question looks the same as every other band guy she falls in love with. Spiky, highlighted hair that flops over one eye. Tight jeans. A wrist cuff. And eyes that look like they may or may not have eyeliner on them.

"He's cute," I say.

"Don't sound so excited," she says, rolling her eyes.

"No, seriously," I say. "He's cute." I pull a book down from her bookshelf and start reading the back cover.

"Have you read that?" she asks. "You can borrow it if you want."

Rielle and I share a love of romance books. It's actually how we met. It was seventh grade, and I'd just transferred to Concordia Prep. I was feeling sorry for myself in the library, looking through the shelves for something to read, when I spotted Rielle. She was sitting with her math book propped up, but I could see the cover of one of my favorite books, *Match Me If You Can*, peeking out from underneath.

I asked her if it was any good. She said it was amazing. I'd already read it, but I wanted to start a dialogue with her and see if she'd offer to let me borrow it. She did, and from that day on, whenever I reread that book, it reminds me of Rielle.

"Thanks," I say, pulling the book off the shelf and putting it in my purse. I lie back on her bed and stare up at the ceiling, willing her mom to call us downstairs. Not that I'm looking forward to dinner. But the sooner we eat, the sooner I can get out of here.

"What's with you?" Rielle asks, still at her desk, still clicking away at her computer.

"What do you mean?"

"You're being weird."

"No, I'm not."

"Yes, you are." She swivels her chair around and faces me, raising her eyebrows. "Out with it. Does it have something to do with Rex?"

I sit up and look at her. "*Rex?* Are you kidding?"

"Well, I don't know!" She reaches over and turns off the song that's playing. "What else could it be? Is it that guy Ira?"

"Isaac," I correct. God. She can't even remember the name of the guy I like? "And no, it's not him."

"Then what is it?"

"I saw you at the mall."

She frowns. "Then why didn't you come over and say hi?"

She doesn't remember. I can't believe this. It's been bothering me for two weeks, and she doesn't even remember. "You told me you were at your grandma's for the weekend."

She laughs, shaking her head like it's some kind of crazy misunderstanding. "I did?"

"Yes." I take a deep breath. "You told me you were away, and then I saw you there. With Anna and Michelle."

She's still laughing, trying to play it off like it's nothing. "I probably just got confused," she says. "When you called, I was probably *getting ready* to go to my grandma's."

"No." I shake my head. "You didn't get confused, Rielle."

"How do you know?"

"Because you didn't. You said your grandma needed help with her arthritis medicine."

She sighs, then stands up and comes and sits next to me on the bed. "Okay, look, the thing is . . . Michelle and Anna feel weird being around you."

"Why?" I've never been particularly close with Michelle and Anna, two girls from Concordia Prep who we hung out with sometimes. They were always best friends, and Rielle and I were always best friends. Our twosomes were already made up. But I guess things have changed. Our twosomes have somehow now become a threesome.

"I don't know." She shrugs. "They just felt like maybe you were going to be different or something. They don't know what to say."

"They don't have to say anything." I'm starting to feel anger bubble up inside me. It's different from the anger I felt that day with Rex. This is more of a real anger, one that I'm more in touch with. "Or they could ask me how things are going, or if there's anything they can do, or how I'm feeling."

Rielle shrugs. "You know how they are." She rolls her

eyes. "Not the sharpest pencils in the box. And kind of self-absorbed." She laughs like this is the funniest thing ever. But I don't feel much like laughing.

"You could have just told me that," I say. "Instead of lying. I would have understood."

"Would you?" she asks. "Would you have really?" She's raising her eyebrows at me like it's a rhetorical question.

"I would have been mad," I say, "but you didn't have to lie to me."

"I'm sorry." She reaches over and pulls me closer to her. "Forgive me?"

"Yeah," I say. But it's not true. I don't forgive her.

Before

Isaac

This night has been a fucking disaster. First, there was that whole weird thing with Kelsey's dad. What the hell is that dude's problem, anyway? I'm a nice guy. Okay, maybe I'm not *exactly* a nice guy, but he doesn't know that. He hasn't even given me a chance. Shouldn't he invite me over for dinner or take me out golfing or some shit and let me be a real screwup before he just decides that I am one? Something is going on with that dude. Something with him and Kelsey. I want to ask her about it, but she's at some dumb dinner with her parents.

And I'm holed up in my room avoiding my dad. He's pissed at me because he saw the scratch on my car that Kelsey put there. He started yelling and freaking out as soon as I got home, which is completely ridiculous. Who cares? It's just a scratch. It can be fixed. No one got hurt, no one's dead, no one even—

My phone beeps. A text from Kelsey.

"Finally done," it says. *"U want to meet up?"*

I race down the hallway and out the door before anyone can say anything to me. My dad took my keys away, but I have spare copies all over the place. My dad is always trying to take my car away.

I drive to Kelsey's house and pick her up, and we end up in the parking lot of the bowling alley.

"Should we go in?" Kelsey asks. She's looking toward the front of the alley doubtfully. There are a bunch of guys standing around the doorway smoking cigarettes and laughing.

"Do *you* think we should go in?" I ask.

"I'm not sure." She bites her lip. "We can't just sit out here."

"Why not?"

"Because what will we do?"

"I can think of lots of things," I say, raising my eyebrows at her. I mean it as a joke, but suddenly she looks really sad. Like, her-eyes-are-filling-up-with-tears kind of sad.

"What's wrong?" I ask.

"Nothing."

"Seriously," I say, "you can tell me."

"No, I can't."

"Yes, you can."

"No, I can't."

"Why not?"

"It's too embarrassing."

"Embarrassing? You want to hear embarrassing? How about the time in eighth grade when Derek Miller pulled my pants down in front of the whole gym class?"

"That's not embarrassing," she says.

"He pulled my boxers down too," I say. "And everyone saw my . . . uh, my junk."

"Your *junk*?" She looks at me and then bursts out laughing.

"What's wrong with 'junk'?" I ask defensively. "And I would have said 'dick,' but I didn't want to insult your delicate sensibilities."

"Please," she says, rolling her eyes. "I think I lost my delicate sensibilities a while ago." This seems to make her a little sad again, and she looks back out the window. "Why did you get kicked out of all your old schools?" she asks.

"Why didn't I get kicked out sooner is the better question." I shift on my seat. From outside, I can hear the sound of the music in the bar, a loud bass line that reverberates in my chest and through the front seat of my car.

"You did a lot of bad things?"

"Bad? Depends on what you mean by 'bad.' I like to think of them as mischievous."

"Like, what did you do?"

"I told you. It was mostly just pranks and stuff. Stupid shit. Spray painting our graduation year on the side of a building, writing 'seniors suck' across their lockers when I was a freshman, stealing chickens and letting them loose in the hallway, that kind of thing."

"Why did you do all that?"

I think about it. "I dunno." I shrug. "Bored, I guess. Trying to get attention."

"Don't you get enough attention being the son of a senator?"

"This is getting way too psychobabble for me," I say. I'm getting a little uncomfortable. Mostly because Kelsey's right. I *do* get a lot of attention just for being a senator's son. So why did I feel the need to do all that stuff?

"We don't have to talk about it," she says.

"No, it's fine." I shrug again. "I don't know. Maybe I wanted attention from my dad. Or maybe I just wanted to show him that he couldn't control me. Who knows? I'm probably totally fucked up."

"Not as fucked up as me," she whispers.

"I doubt that," I say. "You're, like, the least fucked-up person I know."

"How can you say that?" she asks. "You hardly even know me."

"I know you enough," I say. I'm tracing little circles on her hand now. I have no idea how she has this effect on me, but she does. I just want to pull her close and hold her against me.

"Aren't you going to ask me what I did to get kicked out of school?" she asks.

"Is that what you were thinking about before?"

She hesitates. "Yes."

"What did you do to get kicked out of school?"

"How come you've never asked me that before?"

I think about it. "I don't know. I guess I just figured that if you wanted me to know, you'd tell me." She doesn't say anything, just squeezes my hand tight. And then I start to get a little scared. Not that I think she's really dangerous or anything, but who knows? Maybe she is. Maybe she killed a dude or something. Maybe her dad is, like, some kind of controlling, sadistic bastard, not just your run-of-the-mill pain-in-the-ass dad, and so one day she just snapped and—

"I'll tell you," she says. "It's not a big deal."

"Okay." I shrug like I could care less. I wonder if she thinks killing someone is a big deal.

"I wrecked my ex-boyfriend's car."

"You wrecked his car?" I ask. "No wonder you didn't want to drive mine. Good thing I didn't know that, or I never would have let you behind the wheel. But why'd you get kicked out of school for that? Were you drinking or something?" The thought of Kelsey drinking and driving just doesn't make any sense. She's the most in-control person I know.

"No," she says, "it wasn't the car he drove. It was this car he was making for his senior project. It ran on electricity."

"Sounds lame."

"It wasn't," she says. "It was kind of a big deal."

"Why'd you wreck it?"

"Because I found out he was cheating on me with this

really ridiculous girl." She pauses, and I don't say anything. Because sometimes when someone is telling you something really important, it's best to just let there be silence, to really think about what they're saying. A lot of times people think they have to say something all insightful or wise or something to try and make the person feel better. But really, sometimes silence is best.

"And the thing is," she goes on, "I had a feeling that he liked her, even though he always swore up and down that it wasn't true. And so a lot of it . . . I mean, I think a lot of the reason I was doing it was because I was mad at myself. Because I believed him. And because I let myself get close enough to him to care."

I reach across the car and pull her close to me. And then I hold her while she starts to cry.

Before

Kelsey

Okay, so that was pretty humiliating. Crying like that? On Isaac's shoulder over pretty much nothing? Totally ridiculous. Although, it was pretty nice of him to hold me until I stopped. He didn't even care when I got his shirt all wet and disgusting. I'm not a good crier. I try to hold it in as long as I can, and then when it happens, it's like this totally disgusting fountain that I can't control. So gross and embarrassing. I wish I could be one of those girls who tear up and then pull a tissue out of their purse and delicately dab at the corners of their eyes. But I'm not.

This is what I'm thinking about on Monday morning at school. At least, I am until Chloe comes up to me, slams my locker door shut, and then wedges herself in between me and the locker.

"Hey," I say, "I wasn't done in there."

"It happened," she says. Her eyes are darting around, scanning the halls behind me, panic-stricken.

I turn around to see what she's looking at.

"Don't look!" she screams. And then she grabs my arm and pulls me into the gym closet. At least, I'm pretty sure it's the gym closet. I've never been in here before. It's a small room, very closetlike, and it's filled with gym equipment—mats, basketballs, jump ropes—and since my locker is by the gym, it's a pretty good guess. Chloe pulls the string on the lightbulb that's hanging from the ceiling, and a dull glow surrounds us.

"What am I not looking at?" I ask.

"Well, nothing," she says. "I just didn't want anyone seeing you looking around." Her eyes are still darting around the room, even though it's only the two of us.

"Why not?"

"Because then someone might *know*."

"Okay," I say, shaking my head. "We need to start over. What the hell are you talking about?"

"Me and Dave." She pulls a Jolly Rancher out of her bag, unwraps it, and then starts sucking on it nervously.

"What about you and Dave?"

"We hooked up."

"Ohmigod!"

"I know." She's whispering now, and her eyes are huge.

"Why are you looking so scandalized?" I ask. "This is a good thing, right?" I launch myself up onto the stack of gymnastics mats against the wall and sit there, my legs dangling over the side.

"I'm not sure," Chloe says. "And you can't tell anyone! I don't want anyone to know about it."

"Like who?"

"Like any of my friends." She looks around again, like these alleged friends might be hiding behind the shelves of volleyballs, ready to jump out and catch her in the middle of her Dave story.

"Why not? Won't they be happy for you?"

"No," she says. "None of them know that I like him."

I stare at her, and my mouth drops open. "None of your friends know that you like Dave?"

"No."

"Why not?"

"Um, hello," she says, pulling herself up and sitting next to me on the mats. She pulls out another Jolly Rancher and offers it to me. "Because it's embarrassing."

"It is?" I ask, taking the candy and popping it in my mouth. Watermelon. Yum.

"Yeah," she says. "I mean, think about it. If I told my friends I like Dave, they'd always be asking me about it and giving me sympathetic looks when he hooks up with other people, and just . . . ugh. Annoying."

This, I understand. When I first started liking Rex, I

didn't want anyone else to know, even Rielle. Actually, especially Rielle. Rielle's one of those people who's used to getting whatever guy she wants. She doesn't understand why you might want to keep your crush a secret. More than likely she would have wanted me to go for it, which I wasn't ready for. When Rex and I finally did get together, Rielle was shocked, but I played it off like I'd just started liking him.

"Plus I didn't want him finding out," Chloe says, "and my friends kind of have big mouths."

There's a knock on the door to the gym closet, and Chloe and I freeze. I hold a finger to my lips.

The knock comes again, and then Isaac's voice. "Kelsey? Open the door. I saw you go in there."

"Oh," I say, letting out the breath I've been holding. "It's just Isaac."

"Come in!" Chloe calls.

Isaac appears in the doorway, followed by Marshall.

"Hey," Isaac says. It's the first time I've seen him all day, and I smile. He looks gorgeous in a soft-looking navy-blue cashmere sweater and jeans. "What are you guys doing in here?"

"Making out?" Marshall asks hopefully.

"No," I say, "we were just . . ." I try to think of a plausible excuse for why we would be hanging out in a closet. I don't want to tell them Chloe's secret. It's not my place.

"I was telling Kelsey about how I hooked up with my friend Dave," Chloe reports like it's nothing, and then jumps down from the mats.

209

"What?" I screech. "How come you can tell them?" Did she not just remember that she was supposed to be keeping this a secret?

"They're not going to tell anyone," she says. "They don't even know Dave."

"Who's Dave?" Isaac asks.

"Dave Cash?" Marshall asks. "Who graduated last year? That dude's a tool." He's bouncing a basketball on the ground, weaving it between his legs. He actually has really good ball control, which you'd never be able to guess just by looking at him.

"I need a male perspective," Chloe says, turning to Isaac and ignoring Marshall's comment. "What do I do now?"

"You want to hook up with him again?" Isaac asks.

"Yes."

"Oooh, you should go over to his dorm with lingerie on," Marshall says. "And high heels." He leans back on the stack of tumbling mats and looks her up and down. "Maybe under one of those trench coats. You know, like a flasher. Hot."

"Way too obvious," she says, shaking her head. "I don't want him to know how much I like him."

"So you want to keep it casual," Isaac says, nodding. "Invite him out somewhere. But not on a date. To a party or something. A small one, though, so you don't end up getting all drunk and separated from each other."

"A small party! That sounds perfect." Chloe looks over at me. "Can you have one?"

"A party?" Is she crazy? Then I realize she doesn't understand or know anything about my family situation. "No," I say, "I definitely cannot have a party."

"Please?" she says, walking over to me and holding out another Jolly Rancher as a bribe. "Just a few people. Not that many."

"I can have a party," Isaac says.

"You can?" Chloe asks, whirling around and looking at Isaac like he's her savior.

"Sure." He shrugs. "Why not? We can pretend we're working on our project or something, and let my dad take a picture for his website. He'll love it."

"But we won't really be working on the project, will we?" Chloe asks, sounding kind of panicked.

"No," Isaac says. "We'll really be providing a place for you and Dave to get it on."

I push him on the shoulder.

"What about me?" Marshall asks. "Am I invited?"

"Yes, you have to come," Chloe says. "Otherwise, it will be like a double date. And I don't want Dave to think I set it up that way."

"Okay, so it's all settled," Isaac says. "We'll do it this weekend?"

Chloe nods. "But in the afternoon," she says, "so that it doesn't look too obvious." We all go traipsing out of the closet, with Marshall muttering something sarcastic about how fun it is to be the fifth wheel.

• • •

Later that afternoon I get called down to the main office. There's a letter waiting for me there from Concordia Prep saying that they accept our invitation for Face It Down Day and will be sending a select group of students over. Kristin, the president of the student council, writes that she can't wait, and asks me to let her know if there's anything else she can do. Which there isn't, partly because I'm on top of it, and partly because I don't want her getting too involved because then she'll be able to take some of the credit.

When I read the part about her selecting a small group of students, I have a moment of panic. That small group of students better not include anyone I don't like and/or want to avoid, like Rex or Michelle or Anna. But how can I make sure of that?

I text Rielle, inviting her to meet me after school at our fave bakery, Pria's.

"You want something," she says as soon as I walk in.

"No, I don't," I say, putting a fake shocked look on my face. "I'm totally just here out of the goodness of my heart."

"How good is your heart?"

"What do you mean?"

"I mean is it good enough that you'll buy me a cupcake?"

"Of course." I stand next to her in the line in front of the counter. Rielle came right from school, and so she's still wearing her uniform. It's kind of hot out, though, and so she's rolled down the top of her skirt to make it shorter. She's also unbuttoned the bottom of her shirt and tied it in the front, revealing the tiniest bit of stomach. Most of the guys in here can't keep their eyes off her. She's like a schoolgirl fantasy come to life.

We order our cupcakes (cherry jubilee and vanilla for her, chocolate buttercream for me), and head over to the side of the café and sit down at one of the few empty tables.

"So," Rielle says, "how are things?" She gathers her hair up into a ponytail and then takes a bite of her cupcake.

A guy in a suit next to us is practically drooling as he tries to pretend he's not looking at her. Rielle, of course, is oblivious. Not for the first time, I wonder what it would feel like to be like that, to be so beautiful that you don't even realize people are watching you, to be so confident that you don't ever have to worry about being nervous or feeling self-conscious. I've spent what seems like my whole life trying to pretend I'm that way. What would it be like to have it just come naturally?

"I'm good," I say. "You?"

"Excellent." She takes another bite of cupcake.

I decide to cut right to the chase. "So listen," I say, "have you heard about this Face It Down Day thing that we're doing?"

"Sort of," she says. "You're inviting a bunch of us to your school, right?"

"Yeah," I say. "Are you going to come?"

"Of course," she says. "It gets us out of classes for the whole afternoon."

"Awesome," I say. "Any idea who else is coming?"

"Dunno." She shrugs and licks a bite of frosting off her lips. "Probably the usual suspects. Whoever's on Kristin's good side."

"You're on Kristin's good side?"

"For now," she says. "She beat me on a math text last week." Kristin's always been supercompetitive when it comes to grades, and she sees Rielle as her biggest competition. So if she's beating Rielle, she's nice to her. When Rielle beats Kristin, Kristin hates her.

"Perfect," I say. "So can you make sure that Rex doesn't get invited?"

Rielle sets her cupcake down. "Gasp!" she says. "Kelsey! Is it true that you've invited me here to ply me with processed sugar in an effort to get me to agree to some plan you've concocted to make sure certain people you don't want to see don't end up at your event?" She pretends to be outraged.

"Yes," I say. She gives me a look. "Come on," I say, "you knew I was up to something."

She thinks about it. "And how am I supposed to accomplish this crazy task you've laid out?"

"Go to the student council meetings? And make sure you bring up objections to the final list?"

"Ooooh, Kelseyyyyy," she says. "Those meetings are so long and boring."

"Please, Rielle," I say. I think about bringing up the fact that she lied to me a couple weeks ago, but I don't really want to go there if I don't have to.

"Fine," she says finally, "I'll do it. But you are so buying me another cupcake."

The Aftermath

Kelsey

"So you were sent a list of people who would be coming to Face It Down Day?" Dr. Ostrander asks. "From Concordia Prep?"

"Yes." I nod. "It was a list of about fifty students, all different grades, all different types." My heart is beating a million miles a minute, I guess because now we're getting down to it. Now we're going to really talk about what happened that day. And I don't know how it's all going to turn out.

"And you and Isaac went over that list?" Dr. Ostrander asks. He pulls a copy of it out of the file folder in front of him and runs his eyes down the students' names.

"Yes." I nod again. "And then we put an open call out to our school asking for volunteers from Concordia Public. We got a huge response, so we made them all fill out a questionnaire asking them about themselves and why they were so interested in Face It Down Day."

"And you picked fifty students from our school as well?"

"Yes. Isaac and I went through the applications, along with Chloe and Marshall."

"Kelsey had the final say," Isaac reports.

"No, I didn't." It's true, too. I didn't. We all went through the applications together, and we all picked the students together.

"Oh, I'm sorry," Isaac says, giving a sarcastic laugh. "That's right, I got confused. She didn't have the final decision about the students from *our* school. But she did try to keep certain people off the list from Concordia Prep."

"Is that true?" Dr. Ostrander asks.

I want to know how Isaac knows this.

"I told my friend Rielle that we didn't want any drama, and that she should keep that in mind when deciding which Concordia Prep students got invited to Face It Down Day," I say. Semantics, but whatever.

"So you tried to fix it," Isaac says.

"And that's why this Rex person snuck into the school?" Dr. Ostrander asks.

"No, he wasn't . . ." I shake my head because now I'm starting to get confused. And then I feel myself start to tear up. I clear my throat and blink hard because I really, really do not want to start crying now, not when we're so close to finishing up this meeting.

"He didn't sneak into the school," Isaac says. "He was invited." He points at me. "*She* invited him."

"I didn't invite him," I say. "In fact, I didn't want him there at all." It's true. I specifically told Rielle not to bring him.

Isaac snorts. "You see?" he says to Dr. Ostrander. "She's lying."

"About what?" I ask, frustrated.

"Well," Isaac says, talking to Dr. Ostrander, even though I'm the one who asked the question. "You just heard her say that she didn't try to keep certain people out. But now she's trying to say that she didn't want Rex there at all."

I shake my head. "That's not . . . that's not what I said. I told Rielle that I didn't want anyone there who was going to cause drama. But I didn't try to control the list of people who were coming."

"You're lying," Isaac says. "And honestly, I'm sick of going over this again and again and again."

"I'm sorry if we're wasting your precious time, Mr. Brandano," Dr. Ostrander says. "But we're trying to get to the bottom of this whole situation, of why things happened the way they did."

"All right," Isaac says, shaking his head. "I wasn't going to do this. But I can save us all a lot of time and tell you exactly why all of it happened."

My heart stops.

Dr. Ostrander frowns. "What do you mean?"

"I mean," Isaac says, his voice raised, "that we don't have

to have this big conversation about everything. I'm over it." He sighs. "If you want to know what happened, I'll tell you."

He looks at me out of the corner of his eye, and for a second, I pray that he's not going to tell Dr. Ostrander what actually did happen, the real reason shit just completely and totally blew up yesterday, the real lie I told that had nothing to do with people being on the list or not.

"If you want to know the truth," he says, leaning forward like he's getting ready to tell a really good story, "it has to do with Kelsey. And the biggest lie of all."

And that's when I realize the thing about the truth. It always comes out, no matter what you do.

Before

Isaac

If I want to have Kelsey, Chloe, and Marshall over, I'm going to have to smooth things over with my dad. He's still pissed at me for taking my car out the other night.

The one good thing about my dad is that he'll forgive pretty easily. (Notice I didn't say "forget." He never forgets. The dude has an opinion of me that goes back years. I'm actually not even sure if he just decided when I was born that I was a complete fuckup, or if I just did a bunch of stuff when I was younger that he can't get over.)

The hard part is what you have to go through to get that forgiveness. You have to listen to him lecture you. You have to listen to him saying shit that's really not that nice. You have to let him feel like he's imparted some big lesson to you. It makes him feel good about himself, and my dad loves to feel good about himself. He kind of gets off on it.

Which is why I usually never ask him for forgiveness. I don't want to have to go and listen to all that. I would rather have him mad at me. I just don't give a shit.

But I told Chloe I could have people over here, and then I said that maybe we could even get a picture with my dad, and I saw Kelsey's face light up when I said that, and I want Kelsey to be happy, and part of that involves dealing with my dad.

I knock on his office door, and when he calls me in, I stand in front of his desk.

"Hey," I say, "I want to have some people over here on Friday to work on Face It Down Day. Is that okay?"

My dad leans back in his big mahogany chair, relishing this. He loves when I have to come and ask him for something. It's another thing he gets off on.

"Well, I don't know, Isaac," he says. "You haven't really been acting like someone who deserves to have people over."

"I know," I say. "I'm sorry." I look down at the floor like I can't even believe how horrible my behavior has been.

"Yes, well, I don't know if sorry is going to cut it this time. You're sorry a lot. And sometimes that's not good enough. Sometimes we need consequences for our actions."

"So you're not going to let me have them over?"

His phone starts to ring, saving me from some big lecture. "Mow the lawn," he says, "and then I'll consider it."

"Okay," I say, even though we have landscapers who do all that stuff. "Also, if you could stop by, maybe take a picture with us, that would be great."

"Oh?" He looks up, his hand on his phone. God, he loves this shit so much. It's making me really kind of hate him. "Well, I suppose I could do that." He's pretending like it's some kind of big imposition.

"Great." I start to walk toward the door.

"Isaac?" he calls after me.

"Yeah?" I turn around.

He looks at me like he's about to say something, but then he shakes his head. "Nothing." He turns away from me and answers his phone.

Yeah. That's what I thought.

On Friday, Kelsey gets to my house before anyone else.

"So, we need to come up with the questions we're going to be asking and the things we want to talk about on Face It Down Day," she says.

"We have to do that *now*?" We're on the couch in my family room, and no one's home. My dad assured me he would be here at four for the photo op, but that's not for another hour, and everyone else isn't going to be here until around then too. "I can think of other, better things we can do." I wrap my arms around her and pull her down on top of me, kissing her neck. God, she smells good.

"No." She giggles, and disentangles herself from me. "We

need to go over this stuff so that we have something to show your dad when he gets here."

I look at her blankly. "If you think my dad is going to give a shit about the questions we come up with, you're wrong. He's going to take some pictures, hope they get picked up on some news outlet or website, and then he's going to leave."

"I know," she says. "But we have to at least pretend, don't we?"

"No," I say. "Pretending is stupid." I try to kiss her again, but she pushes me away.

"Okay, okay," I grumble, and sit up. I reach over and pick up a chip from the bowl on the coffee table. When my mom found out I was having friends over, she made the house-keeper put together a tray of snacks for us, which she left in the refrigerator. Technically, no one's here yet, but I'm hungry. So I pulled out the thing of snacks. Of course, the chips are cold, which is kind of weird. But my mom must have figured I was too lazy to open up a bag of chips and put them in a bowl.

"So what should we ask about?" Kelsey asks, her pen poised over her notebook.

"Sex."

"Sex?"

"Yeah." I shrug. "Sex is universal. Everyone is worried about it."

"I don't know." She reaches over and grabs a cracker. "I mean, isn't that a little racy for something like this?"

"You don't want to push the envelope?"

"No." She shakes her head. "I want to play it safe."

"Well, then maybe we should talk about—"

The doorbell rings.

"Ohmigod," she says, standing up and smoothing down her skirt. "That's not your dad, is it?"

"Why would my dad be ringing the doorbell at his own house?" I ask. She relaxes. "It's probably one of our friends getting here early."

I cross the room and peer out the front windows. Marshall's standing on the porch holding a big package wrapped in foil. Hmmm.

"What do you know about Marshall?" I ask.

"What do you mean?" Kelsey comes over to the window, and we watch as Marshall picks up one side of the foil-wrapped package and peeks under it, then pats the foil back down. He rings the doorbell again.

"I mean, do we know anything about his political beliefs?" I ask, giving her a mock serious look. "He's standing out there holding some kind of mysterious package, so I just want to make sure that—"

Kelsey laughs. "He's not dangerous," he says.

The doorbell rings for the third time.

"Okay, okay," I say, shaking my head and walking toward the front hall. Geez. Doesn't this dude know it's impolite to ring the doorbell more than once?

"Yo, what took you so long?" he asks when I open the door. He walks into the front hallway without waiting to be invited in.

"Come on in," I say sarcastically, shutting the door behind him.

"Here," he says, shoving the package into my hands. Although, now that it's in my hands, I can see it's not a package. It's a plate covered in foil.

"It's a chocolate sheet cake," Marshall says, ruining the suspense. "I made it myself. Well, not from scratch. Used a mix. Betty Crocker." He must mistake my incredulous look as surprise at the fact that he made a cake out of a mix, not that he made a cake at all, because then he says, "What? It's just as good." He sounds all defensive.

"Why are you here so early?" I ask. "And why did you make a cake? I mean, not to be a dick, but—"

"No, it's fine." Then he sighs like he can't believe he's being forced to explain himself. "I got here early so I could see if you needed help with anything," he says. "And I brought a cake because it's polite to bring something when you're invited over to someone's house, Isaac."

Apparently, now he's all up on decorum, despite the fact that he rang my doorbell three times. He's also obviously crazy. But whatever. "Fine," I say, looking at the huge cake doubtfully. "Let's take this into the kitchen."

"Good," he says. "I'm starving." He follows me into the family room. "Hey, Kels," he says when he sees her. Kels?

"Hey, Marsh," she says, obviously not caring that he's shortened her name. "What's up?"

"Nothin'." He shrugs. "Brought a cake."

"Great," she says. "I love cake."

I usually love cake too, but not when it comes at the expense of making out with my girlfriend.

"Isaac's going to slice it up," Marshall reports.

"I am?"

"Yeah." He looks at me, confused. "Aren't you hungry?"

Not for this cake. "Well, shouldn't we wait until—"

"Sounds perfect," Kelsey says, standing up from the couch. "I could use a break."

"Okay," I say, "I guess we're having cake now."

"And milk," Marshall says. He walks into the kitchen and sits down at our breakfast bar.

"Duh," Kelsey says, pulling it out of the refrigerator. She grabs a few glasses from the cupboard overhead.

"I guess we're having cake and milk," I say. I take a knife out of the drawer and pull the foil back. "Jesus," I say, "what the fuck happened to this cake?"

"What?" Marshall screeches, running over and looking at it. "Oh, yeah. It got a little smushed."

"A little smushed?" I ask. "That shit does not look just a little smushed." One whole side of the cake is pushed down, almost to the plate.

"Well, it fell a little while it was cooking," Marshall says. "And then when I was bringing it over here, it got jostled in the car."

"How come the frosting's all runny?" I ask, peering down at it. I'm starting to think it might not be the best idea to eat this. Who knows what kind of infectious diseases are lurking in there?

"I had to put the frosting on before the cake cooled," Marshall says, "because I didn't want to be late."

I look at the clock on the microwave. "You're an hour early."

"See?" Marshall says, grinning. "My haste paid off. I made it."

"I'm sure it tastes delicious," Kelsey says. She has plates out now, and she sets them on the counter, waiting for me to cut the cake. I have to admit that I kind of like having her here in my kitchen, taking care of things. It's like we're married or something. I've never felt that way about a girl before. The only thing that's messing up this whole scenario is that Marshall's here. And, of course, that this cake looks like something you'd see on one of those reality cooking shows where everything goes horribly wrong.

My dad walks into the kitchen then, ruining my little domestic fantasy even more.

"Hello, everyone," he says. He nods at me. "Isaac."

"Hi," I say. "This is Marshall. And you remember Kelsey."

"Hello," my dad says again, all smiles. He puts his briefcase down on the counter. "Isaac tells me you're all working on a new group for school?"

"Face It Down," Marshall reports. He leans over and picks the knife up off the counter and cuts a huge piece of cake. He slides it onto his plate and then licks a stray bit of frosting off his finger. Kelsey looks appalled.

"Yes," she says, a little too loud, I guess so that she can try and distract my dad from Marshall's bad table manners. "Isaac and I were just going over some questions we're planning to ask the students from Concordia Prep."

"Sounds great," my dad says. "I'd love to take some pictures for the school newspaper if you need them."

I roll my eyes. It's so typical of my dad, trying to pretend like he's doing us some big favor. Which, technically, I guess he is. But you can bet those pictures are somehow going to end up on his website or in the local newspaper. My dad doesn't pose for any photos that aren't going to further his political agenda.

"That sounds great," Kelsey breathes. How can she be taken in by this? Doesn't she remember the first day of school, when she was so mean to me just because she thought I was a stuck-up jerk? Can't she see that my dad actually *is* a stuck-up jerk?

"Should we do it now?" my dad asks. "We could set up around the table."

Obviously, he has somewhere to be.

"But we're having cake," Marshall says through a mouthful of chocolate. "You want some, Mr. Brandano?"

This kid's the best. I love that he called my dad "Mr." instead of "Senator" and that he's offering him his ghetto cake.

"Cake?" My dad looks confused.

"Oh yeah," I say, "Marshall made this delicious chocolate cake, didn't you, Marshall?"

227

"Yup." He takes another big bite. "You should have some, for real. It's wonderful."

My dad's looking at the cake doubtfully. "Are your parents registered to vote, Marshall?" he asks.

Marshall looks confused. "Yeah," he says, and swallows his cake.

My dad reaches over and pulls a plate off the stack that Kelsey set out. "I'd love a piece," he says.

"Milk?" I offer.

"Please."

Kelsey pours him a big glass, and as she does I catch her eye over the glass. She smiles at me, and I smile at her, and I know we're both thinking the same thing—that it's going to be hilarious watching Marshall interact with my dad. And I'm pretty sure that's the moment that I realize I'm falling in love with her.

Before

Kelsey

Isaac's dad takes tons of pictures with us, on our cameras and his, and it's all totally fake. Like, *really* fake. We spread out all our notebooks and stuff on the dining room table, and then Senator Brandano pretends like we're all working together. He even loosens his tie before he does it, like he's trying to pretend that he's just relaxing at home with his son and his friends. It's all very scandalous.

But I don't care, because now I have a picture of me and the senator working together. Isaac even made sure to take a picture of just the two of us bent over a binder, looking very intent. I wonder if attaching it to my college applications is going a little too far, but I don't think you can really go too far when it comes to important things like that. And plus don't they always say that a picture is worth a thousand words?

Anyway, right after Senator Brandano left, Chloe showed up with that guy Dave. I knew things might be awkward between the two of them, since Chloe led me to believe that would be the case, but I really had no idea just exactly how awkward they would be. I mean, I kind of thought she was exaggerating.

"So," I say. We're all sitting in the family room—me, Isaac, Chloe, Dave, and Marshall—and so far the conversation hasn't been so great. After asking Dave the usual "How do you like college?" questions, no one's really come up with anything much to say.

"Eat your cake, Dave," Marshall says. Everyone has a piece of cake sitting in front of them on the coffee table. But no one's eating any. Probably because of the melted frosting.

"You should," Isaac says. "It's good." He reaches over and picks up his plate, and then I do the same with mine. I take a bite. The cake *is* actually really good, although I'm not sure I should be having a second piece. But I didn't want to be rude. And besides, there's so much of it.

"Wow," I say. "Marshall, this is delicious." He beams.

"Oh, great," Chloe babbles. "I love cake. Cake is the best."

"Do you like cake, Dave, my man?" Marshall asks. Marshall is on his fourth piece of cake. His lips are coated with crumbs, and there's a big smear of chocolate frosting on his shirt. This isn't stopping him, though. In fact, the more chocolate he eats, the more he seems to want.

"I like cake," Dave says. "Who doesn't?"

Marshall starts talking to him about different kinds of cake, and what kind of desserts they have in the dining halls at college. Then he asks Dave if there are a lot of hot college girls at his school. Which is awkward since Dave just hooked up with Chloe. Which Marshall knows. Doesn't he know better than to bring that up? Dave shifts on the couch and tries to answer the questions, all the while shooting Chloe nervous looks out of the corner of his eye.

"Oh my God," Isaac whispers into my ear, leaning into me on the couch. "What should we do?"

"What do you mean?"

"I mean, this is about to turn into a big debacle," he says. I can feel his breath on my neck, and a little shiver runs up my spine.

"What kind of debacle?" I ask.

"The kind where everyone just sits around being awkward, and then when they leave, they all talk about how lame it was," he says.

Hmmm. He's right. What were we thinking, planning an afternoon hangout with five people to try and get Chloe together with Dave? I know she didn't want it to seem too obvious, but come on. Hanging out in the middle of the day eating cake? That's, like, the least romantic thing ever. Maybe I should have a talk with her about being a little more assertive.

"How do we fix it?" I whisper to Isaac.

"Play spin the bottle?" he asks, one side of his mouth sliding up into a grin.

I grin back, and he leans over and gives me a kiss.

In the end, Isaac pulls out the Wii and we all start playing. It's actually pretty fun. We get into a supercompetitive game of Dance Dance Revolution and then move on to Mario Kart. The conversation is flowing, and Chloe is actually starting to loosen up, flirting and having fun.

And then, right in the middle of this weird jumping game where you have to jump over things that are being thrown at you, Marshall suddenly grabs his stomach and goes, "Uh-oh."

"What uh-oh?" Isaac says, sounding concerned. He hits the button to pause the game.

"I dunno," Marshall says, "I just . . . I feel like maybe I'm going to . . ." And then he leans over and pukes all over the floor.

"Gross," Dave says.

"Gross," Chloe says.

"Gross," I say. And then I feel bad, so I add, "Are you okay?" I'm trying not to look at the puke.

"I'll get some paper towels and a mop," Isaac says, then disappears into the kitchen.

Dave throws his Wii controller down onto the couch. "I should get going," he says.

"Already?" Chloe asks. She looks a little panicked. "We just got here."

"I think I'm going to throw up again," Marshall says. He falls onto the couch clutching his stomach. He's looking a little green in the face.

"You ready, Chloe?" Dave asks.

"Um, yeah." She stands up and starts to follow him toward the door. "I'll text you later, okay, Kels?"

"Okay." Even though the whole group hangout thing didn't go so well, I'm psyched that she's going to be texting me. My first public school friend! Well, besides Isaac. But he's my boyfriend. At least, I think he is. We still haven't had the whole "we're officially together" talk yet. But we spend so much time together. There's no way he would have time to see anyone else. Which must mean we're boyfriend/girlfriend, right?

But maybe it's not a time thing. Maybe he just wants to keep his options open, like in case someone better comes along. Or maybe he's one of those guys who doesn't do the whole girlfriend thing. Maybe he just dates girls and doesn't ever make it official. That way when he cheats on you, you can't really call it cheating, because—

"I don't feel so good," Marshall moans.

"Maybe you should go lie down in the guest room," Isaac says. He's back with the mop.

"I think I should," Marshall says. He stands up and wobbles toward the hallway.

"It's the second door on the right," Isaac calls. "And if you get sick again, use the guest bathroom that's attached, okay?"

Marshall nods, then goes stumbling down the hall.

"Well," Isaac says, "do you see why I wanted it to just be me and you? Everyone felt awkward, and the afternoon ended with me cleaning up puke."

"I don't feel awkward," I say, lying back on the couch and propping my feet up on the ottoman.

"That's because you're not cleaning up puke." He grins.

When the floor is clean again, we check on Marshall, who's sprawled out on the bed in the guest room snoring. And then Isaac takes my hand and pulls me down the hall toward his room.

"Should we be going to your room?" I ask, suddenly nervous.

"Why not?"

"Won't your dad care?" I ask.

"My dad left."

Oh. Right.

His room is totally clean, neat as a pin. He kisses me, and his lips feel amazing. The kisses intensify, until finally, he's pulling me down on the bed next to him. I sink into the softness, and then his hands are moving up and over my shirt.

We make out for a few minutes, until I pull back.

"Wait," I say, sitting up. My body's on fire, and my head's all cloudy.

"It's okay," he says, rolling over onto his back and looking up at the ceiling. "We can stop."

"No, it's not that," I say. "I mean, it is that, but . . ." I swallow hard and look out the window.

"What?" he asks, sitting up next to me. "What's wrong?"

I don't know what's wrong. I'm just having all this weirdness, thinking about what happened with Rex, and how I'm here now with Isaac, and just . . . I don't know. "What's going on with us?" I ask.

"What do you mean?" Isaac asks, looking confused.

"I mean, are you my boyfriend?"

He frowns. "I never thought about it."

"You never *thought* about it?" I start to get up from the bed, but he grabs me and pulls me back down.

"Hey," he says, "what's going on?"

"Nothing," I say. "I just would have hoped that you would have thought about it by now. I mean, we've been spending pretty much every second together."

"Yes," he says, his brown eyes meeting mine. "We're together. And I didn't mean that I haven't thought about it because I didn't want to be your boyfriend. I just meant that I assumed you were my girlfriend, and so I wasn't spending a lot of time thinking about it."

"And why would you assume that?" Suddenly I'm all emotional. I feel like I want to pick a fight with him, and I don't understand why.

"Um, because of what you just said? That we've been spending every single moment together since I kissed you that day outside the mall?" He's looking at me sort of worried, like he doesn't understand why I'm all upset. Which makes two of us.

"That's the problem with you," I say, still angry at him for no reason. "You're always just *assuming* things. You're always just taking it for granted that things are going to be the way that you want them."

"I'm sorry," he says, shaking his head. "I don't understand why you're—"

"I want to go home," I say.

"Okay." But he doesn't move.

"You have to drive me home," I tell him.

"First you're going to tell me what this is all about."

"It's about you just assuming we were together and not even thinking that maybe I have a say in it too."

"No, it's not," he says.

"It's not?"

"No." He shakes his head. "I'm not stupid, Kelsey. You're upset, I can see that, but it has to do with more than me. What's going on?"

I don't say anything. Because the truth is, I don't know.

He takes my face in his hands and says, "Look at me."

I raise my eyes to meet his. It's hard because it makes me feel really close to him. I feel like he's looking into my soul, like he's the first person who can see the real me. "I am falling in love with you," he says. "And I am not Rex. Okay?"

I nod. And then he kisses me again.

And again.

And again and again and again. His hands are everywhere, and so are mine, and my body is melting into his, responding to his touch, falling into the moment. And when he whispers in my ear, when he asks me if I've ever done this before, I tell him I haven't.

I lie.

The Aftermath

Isaac

"Can I talk to you alone, please?" Kelsey hisses.

"Who? Me?" I look at her with a faux innocent look on my face, like I have no idea what she'd need to talk to me about.

"Yes, you." She gives Dr. Ostrander a smile. But he's not smiling back. Probably he can't figure out why she wants to talk to me alone. Probably he knows she's up to something.

"Why?" I ask, just to be mean. Which isn't very nice. I mean, I don't want to be an asshole just to be an asshole. Actually, when I think about it, that's not even true. I *do* want to be an asshole just to be an asshole. I mean, why shouldn't I? I fell in love with her, and she shit all over me.

"Because I think we should talk for a second. In private."
She looks at Dr. Ostrander, and then she changes her voice
into the voice she uses with adults when she wants to get something from them. "Dr. Ostrander," she says, "would you mind
giving me and Isaac a moment alone?"

"You want me to *leave* my *office*?" Dr. Ostrander looks very
offended. I would be too, if I were him. It's a really nice office.
He probably had to go through years and years of boring-ass
classes to be able to get the job that gave him this office. And
so I'm sure the last thing he wants is snot-nosed kids telling
him to get out of it.

"Of course not," I say, mirroring Dr. Ostrander's same
offended look. "We would never ask you to leave your own
office. That would be disrespectful." I shoot Kelsey a look like
she should know better.

"Oh, now you're worried about being disrespectful," she
says. "Where was your sense of decorum when you were punching out Rex?"

"I didn't punch him out," I say. "And honestly, I don't think
we should be talking about that. We're getting ahead of ourselves. We should go back to the reason I was mad at him in
the first place, the reason you told Rielle to keep him away."

She's out of her seat in a flash. "Isaac," she says. "Outside.
Now."

I sigh like it's a big inconvenience, then put my hands in the
air, palms up, as if to say to Dr. Ostrander, *What can you do?
This girl's obviously crazy.*

"Isaac and I have to talk about a, um, personal matter," Kelsey says. "We'll be right back."

I follow her out into the hall. When I was in the office, I was enjoying making her upset, making her nervous, making her squirm. But now that we're out of there, I just feel beaten down again.

"What the fuck are you doing?" she says, her eyes flashing.

"What do you mean?" I put a confused look on my face.

"You know exactly what I mean!" Her face is flushed, and she pushes her hair back. "You can't just go in there and start talking about my sex life."

"Oh, now you have a sex life," I say. "That's so interesting, because last time I checked, you said you didn't."

Her eyes blaze with anger, and for a long moment we just stand there looking at each other. It's like a face-off, and whoever blinks first is going to lose. She wants me to promise that I'm not going to bring up the real reason things got out of control on Face It Down Day, and I want her to give up and go back into the office. She knows there's a chance I won't actually tell Dr. Ostrander what happened, but she can't be sure, and so she's frozen out here.

Then suddenly her face crumples, and she slides down the wall and onto the floor. There's a run in her stocking, and she traces it with her finger, looking at it in confusion like she can't believe it's there.

"What happened?" she whispers.

"What?"

"What happened?"

"With us? Um, you lied to me. And then you got caught." It's more complicated than that, obviously. Because the truth is, I wouldn't care if she lied to me, except for the fact that I love her. And once you love someone, you can't really put up with them lying to you. It just doesn't work. It makes things into a big mess. It makes you start running around punching people in front of the nightly news cameras.

"When did things get so complicated?" she asks. "I just . . ." She looks frustrated now. "I just want things to go back to being *easy*."

"They were never easy," I say. And then I sit down next to her. She turns and looks at me. "You can't forgive me?"

I think about it. "No," I say.

She nods like she already knows. But it's the first time she's asked me this, and so I think about it again, *really* think about it instead of just giving in to the fact that I want to punish her, that I want to hurt her as much as she hurt me.

"Maybe," I say. She looks at me, her eyes hopeful. "But first you have to tell me exactly what happened. Everything. The complete truth."

"Everything?"

"Yes."

She looks nervous, but then she nods. And then she starts to talk.

Before

Kelsey

I didn't sleep with Isaac. Or, actually, *he* didn't sleep with *me*. I think it was because I told him I was a virgin. The weird thing is, I didn't even know that I was lying. I mean, I *did* know I was lying, but to me, it kind of wasn't a lie. I don't count sleeping with Rex as sleeping with someone. Why would I? I just want to forget about it.

I wouldn't have slept with Isaac anyway. At least, I don't think I would have.

"I don't want to make you do something you're not ready for," he said, kissing my forehead. "We have all the time in the world."

And I believed him.

The next day, Isaac and I are supposed to get together at Barnes & Noble with Chloe and Marshall to come up with some questions for Face It Down Day. But when my mom drops me off, Isaac isn't there yet, leaving me to deal with Marshall and Chloe. Who are not in good moods.

"Yesterday was a disaster," Chloe moans. She puts her head down on the table and looks up at me forlornly. Her curly hair is a big mess, and there are dark circles under her eyes.

"You're telling me," Marshall says. "I spent the whole night puking my guts out." He still looks a little green.

"Shouldn't you have stayed home?" I ask, inching my chair away from him. I know he probably just got sick from all the cake and all the jumping, but if that was true, wouldn't he have only thrown up once? Why was he puking all night? I knew that cake was sketchy. Hopefully, I'm okay. Sometimes food poisoning can take days to show up. Not that I was Googling all night or anything.

"No," he says, "I didn't want to let you guys down. Plus I need to start studying for the math test I have on Monday."

"You need to study all weekend?" Chloe asks, lifting her head.

"Yes," Marshall says. "I need to get a good grade if I'm going to pass the class."

Wow. I admire his fortitude, at least. He doesn't seem like the type to put his academics above his physical well-being, but whatever.

"I'd rather be throwing up than have a broken heart," Chloe says. She throws her head back down on the table and closes her eyes like she can't even take being alive.

"Your heart is broken?" Marshall asks. "Why?"

Chloe keeps her head on the table but moves her eyes so that they're on Marshall. "Were you even *there* yesterday? Did you even *see* what happened with me and Dave?"

"You guys seemed in love," Marshall says, shrugging.

"We aren't in love!" Chloe yells. "We hooked up once!"

"Guys," I say, "please, can we focus?"

"I don't think so," Chloe moans.

"I can, Kelsey," Marshall says, pulling a pencil from behind his ear and licking the tip. "I can focus."

"Good." I nod. "Now, listen, the Concordia Prep students are going to be here in two weeks. And we need to come up with some good questions to ask them, some topics of conversation to get everyone talking."

"How about 'What's your favorite color?'" Marshall asks. He sets his pencil down, then pulls out a thermos and a Styrofoam cup. He unscrews the top of the thermos and starts pouring hot water into the cup.

"Well, um, that's a good way to get to know someone," I say. "But we're looking for something a little more in-depth."

"Dave's favorite color is orange," Chloe says. "Do you know how hard it is to find cute clothes that are orange?"

Marshall takes out a tea bag and starts dipping it into his cup of hot water. He picks up the cup and takes a sip. "Hey, we could ask people about how they lost their virginity," he says.

I feel my face flame hot. Chloe catches my eye over the

table, and she raises her eyebrows. I look away quickly and then say, "That's good. But I don't think we should ask specific questions like that. Maybe something a little more generic, but still along those same lines, like how everyone feels about sexuality and the pressures teenagers are facing." I make a note on my paper about that.

"Good question, Marshall," Chloe says. She's still looking at me with that curious look, and I wonder if she can tell just from looking at me that something almost happened with me and Isaac yesterday. Or maybe she can just tell that there's a situation with me and sex and secrets and—

Isaac comes walking up to the table. He's wearing a crisp white T-shirt under a navy zip-up hoodie, and a pair of black track pants with a white stripe up the side.

"Whoa," Marshall says. "Looks like you're slumming it today, huh, Brandano?"

He gives Marshall an easy grin as he slides into the chair next to me. "I slept in," he says, "and I'm just trying to fit in with the unwashed masses."

I wonder if things are going to be weird and different between us now, but Isaac leans over and kisses me briefly on the lips. Chloe's eyebrows go up even more, and she gives me a look. A *"We'll talk later"* kind of look.

"So, what'd I miss?" Isaac asks.

"We were just talking about virginity," Marshall says. He takes another sip of his tea.

Isaac gives me a look.

"No, we weren't," I say quickly. "We were just talking about how we can bring up sex as a topic of conversation when we have the kids from Concordia Prep here in a couple of weeks."

"Good idea," Isaac says.

"Yup," I say, deciding it's time to change the subject. "Good idea, so let's think of other things. You know, um, besides sex."

"How about relationships?" Chloe asks. "Broken hearts, that kind of thing?"

"That's good," I say, writing it down. "That's really good."

"Want some tea?" Marshall asks Isaac, holding the cup out.

"Um, no," Isaac says. "That's okay, bro."

"Kelsey?" Marshall asks.

"No, thanks." Doesn't he know that no one's going to be too psyched to share a drink with him when he was just puking his guts out all over the place?

But when he offers it to Chloe, she asks, "Is it caffeine free?"

"Yes," Marshall says.

"Then no."

These people are crazy, and I love them.

We brainstorm for a little longer, and then Isaac and I decide that later we'll type the questions up into one document and then the four of us will meet up again next week to go over them.

"Let's go have lunch," Chloe says on the way out. "You want to?"

"Sure." I turn around to ask Isaac and Marshall if they're up for it.

"Unh-uh," she says, shaking her head. "Just you and me."

"Um, okay," I say, a little nervous about why she wants to get me alone. "Is that okay?" I ask Isaac. "I know we had lunch plans, but—"

"Fine with me," Isaac says. He slings his arm over Marshall's shoulders. "Looks like it's just you and me for lunch, Marsh."

"Can we go to Chili's?" Marshall asks him. "I'm in the mood for Mexican."

Chloe and I decide to walk over to McDonald's because it's close and cheap, and because it's a gorgeous day out. On the way over she immediately starts in on me.

"So," she says, "you and Isaac had sex last night?"

"No!" I say.

She raises her eyebrows at me skeptically.

"I swear," I say, shaking my head emphatically, like that will make her believe it. "We didn't."

"So then what was all that weirdness just now?" she asks.

"What weirdness?" I look down at my feet, pretending that I'm superfocused on putting one foot in front of the other. It helps that the shoes I'm wearing are superhard to walk in.

"Oh, please," she says. "You freaked out when Marshall brought up sex."

"I didn't freak out," I say. I love Chloe. But talk about being dramatic. I mean, I most definitely didn't freak out. Yes, I might have, you know, had a reaction. But it was slight.

"You definitely acted weird," she says, "and I saw the look Isaac gave you when he came in."

Isaac gave me a look? I want to ask her what kind of look, but I don't want to add fuel to the fire. "It's nothing," I say. "It's just that yesterday we were making out, and things got a little, um, heated."

"But you didn't?"

"No."

"But you wanted to." She grins.

I think about it. "Not really," I say. "I mean, I did, like, hormonally." She laughs. "But we haven't been together that long. And the last thing I need is to get myself into another situation where sex complicates everything."

The words are out of my mouth before I realize I've said them, and I quickly try to figure out a way to backpedal. "I mean, not *another* situation, just a—"

"Please," Chloe says. "Save it." We're at McDonald's now, and she reaches out and opens the glass doors. The smell of salty French fries assaults my nose, and the cool air of the restaurant makes me shiver. "Who'd you sleep with?"

"Shh!" I say, looking around to see if anyone I know is here. The last thing I need is rumors starting up about my sex life. "No one." I start hustling her up to the counter.

"Don't lie," she says, shaking her head. "I hate liars."

Me too. Or at least, I thought I did. Can you hate something that you, yourself, are? Actually, I think you can. It's called being a hypocrite.

"It . . . there was a guy at my old school," I say. "My ex-boyfriend."

247

"The one whose car you wrecked?"

I nod.

"Ahhh." She gives me a knowing look. "That story makes so much more sense now. Guys are such dicks." She raises her eyes up to the menu above the cash registers.

I love that she's not making a big deal of my revelation, or pushing for a lot of details. It makes me feel like she wants to know stuff about my life because she wants to get to know me better, not because she's looking for gossip to tell her friends. It's a nice change from my friends at Concordia Prep.

The line shuffles forward, and when it's our turn, Chloe orders a fish sandwich, fries, Diet Coke, and a large milk shake. Wow. I have to get a Big Mac, fries, lemonade, and an apple pie to try and keep up. Anytime I eat junk food with Rielle, she usually eats a few bites and then claims to be full. Her only real food weakness is cupcakes, hence the reason I took her to Pria's Bakery the other day. I make a mental note to put body image issues on the list of things to bring up on Face It Down Day.

"So what's up with you and Dave?" I ask as Chloe and I sit down at a table near the middle of the restaurant. I unwrap my straw and slide it into my lemonade.

"I don't know," she says. "It's been all awkward ever since we hooked up. I mean, he came to Isaac's and everything, which I thought was a good sign, but after we left he took me right home. It's like now that we hooked up, he doesn't know how to act."

"Well," I say, and take a sip of my drink, "maybe it's going to be up to you to take the lead."

"What do you mean?" she asks, ripping open a ketchup packet.

"I mean, what do *you* want?"

"I want to be with him," she says. "That's all I've ever wanted."

"Then why don't you tell him?"

"I told you," she says. "I can't."

"Why?"

"Because then everything will change between us."

"Everything's already changed between you guys," I point out. "I mean, it sounds like things are really weird."

"True," she admits. She pulls a fry through the pile of ketchup on her tray and pops it in her mouth.

"And besides," I say, "didn't you just say that you hate liars?"

"Yeah." She looks uncomfortable, and she leans back in her chair and pushes her long, curly blond hair away from her face. "But I'm not lying to him."

"You're not?"

"No. I mean, he's never actually come out and asked me if I like him."

"But lying by omission is the same as lying," I tell her.

She nods. "You're right," she says, "and I do hate liars. It's just really hard, you know?"

"Yeah."

"But I think maybe I will tell him." She grins at me, and I grin back.

But for the rest of lunch, all I can think about is how I told her that she shouldn't lie to Dave. Even though I'm doing that exact same thing to Isaac.

Before

Isaac

Over the next couple of weeks things are pretty hectic. For some reason it seems like every teacher has decided to shift into another gear and pile on the homework. Not to mention my dad's in the midst of some big school tour, where he visits a bunch of schools, talking about the need for good teachers and a shift in educational standards. He's been trotting me out to talk about the difference between private school and public school. I do my job, and I do it with a smile on my face, not enjoying it but not really minding it either. I look at it as just playing the game.

Besides, I'm happy. And I'm pretty sure it's because of Kelsey. We're spending every spare moment together, and it's the easiest relationship I've ever had with a girl. Not that I've had many relationships. But still. A lot of times we'll just be hanging out at my house, doing our homework, watching TV, whatever, and it's okay to just *be*. We don't have to keep talking or trying to make sure the other one's entertained or anything. It's just perfectly natural for us to coexist.

I might be the happiest I've ever been.

This is what I'm thinking about on the day before Face It Down Day as I'm whistling down the hallway at school. I'm late for gym, so I'm kind of rushing. I like to meet Kelsey as soon as we're done changing, so that we can do our warm-up run together. I know. Who would have thought that I would turn into such a sap? Doing a warm-up run together? It's the kind of thing that used to make me roll my eyes and mime a gagging motion. But now it just seems right.

I'm debating whether it would be totally uncool to start running toward the locker room when someone steps in front of me.

"Whoa," I say, putting my hands on the person's shoulders to avoid barreling into them. "Sorry."

"I'm sure you are," the person says, sounding sarcastic. I take a step back. And that's when I realize it's Marina.

"Hey, Marina," I say, trying to sound polite and not give away the fact that inside, I'm kind of terrified. Marina and I haven't really talked since that day when she stomped out of our meeting. She never came to another Face It Down meeting, and we never really asked her why. I mean, it was pretty obvious.

In fact, if you want to know the truth, Marina and I haven't really talked since that night at the beach last month. The night I kissed her. She sent me a couple of texts, but I never replied, and then I started dating Kelsey. I know I should have talked to her—I've been *meaning* to talk to her—but there just never seemed like a good time. She was always surrounded by her friends, and the couple of times I did try to approach her after her blowup at the meeting, she would see me coming and then turn on her heel and stalk away. After a little while I just assumed she was so mad at me that she didn't want anything to do with me. Which, I'm sorry to say, made me kind of relieved.

"Hi, Isaac," she says, giving me a fake smile. "How are things?"

"Fine," I say, looking behind her nervously. "How are things with you?"

"Things are great with me," she says. "I have a new boyfriend."

A new boyfriend? I'm assuming she means new as in she just got him, not new as in I was her old boyfriend. She can't think I was her boyfriend, can she? I mean, we only hung out once. "That's great," I say, deciding it's best not to think about it. "I'm happy for you."

"And I'm happy for *you*," she says. "Rushing off to gym, are we? So that you and Kelsey can do your little warm-up run together?"

Wow. I wonder if anyone else has noticed we do that. "Well, I'm rushing off to gym because I don't want to be late." I force a little laugh and decide to leave the warm-up run part out of it.

"Is there a reason you didn't pick me to come to Face It Down Day?" she asks.

The response to Face It Down Day has been insane. So many kids wanted to come, and we got a ton of applications. Kelsey, Chloe, Marshall, and I spent a bunch of time going through them, picking out the kids we thought were really going to get something out of it, not just the ones who were looking for a free pass out of class. We also picked a pretty diverse group because getting a good group is really important. Especially since thanks to my dad's involvement, and the fact that he's been talking up Face It Down at all the schools he's been visiting, there's going to be a camera crew here tomorrow from the local news.

"You submitted an application?" I ask, trying to look confused. The truth is, when we saw Marina's application, we didn't really read it. There was no way we were going to let her in.

"Yes," she says, "and I would hate to think that I wasn't picked just because you and I have a history. I don't think that the NBC affiliate would like to cover that angle of the story, do you? Especially since the day is supposed to be about bringing students together, not tearing them apart."

My mouth drops open, but I quickly shut it. Is she . . . she's not *threatening* me, is she? Like saying that she might start some kind of *scene* or something while the reporters are here? That would be so fucked up.

"Huh," I say, "yeah, well, you weren't not picked because

me and you have a history. We don't really have that much of a history."

Her face gets all angry then, and I realize I shouldn't have said that last part, about us not having a history. That was a bad idea. Obviously, she thinks we do have a history. And that's all that matters. And now I've angered her even more.

"Really?" she says. "Because I think kissing me and then refusing to talk to me is a history. A very interesting history." She takes a step toward me. She's wearing these very tall black boots with a very skinny, sharp heel. They look like the type of shoes you see on the covers of crime novels about female serial killers, the kind that usually have blood dripping off the bottom.

The warning bell rings, signaling that we only have thirty seconds to get to gym. Which doesn't seem like it's going to be happening. I don't want to be late, but I also don't want any kind of *Fatal Attraction* thing to be going on here either. Keeping my life is definitely preferable to keeping my attendance record.

"I didn't refuse to talk to you," I say. "You, um, you didn't seem like you wanted to talk to me."

"When did you try?"

"A bunch of times," I say. "I tried to come up to you, but you were always walking away."

She leans back against the row of lockers and pouts her bottom lip. "I wanted to make really sure that you wanted to talk to me. You know, about what happened."

"Right," I say, "about what happened. That's why I wanted to talk. You know, to explain."

"So explain."

There's an alarm going off inside me, some kind of crazy-girl radar. And I've learned that in these instances, it's best to trust my instincts. "Um, well," I say slowly, "I wanted to talk to let you know that me and Kelsey started going out, and that I was really sorry that I kissed you that night. I was drunk, and it wasn't right of me to lead you on like that."

This is the truth. The complete and total truth. I *do* wish I had talked to her, I *was* drunk that night, and me and Kelsey *are* together. But obviously, honesty isn't what Marina's looking for.

"So you did keep me out of Face It Down Day because of our history!" she yells. "You didn't want me around because you thought I was going to stalk you!"

"No!" I say. Although, now I *am* a little scared that she's going to stalk me. But I wasn't at the time. Well, not that much.

She turns and starts to stomp down the hall, but I run after her. "Marina!" I say like some sort of crazy person. "Wait!"

She turns around. "Yes, Isaac? Do you have something to say that is going to make this situation any better?"

God, this chick has really gone off the reservation. "I just wanted to say . . . um, I hope we can be friends." This is a lie. I don't want to be friends with her. But I'm trying to calm her down.

"I don't think that's going to be possible," she says. "I'm not friends with people who are so blatantly manipulative. My therapist doesn't think it's good for my self-esteem."

Figures that she has a therapist. Not that there's anything wrong with therapy. My dad's always trying to foist that shit on me. But in my experience, there are two kinds of therapists. The kind that actually tries to help you and makes you work on your issues, and the kind that coddles you and doesn't make you do any real work so that you keep coming back. I'll bet that Marina's therapist is the second kind, the kind that makes her feel like everyone around here is just so manipulative, and that she's the victim in every situation.

"I'm not trying to manipulate you," I say. "See you around." And then I start to walk away from her. Because this chick is crazy. And also because I'm late for my run with Kelsey.

"I think the news channel is going to be really upset about all of this!" she yells after me.

I keep walking, pretending I don't hear her. But then I remember Kelsey. And how important this is to her. How she's pretty much banking on Face It Down Day going well so that she can get into a good college. How she really, really wants it to go perfectly, how she can't wait for it to happen.

And so I sigh. And turn around. And I say, "Marina, would you like to come to Face It Down Day tomorrow?" I can deal with her for one day. Then after that, she won't have any power over me—the news story will have already run.

"I don't know," she says, pretending to think about it just because she wants to torture me. I wonder what her therapist would think about that kind of blatantly manipulative behavior. Probably he'd tell her she was a victim. "I mean, you didn't

257

want me there in the first place. I don't want to be anyone's second choice."

She says it vaguely threatening, like I better not break up with Kelsey and expect her to have just waited around for me. I wonder if maybe I'm going to need to borrow my dad's security detail.

"Oh, you're not a second choice," I say. "I really, really want you there."

"Great," she says, deciding to believe it. "Now walk me to gym."

And since I want to keep things calm, I do.

"I just don't understand why we had to run with her," Kelsey says once gym class is over and we're on our way through the halls, dodging the other kids as we make our way to second period. "It was weird, having her there during our warm-up."

"Um, hello," I say, "did you not hear the part about how she threatened me with creating some kind of scene tomorrow?"

"Isaac," she says, "we can't bow to that kind of thing! Do you want to be beholden to Marina Ruiz for the rest of your life?"

"I don't think it's going to be for the rest of my life," I say. "It's just going to be until tomorrow."

"I just hate thinking that that girl is pulling one over on us," she says.

"She's not pulling one over on us," I say. I put my arms around her waist and pull her close to me. I bury my face in her neck, which makes her laugh. I love making her laugh. "And it's just until tomorrow."

"I don't like thinking about her being there."

"I know, but you're not even going to be thinking about her," I say. "You're going to be having too much fun being famous."

She laughs again, and I kiss her, and then we walk down the hall, together and happy.

Before

Kelsey

On the morning of Face It Down Day the sky is overcast, and it looks like it's going to rain. I'm not upset. In fact, it actually makes me happy because I feel like it's fitting for what we're about to do. I mean, we're going to be dealing with some pretty heavy subjects, and so I feel like the weather should be heavy too. What would be really cool would be if later, when we were done, the clouds parted and the sun came out. Of course, that kind of stuff only happens in movies. But still. It's cool to think about.

"Do I look okay?" I ask Isaac nervously. We're standing outside the gym before second period. Everyone else is in class, so the hallways and the gym are empty. But the students from both our school and Concordia Prep should be here in about twenty minutes.

"You look beautiful," Isaac says, leaning down and giving me a kiss.

"You have to say that. You're my boyfriend."

"I would say it even if I wasn't your boyfriend, because it's true," he says, looking at me. He pushes some hair back from my face. "Kelsey, you need to relax. Everything is going to be fine."

I nod and smooth down the skirt I'm wearing. It's white, knee length, with ruffle detail on the bottom. I've paired it with a flowing black-and-white blouse with a geometric pattern, black high heels, and big gold hoop earrings. My hair is pulled back in a bun. I'm hoping the outfit makes me look responsible, but with a touch of young and funky.

"Ohmigod," I say, grabbing Isaac's arm. "I just remembered something."

"What?"

"White doesn't look good on camera." I feel the blood drain from my face. "It doesn't show up. I saw it on one of those 'behind the scenes of your favorite reality shows' specials. There was that girl, Ally or whatever, who was on *In the House*, and she was talking about how they couldn't wear white because—"

"Kelsey," Isaac says. He reaches out and puts a finger over my lips. "Re. Lax. Deep breaths. You are going to look fine on camera. Everything's going to be fine. Okay?"

"Okay." I nod. "Right. You're right."

There's the sound of a car outside, and I look down the hall and through the front doors to see the 7 News van pulling into the traffic circle. I open my mouth and look at Isaac so I can start freaking out again, but he gives me a look. "Okay," I say, forcing my shoulders back and giving him a smile. "Let's go out and meet them."

The camera crew and the newswoman are actually really nice. Her name's Brianna, and she instantly makes me feel at ease. The best part is that they're not going to interview me and Isaac right away. They're just going to observe and film some of the day, and then talk to us later.

They're going to ask everyone to sign a release on their way in, to make sure every student is comfortable being filmed. They just want to sort of highlight the day and the purpose of the event, not embarrass anyone on television.

When the bell rings at the end of second period, the students from our school who have been chosen to participate start to file down to the gym. Chloe and Marshall are working the door and are in charge of checking everyone's student ID against the master list.

As people start filing in I hand them the packet that Isaac and I put together, about what we're hoping to accomplish and how they're participating in something important and wonderful. Yes, it's a little cheesy, but this whole thing is a little cheesy. Besides, sometimes a little cheese is okay.

Brianna and the camera crew are over by the door, filming

the kids as they come in. Which I thought might be a distraction, but really, all it's doing is giving the air a sense of excitement. The kids are excited that they're going to be on the news, and Brianna is even asking some of them if they're excited about Face It Down Day, what they're hoping to get out of it, etc.

Everything is going great until I hear a commotion from the table by the door where Chloe's checking people in.

"You're not on the list," I hear her say, and then it sounds like there's some kind of scuffle, and then someone says, "Hey, hey, hey!"

Isaac and I lock eyes across the gym and then both head for the door.

Marina is standing there, her cell phone out, her foot tapping against the floor. "This is ridiculous," she says, waving her phone around. "I'm going to the media with this."

"I'm sorry," Chloe's saying, shrugging, "but you're not on the list."

Brianna's cameraman swings his camera over and starts to film the drama. Great, just great.

I give Isaac a nudge in the ribs. No, I don't like the idea of another girl being obsessed with my boyfriend, but when it comes to defusing possible horrible situations, I'm not above using him.

"Hey," Isaac says easily, walking up to the table. "What's going on here?"

"Oh, Isaac," Marina says, practically throwing herself at him in relief. "This girl"—she wrinkles up her nose in distaste at Chloe—"said that I'm not on the list. And then I said that was impossible."

"No, you didn't," Chloe says. "You said, 'You skank whore, my name is on that list, and I'm going in no matter what you say.'"

Yikes.

"She's in," Isaac says.

"She's *in*?" Chloe asks. The cameraman is moving the camera back and forth between the two of them like he's capturing some big moment. Which, I guess, in a way he is.

"Yes," I say, "of course she is." I give Chloe a *"We'll talk about this later"* look.

"Okay," Chloe says. "But if you ask me, she's not really in the spirit of the day with the kind of language she's been—"

"Kelsey!" someone yells. I turn and see Rielle at the back of the sea of students who are now waiting to get into the gym. The students from Concordia Prep have arrived. Wow. There are a lot of them. My stomach flips nervously.

"Hey," I say, waving back to her. Then I turn away and start to head back into the gym because I don't want her to think that she can cut the line. But she obviously doesn't get the message, because the next thing I know, she's elbowing her way through the crowd toward me. Elbowing along with her are Anna and Michelle. Which is weird, since I specifically told Rielle not to bring them. Whatever. Can't worry about that now, la la la. I paste a smile on my face for the cameras.

"You can't cut the line," Marina says all bitchy-like, once Rielle's at the check-in table. Then she turns her attention back to Chloe. "Can you please write my name on the list? I want it to be official that I was here."

"Don't worry," Chloe tells her, giving her a fake-sweet smile. "It will be official."

"Write. It. Down," Marina says. She taps one manicured finger against the paper. "I'm not moving until you do."

"Excuse me," Rielle says, shaking her head like she can't believe what's happening. "But who are you?"

"Excuse *me*," Marina says. "But who are *you*?"

Rielle looks shocked. Probably because there's a girl standing in front of her in nondesigner shoes asking her who she is. Rielle's definitely not used to that kind of treatment. "I'm Kelsey Romano's best friend," Rielle says. Which is kind of true and kind of not. "Which means I can cut the line if I want to."

"*You're* Kelsey's best friend? Wow, you must be really proud of her for stealing my boyfriend." Marina sneers. "I mean, with friends like that . . ."

Rielle's eyes meet mine, confused. I never told her about Isaac kissing Marina. No way she needed to know that. She would have just gotten even weirder about him, and about how I wasn't ready to start dating anyone.

"I don't know what you're talking about," Rielle says, shifting her gaze back to Marina. "But I do know that I've decided to ignore you now." She turns to Chloe. "I'm Rielle Marsh," she says. "From Concordia Prep. Checking in."

"You cut the line," Chloe says apologetically. "We're not really supposed to be letting people do that."

"Are you going to write my name down on that list or not, Chloe?" Marina demands.

"Give it up," Rielle says. "She's busy." She steps in front of Marina, and as she does she kind of elbows her in the side, muscling her out of the way. So then Marina pushes Rielle back even harder. It must take Rielle by surprise because she stumbles backward into Anna.

"Hey," Anna says to Marina, stepping in front of Rielle. "Get your fucking hands off of her."

Ohmigod, ohmigod, ohmigod. This is definitely not good. This is definitely not good at all. I take a step toward the chaos, hoping I'll be able to defuse it. But before I can say anything, Marina pushes Anna. "Don't tell me to get my fucking hands off anyone," she screams.

And then, in the blink of an eye, Michelle and Anna both descend on Marina, pushing her into the table. Chloe stands up, and all the name tags fall to the ground. A couple of girls I don't recognize get involved, trying to pry everyone apart, but before they can, Marina grabs Michelle's hair and pulls hard.

"Guys, guys, guys," I say, stepping in front of the table. I put my arms around Marina and try to pull her back, but she struggles, and as she does her fist connects with Michelle's shoulder.

"Don't touch her," Anna yells, then reaches out and slaps at Marina's face.

"Get off me!" Marina screams. She leans backward, trying to shake me off of her, and as she does her heels slip on the floor of the gym, and she falls on her butt. Hard. She sits up, looking a little dazed.

"Oh my God," I say, kneeling down next to her. "Are you okay?"

"I don't know," she says. "I feel a little faint." And then she kind of swoons and falls back onto the gym floor.

Isaac rushes over and pulls her off to the side of the gym, and a couple of other kids from our school go over there to see if everything's okay. "It's all right," I hear Isaac saying to Marina. "Just take a deep breath." He's going to have to get her to the nurse to make sure she's okay. I mean, she hit her tailbone really hard, and you never know what could—

"Wow," Rielle says, coming up behind me. "Who was that psycho bitch?" She shudders like she can't believe how crazy Marina is, and then smooths back a strand of hair that's escaped from her French braid.

"Rielle," I say, crossing my arms over my chest, "what the *hell* are you *doing*?"

"Relax," she says, rolling her eyes. She must have rescued her name tag from the floor, because she's holding it in her hand. She peels the backing off and slaps it onto her shirt.

"I told you not to bring Michelle and Anna," I say.

She shrugs. "It wasn't as easy as I thought it was going to be to keep people out."

"It wasn't as easy as you thought it would be to keep people out?" I repeat incredulously. Is she kidding me? She knew how important this was to me. She *knew* I really needed this day to go well.

But I don't have a chance to question her further, because Anna and Michelle come over, asking her if she's okay. Neither one of them says a word to me. Then the three of them head up the bleachers, where they sit down next to each other, chattering and giggling about what just happened.

I look over to the other side of the gym, where Marina's being led out of the gym toward the nurse's office, flanked by two girls I don't recognize.

"Jesus," Isaac says, walking up to me and shaking his head. "What the fuck was that?"

"I have no idea," I say. I take a couple of deep breaths, trying to slow my heart rate down.

"That's your best friend?" Isaac asks, sounding incredulous that anyone who could start as much drama as Rielle just did could be my friend.

"Yes," I say. "Well, she used to be, at least. Now I'm not so—"

But then I stop talking.

Because the kids from Concordia Prep are starting to file into the gym. And one of them is Rex.

My face gets all hot, and there's a rushing noise in my ears, and for a second I'm afraid Marina's not the only one who might faint. But then I take some deep breaths and tell myself that's ridiculous, that I'm not going to faint just from seeing Rex. I mean, that would be crazy.

He meets my eyes across the gym, and I'm nervous he's

going to come over and say something to me. But then he just gives me a dirty look, his face narrowing into a scowl, and moves up the bleachers, where he disappears into the crowd.

"Who was that?" Isaac asks, his voice sharp.

"That was Rex," I say, my stomach flipping. I feel a little nauseous.

"What the fuck is *he* doing here?" Isaac asks. He looks like he's about one second away from going after him.

"I don't know," I say. "I told Rielle not to let him in." I grab the sleeve of his shirt. The room feels like it's spinning, and I think maybe I'm having a panic attack.

"Hey, hey, hey," Isaac says. He puts his arms around my waist and leans his forehead against mine. "Relax."

"Relax?" I ask. "How can I relax? The news crew just got footage of a girl fight, and now Rex is here."

"Ehhh," Isaac says, "we can spin the stuff with the girls, like, 'Oh, look, they were fighting when they got here, but when they left, they were friends.' And as for Rex, just ignore him."

I nod. He's right. I've worked too hard to let a few mishaps ruin this day. I need to get it together. So once everyone is settled into the bleachers, I make my way up to the microphone that's set up in the front of the gym, and speak into it in a loud, clear voice. "I'm Kelsey Romano," I say. "Welcome to Face It Down Day."

After I give my welcome speech, we break up into groups and sit down on the folding chairs that are set up throughout the gym. We each have an index card with a question printed on it, and the plan is for each person to go around the circle, read their question, and then have everyone answer it. The point is to be as honest as possible.

In my group there are two guys from Concordia Public who I don't know, and a freshman girl and a sophomore girl from Concordia Prep who I also don't know.

We all stare at each other and play with our cards, looking around the circle awkwardly.

"So, I guess I'll go first," I say. I don't really want to go first, since that's kind of embarrassing. But I *am* in charge, so I guess I have to. Also, if I read my card first, does that mean I have to actually answer first? Hmm. I really should have made the rules of circle time a little more clear. "Oh!" I say. "Actually, maybe we should go around and introduce ourselves first."

It doesn't take long. The kids from Concordia Public are Jensen and Max, and the girls from Concordia Prep are Eva and Claudette. Well. Okay, then. Guess I'll just jump right in.

"'What is something about you that, if they knew, would shock your fellow students based on how you think they perceive you?'" I read off the card.

Then I give everyone a friendly, welcoming smile, hoping it will inspire at least one of them to talk. I've decided the least they can do is go first. I mean, I planned the whole damn day.

But everyone just looks at each other shyly, not saying anything. Out of the corner of my eye I can see Brianna and her crew making their way around the gym.

"Well," I say, clearing my throat, "I guess I'll start. Um,

well, a lot of people think that I'm totally in control because of how I present myself. I always keep my grades high, I study, I seem like I have it all together." I take a deep breath. "But if I'm being completely honest, I never feel in control. I always feel like I'm a second away from losing everything."

Claudette nods. "I know what that's like," she says. "I mean, not the control part, but to have everyone perceive you to be different than what you really are. Everyone thinks that I'm so popular, and that I'm so lucky because I have a lot of friends." She looks down at her hands and twists them in her lap nervously. "But the truth is, my friends aren't really all that great. I have a lot of friends, but not a lot of close friends."

We continue around the circle, and actually get a pretty good discussion going about perception, high school, and how weird it is to spend so much time with people who are convinced they know who you are, when really they have no idea.

We're getting ready to move on and have someone else read the question on their card, when I hear a commotion coming from the other side of the gym.

I look over to where it's coming from, and I see Isaac stand up. His folding chair goes clattering to the ground. I can't really hear what he's saying, but I think it's something about shutting your mouth. He sounds angry.

I stand up so that I can get a better look at what's going on. And that's when I realize that Isaac is in the same group as Rex. What? *Why?* Why, why, why would he put himself in the same group as Rex? But even as I'm asking myself the question

I already know the answer. He did it because he was looking out for me. He wanted to keep an eye on Rex, to make sure he could keep him away from me so that I wouldn't get upset.

"Dude, knock it off," Rex says. "Why are you getting so fucking worked up?"

"Because you're a fucking liar," Isaac says. He takes a step toward him, looking like he wants to punch him in the face.

What are they talking about? I wonder. And then that nauseous feeling comes back to my stomach. Because I'm remembering something. The question Marshall came up with. The one about sex, and how it can complicate things, and if it's ever complicated a situation for you, even if it was because you decided to wait.

Oh no, oh no, oh no, oh no.

I rush over to the other side of the gym, hoping I can get there in time.

"Kelsey," Isaac says when he sees me. "Tell him I know the truth, that he can't lie to me." His eyes are flashing.

"This is your boyfriend?" Rex asks, his eyebrows folding into a V. At first he looks angry, but then his face relaxes into a look of arrogant amusement. "Did you tell him how you went psycho bitch and wrecked my car?"

"Don't call her that," Isaac says. "Don't you say anything to her!" He takes another step toward Rex, and I step in front of him, putting my hand on his chest and pushing him back.

"Stop," I say. "Please, just stop."

"Oh, I get it," Rex says. He stands up and grins. "You

thought you were the first one to sleep with her. Sorry to burst your bubble, pretty boy, but I already took the prize."

And that's when Isaac steps around me and punches Rex in the face.

After that everything becomes kind of a blur. Marshall rushes over with a couple of guys from the football team and pulls Isaac off of Rex, who starts freaking out about his face, saying that he needs an ambulance. The nurse comes to the gym. The principal comes to the gym. A bunch of teachers come to the gym. A couple of freshman girls start crying.

All the kids are out of their groups now, milling about, chattering excitedly.

I'm looking around trying to find Isaac, but I've lost him in the chaos.

"Hey," Rielle says, coming up to me. "Ohmigod, what the hell was *that*?" Her eyes are shining excitedly. "How cool is this?"

"How *cool* is this?" I ask her. "Are you fucking crazy?" She looks taken aback, probably because I've never talked to her like that before. "How could you let Rex come here when I specifically told you not to?"

"Kelsey," she says, sighing. "I told you it was going to be hard to keep certain people away." She shrugs. "I wasn't even in charge of it. Kristin was—you know that."

"You could have warned me," I say. I'm starting to cry now. "You could have told me that he was going to be here."

"Told you he was going to be here?" she says. "Why would

I do that when you kept talking and talking about how over him you were?"

"I never said that!"

"Yes, you did."

"No, I didn't. I told you that I didn't want him to come." But now my thoughts are all a mess, a mixed-up tangle of emotions. I can't figure out what I told her and what I didn't. I know I was going out of my way to make her think that I was over Rex, because I didn't want her to think that I was crazy. And I *am* over Rex, but that doesn't mean that I wanted him—

Out of the corner of my eye I see Isaac angrily pushing his way through the crowd toward the door, and I leave Rielle standing there and start running after him.

"Isaac!" I yell. "Isaac!"

I push past Brianna, who's interviewing one of the students from Concordia Prep about what just happened. But I can't worry about that now. I have to get to Isaac.

He's pushing through the front doors and out into the parking lot. I run after him. He's going too fast, though, and my high heels are making it hard to catch up. So I reach down and pull them off.

"Isaac!" I yell. I keep running, in my bare feet, finally catching up to him at the edge of the traffic circle.

"Is it true?" he asks, not stopping.

I think about lying. I want to lie, I do. But I can't. I keep running, trying to keep up with him. "Isaac," I say, "please, can we go somewhere? Let's leave, let's talk, I can explain. It wasn't—"

He stops and looks at me, his eyes angry and hurt. "Is. It. True?"

"Why does it matter?" I try. It's a stupid thing to say, but I'm desperate. "You're not a virgin."

"It *doesn't* matter," he says. But then he shakes his head like I'm trying to confuse him with the semantics of it. Which I am. "I mean, I don't care if you slept with him or not. I care if you lied about it." He looks at me, waiting for me to deny it. But I don't. "Did you?" he asks. "Did you lie?"

I still don't say anything. There's the sound of an ambulance wailing in the distance, probably coming for Rex.

"Did. You. Lie?"

"Yes," I whisper.

"I'm going to walk away now," he says. He starts to walk, and so do I. And then he turns around. "Do *not*," he says quietly, "follow me."

And so I stop. And watch as he walks to the student parking lot, gets in his car, and drives away.

The Aftermath

Isaac

Kelsey's still talking when Dr. Ostrander's secretary comes out in the hallway looking for us. "Dr. Ostrander wants to know if you're coming back in," she says. She looks kind of nervous, like if we don't come back in, Dr. Ostrander's going to take it out on her.

"Yes," I say, giving her what I hope is a reassuring smile. "We'll just be one more second."

She disappears, and I stand up. "We should go back in," I say to Kelsey.

She nods, then stands up, looking disappointed. She's been talking for the past fifteen minutes, trying to explain to me why she didn't tell me about her and Rex, telling me it was because she'd just wanted to forget the whole thing happened. Which makes sense. And I know now she's hoping I'll say something, that I'll forgive her for lying. And the thing is, I *want* to forgive her. I do. I want it—I want *her*—more than I've ever wanted anything in my life. But how can I be sure she won't lie to me again?

"I wouldn't have cared," I say to her. "It wouldn't have made me want you less. I wouldn't have looked at you differently."

"I know," she says, "which is why it's stupid that I even lied about it in the first place, I just . . ." She shakes her head. "I didn't know how to deal with it. I just wanted to forget that whole part of my life, pretend that it didn't happen."

"But it *did* happen," I say. "And me and you were together, and you should have—"

The door to the office opens, and Dr. Ostrander sticks his head out. "Are you two finished?" he asks. "This sort of behavior is completely unacceptable, making me wait during a disciplinary meeting."

"Yes," I say. "We were just finishing up."

I start walking back into the office, Kelsey following behind me.

The Aftermath

Kelsey

I'm following Isaac back into Dr. Ostrander's office, and when I get in there, it becomes completely obvious what I need to do.

And so as soon as the door shuts, I take a deep breath, look Dr. Ostrander right in the eye, and say, "Dr. Ostrander, this whole thing was my fault. Isaac had nothing to do with it."

Dr. Ostrander raises his eyebrows.

"Seriously," I say. "You should send him home."

Isaac shakes his head. "No," he says, "it's not her fault. I'm the one who hit Rex, and I'm the one who started the whole thing with Marina."

"But I lied to you," I say to him. "Dr. Ostrander—"

"Enough," Dr. Ostrander says, holding his hand up and

silencing us both. He looks at the clock and sighs, then takes his glasses off and rubs his eyes like he can't believe what he's dealing with. "It's getting late. I need to think about this and talk to your principal. I'll let you know what the next steps will be tomorrow."

That's it? That's *it*? We spent hours here talking about all this stuff, and now he's going to let us know about next steps *tomorrow*?

"No," I say, shaking my head emphatically. "I think Isaac should go home, and you and I should keep talking."

"There's nothing left to talk about," Dr. Ostrander says. His face is drawn, and his eyes look tired from the time we've spent sitting in this office. "The two of you can't seem to agree on anything, and when it comes down to it, I'm not sure the specifics matter."

"Of course the specifics matter!" I say. "Why else have we been talking about it?"

Dr. Ostrander gives me a look, and Isaac squeezes my hand, I guess in a warning that pissing off the superintendent right before he's going to decide our fate might not be the best idea. "I'm sorry," I say, hoping my face looks apologetic. "Whatever you think is best."

I pick my purse up from where I left it on the chair and then head outside. My stomach is in knots, and my throat is dry. I hate not knowing what's going to happen. It makes me way too anxious.

"Um, do you have a ride home?" Isaac asks. I turn around.

He's standing behind me on the sidewalk, not really looking me in the eye, and sounding awkward.

"I'm supposed to call my mom when I'm done," I say. "She's going to pick me up." I pull my cell out of my bag, hoping he's going to insist that I let him drive me home. I'm just realizing that after we get whatever punishment Dr. Ostrander decides on, there will be no reason for me and Isaac to really talk. And so I want to prolong this moment, of him being here, with me, as long as I can.

He nods, and we stand there for a second not saying anything. Finally I start to scroll through my contact list until I find my mom's number. I'm just about to hit the call button when Isaac speaks.

"Why did you do that?" He shoves his hands in his pockets and looks at me.

"Do what?"

"Take the blame like that? It wasn't true. It's not all your fault."

"Yes, it is," I say. I plop down on the high stone wall in front of the superintendent's office, and then lie back, kicking my shoes off into the grass. I look up at the clouds as they blow across the sky. "If I hadn't lied to you, you wouldn't have flipped out on Rex."

Isaac pulls himself up on the stone wall next to me. I can feel his leg touching mine as he lies down beside me. "If I hadn't kissed Marina, she wouldn't have flipped out on *you*. We both made mistakes."

"Mine was bigger," I say, feeling myself start to choke up. I'm always making mistakes. With Rex. With school. With my family. And now with Isaac.

The urge to get up and run away flows through my body, threatening to take over. Talking about this stuff is way too painful. But walking away from him is even more painful, and so we just lie there for a second, not saying anything. I can hear Isaac breathing beside me, softly. I close my eyes. I can feel his leg against mine, and as long as we're not talking, I can almost pretend that none of this ever happened.

Isaac talks first. "Why'd you do it?"

"Do what?"

"Lie."

"I told you," I say. "Admitting it made me feel vulnerable somehow, like if I said out loud that Rex and I had sex, it made me more pathetic. Because of what he did to me." I sit up, and Isaac sits up too. I cross my legs in front of me, and he does the same. "The truth is," I say, "I wasn't really lying to you. I was lying to myself. And it wasn't even about the virginity. I know you don't care about that."

"Good," he says. "Because I don't." He's looking at me, but I can't meet his eyes. I'm staring down at the grass when I feel his hand brushing my hair away from my face. "Hey," he says, "look at me."

He leans down toward me, and I tilt my head up, and he's right there, so close, and I'm reminded of the first day I met him, in the gym, when I thought he was conceited and arrogant and a total jerk. I was wrong about him. And it breaks my heart to realize that he was wrong about me. He thought he could trust me.

"Kelsey," he says, "I'm sorry for the way I was acting in there, treating you like I thought it was all your fault, bringing up personal stuff in front of Dr. Ostrander. It's just . . ." He trails off and takes a deep breath, and it's almost like I can see the anger he's been carrying turn into sadness. "You don't understand how I feel about you. You were the first girl I ever really loved, that I ever let myself believe I could actually be with. And then when I found out you lied, it was so horrible. I was so angry, and all I knew how to do was push you away and lash out."

"I'm sorry," I say, my voice catching. "Isaac, I really am."

His hand reaches up and strokes my hair again. "You need to learn to let go a little bit," he says. "Let your guard down. You can't control everything all the time."

I think about it. "You think that's why I lied?"

"I think that's part of it," he says, nodding. "You wanted to be in control of every aspect of our relationship, including how your past was going to affect us. But honestly, that's not how life works. Life's messy. There are broken hearts and ex-boyfriends." He grins. "And school activities that end with fistfights and ambulances."

I laugh.

"Besides, what's the worst that can happen?" he asks. "If you let go? Things don't go exactly as you planned? Oh, boo hoo. Everything always ends up working out the way it's supposed to anyway."

I think about it. And I realize he's right. This whole time I've been trying to pretend to be this girl who has it all together, who hasn't made any mistakes, but in the process, I lost myself, who I really am, who I want to be.

I turn away from Isaac and look back across the parking lot, toward the trees that line the sidewalk. It's too hard to be close to him, to look in his eyes, to see the hurt there. "You're right," I say. "And the worst part is that I tried so hard to hold on to you, and I lost you." He doesn't say anything. I take a deep breath. "But you tried to control things too," I say.

"I did?"

"Yeah," I say, "you tried to control your emotions, to pretend that you didn't love me anymore just because of one stupid lie."

He opens his mouth, probably to deny it. But right before he's about to talk, he shuts his mouth. And then he nods.

"You're right," he says.

"I am?"

"Yes," he says, "I did try to control my emotions." He reaches over and takes my hand. "But you didn't lose me." His fingers intertwine with mine, and electricity zings up my fingers and through my body, and for a moment I can't catch my breath.

I turn back toward him, slowly, trying to keep my heart calm. "I didn't?"

"No," he says. "You're never going to lose me."

"How can you say that?" I ask. "After how I lied?"

"Because I know you," he says. "The real you. And I

understand why you did it." He pauses, then tilts his head like he's thinking about something. "And besides, I'd hate to give that asshole Rex the satisfaction of having anything to do with us being apart."

I laugh then, the first time I've laughed or felt anything except a twisting in my stomach since yesterday. Isaac wraps his arms around me, pulling me close, and I bury my face against his neck, feeling the smoothness of his skin against my cheek.

I tilt my head up slightly, and then his lips are on mine. We kiss for what seems like forever, and everything else disappears as I get lost in being close to him. Finally, when we pull apart, Isaac sits up and hops off the wall. "Come on," he says, holding his hand out to me. "I'll buy you a lemonade."

I take his hand and follow him to his car.

We go to a convenience store and sit on the curb of the parking lot, drinking Snapples and snacking on chips. I kick my high heels off, and we just sit there, eating and talking and ignoring the dirty looks we're getting from people who have to step over us as they come in and out of the store.

As Isaac drives me home he asks, "You going to be okay? Talking to your parents about everything?" We're on my street, and I can see my house in the distance. The driveway's empty, which means my parents are out, giving me a little reprieve until I have to talk about everything that happened at the meeting.

"Yeah." I nod. "I'll be okay."

He walks me to the door, then pulls me close, wrapping his arms around my waist and kissing me before he lets me go.

"I love you," he whispers in my ear.

"I love you, too," I say, the words sending a delicious shiver up my spine.

"I'll text you later," he says, and heads back toward his car. I watch him go, standing on the porch until he disappears around the corner.

Once I'm inside, I head up to my room and drop my bag on the floor, thinking about how crazy the last twenty-four hours have been. The weird thing is, I'm not that worried about it anymore. I know that no matter what happens, I'll be okay.

I brush my hair, tie it back into a ponytail, and change out of my skirt and into soft gray yoga pants and a white hoodie.

I look around my room, running my hand over the books on my bookshelf, stopping when my finger rests on a baby-blue hardcover. It's the book I was reading when everything happened with Rex, the one that I haven't been able to finish. I pull it down and trace the embossed letters on the cover.

I lie down on my bed and open the book. And then, finally, I take a deep breath and start to read.

Read on for a peek at
right of way

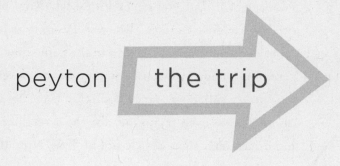

peyton | the trip

Saturday, June 26, 10:03 a.m.
Siesta Key, Florida

I'm a traitor to my generation. Seriously. All we hear about these days is how we're supposed to be strong women and not depend on anyone else and blah blah blah. And now look what I've done.

"Are you sure there's no way you can come?" I say into my phone. I'm crouching behind some bushes outside the Siesta Key Yacht Club, which is not comfortable. At all. The bushes are prickly, there are bees floating around, and the ground is kind of wet. Which makes no sense. I thought it never rained in Florida. Isn't it called the Sunshine State?

"I'm sorry," my best friend, Brooklyn, says on the other end of the line. "I'm so sorry, but there's no way I can come now. My parents found out, and they're freaking out. And honestly, Peyton, I kind of think you should just forget the whole thing. I mean, what if my parents call your parents?"

My heart leaps into my throat. "Are they going to?"

"I don't know. My mom said she wouldn't as long as I talked you out of it, but you never know what my mom's going to do. She's a loose cannon." It's true. Brooklyn's mom really is a loose cannon. One time last year she came down to our school screaming about women's equality on the wrestling team. It was pretty ridiculous, since Brooklyn is totally unathletic, and no girls were even trying out for the wrestling team. But her mom had read some article about Title Nine that had gotten her all riled up.

"But what am I supposed to do?" I ask. "My parents already left. I can't call and tell them I don't have a way to get back to Connecticut. They'll be pissed."

Brooklyn and I had this whole thing planned out. She was going to fly down to Florida from Connecticut, and meet me here, in Siesta Key, at my uncle's wedding. Then we were going to rent a car and drive to North Carolina, where we were going to spend the summer. It was a very simple two-part plan. One, she takes a plane down here. Two, we rent a car and go to North Carolina. Leave it to her parents to wreck everything.

"You're going to have to call your mom or something," Brooklyn says. "It'll suck, yeah, but what else are you going to do?"

I don't say anything. My eyes fill with hot tears. There's a bee buzzing near my face, and I don't even bother to swat it away. I really, really do not want to call my parents. And not just because they're going to be pissed. But because it's going to mean that I have to go home, and I really, really do not want to do that.

Brooklyn sighs.

"Look," she says finally. "Is there any way you can book a flight to North Carolina? And maybe get a ride to the airport?"

"I don't have a credit card. Or any money, really."

"Can you ask Courtney for help?"

"I could ask her, I guess, but I don't know if she has any money either." I stand up and scan the outdoor tables for my cousin. I don't see her dark hair anywhere. I look for her boyfriend, Jordan, but I don't see him either. In fact, I don't see *anyone* I recognize. Most people have already left the brunch and gone home. The wedding was yesterday, and the festivities are over.

I guess I could call Courtney, I think, taking a step back toward the tables that are set up on the lawn of the yacht club. But who knows if she would tell my parents? Or her dad? I mean, I trust her, but—

My eyes stop scanning the crowd as they land on the only person I recognize who's still at the brunch. The only person I don't want to see. Jace Renault. He looks up from the table where he's sitting, talking to some older couple that he probably just met. The old lady is laughing at something Jace is saying. Which isn't surprising. Jace is charming like that. Ugh.

He catches my eye, and I quickly turn away.

"Brooklyn," I say. "Please, can you lend me the money for a plane ticket? I'll pay you back, I promise."

"Peyton, you know I would if I could, but my mom took my credit card away."

"I can't believe this," I say. "I planned so hard so no one would find out, and now—"

There's a tap on my shoulder. I turn around. Jace is standing there, a huge smile on his face. "Hello," he says.

I turn and start to walk away from him. "Who's that?" Brooklyn asks.

"That's no one," I say loudly, hoping that Jace will get the message to go away. But of course he doesn't. He just starts to follow me as I walk through the grass of the club back toward my room. He's doing a good job keeping up, since I'm having a little trouble walking. My shoes keep slipping on the wet grass.

"You really shouldn't be walking through here," he says conversationally. "I don't think the groundskeepers are going to be too thrilled with all the divots you're making."

"Who the hell is that?" Brooklyn asks. "Is that Jace?"

"No," I say.

"Yes, it is."

"No, it isn't."

"Yes, it is!"

"No. It. Isn't."

"No it isn't what?" Jace asks from next to me. He's caught up to me now.

He really is like some kind of gnat that I can't get away from. I knew there would be pests and bugs in Florida; I just didn't expect them to be six foot two and of the human variety.

"I'll call you back," I say to Brooklyn. I hang up the phone and whirl around. "What do you want?" I ask.

He shrugs. "I don't know," he says. "I saw you staring at me, and you looked upset."

"I wasn't staring at you!" I say. "I was looking for Courtney." I smooth down my dress. "And I'm not upset."

"Courtney and Jordan left a little while ago," he says.

"Do you know where they went?" I ask, my heart sinking.

"I'm not sure." He shrugs like it doesn't matter. And I guess to him, it doesn't. He's not the one who's stranded at some wedding in Florida with no way to get to North Carolina. "Why?"

"None of your business." I'm walking again, looking down at my phone, scrolling through my contacts. I wonder if there's someone I can call—someone who might be willing to help me. Why didn't I make more of an effort to get to know someone at the wedding? Why didn't I befriend some nice old lady who would be able to take me somewhere—preferably a senile one who would be too out of it to ask any questions? *Because you were too busy with Jace.*

"Do you need a ride or something?" Jace asks.

I snort.

"What's so funny?"

"I just think it's kind of hilarious that suddenly you're so concerned about my well-being after what you did to me last night."

"Peyton—" he starts, his voice softening. But I'm not in the mood.

"Stop." I hold my hand up. "I don't want to hear it. And I don't need a ride. So just go away."

"Then how are you getting to the airport?"

"I'm not going to the airport." God, he's so annoying. How can he think that after what happened between us last night that I would get into a car with him? Is he crazy?

Although I guess when I really think about it, it's actually not that surprising.

Anyone who is as good-looking as Jace is usually completely out of touch with reality. It's like they think their looks give them the right to just go around saying whatever they want to say, and doing whatever they want to do. As if the fact that they're six foot two and broad-shouldered with dark hair and gorgeous, deep-blue eyes gives them the right to get away with anything.

"If you're not going to the airport, then where are you going?"

I keep ignoring him, continuing through the grass in these stupid high heels, trying to get back to my room. And he keeps following me, still not having any trouble keeping up. I glance down at his feet. He's wearing sneakers. Of course he is. Jace Renault would never do anything as, you know, *polite* as wearing dress shoes to a wedding. Although technically he's wearing them to the brunch the day after the wedding. But still. Proper attire should be worn. Proper attire that doesn't include sneakers.

I'm so caught up in looking at his feet that I don't realize that my own shoes are sinking farther into the wet grass, and so when I slip, I'm halfway to the ground before I feel his arms grabbing me around the waist.

He's so close that I can feel his breath on my neck as he lifts me up, and it sends delicious little shivers up and down my spine. He looks at me, his eyes right on mine, and I swallow hard. If this were a movie, this would be the moment he'd kiss me, the moment he'd push my hair back from my face and brush his lips softly against mine, telling me he was sorry for everything that happened last night and over the spring, that he had an explanation for the whole thing, that everything was going to be okay. But this isn't a movie. This is my life.

And so instead of kissing me, Jace waits until I'm upright and then he says, "Those shoes are pretty ridiculous."

"These shoes," I say, "cost four hundred dollars."

"Well, you got ripped off."

"I didn't ask you."

He keeps following me, all the way back to my hotel room. What is *wrong* with him? Like it's not enough that he stomped all over my heart? Now he has to keep torturing me with his nearness? When we get to the outside of the suite I'm staying in, I unlock the door and push it open.

"Well, thanks for walking me back to my room," I say, all sarcastic.

But he doesn't seem to notice. In fact, he just peers over my shoulder into the sitting area of my room. "Jesus, Peyton," he says, looking at the mound of bags that are stacked neatly in the middle of the floor. "How long did you plan on staying? A few months? I knew you were high maintenance, but that much luggage is a little crazy, don't you think?"

"I'm not high maintenance!"

He shrugs, as if to say I am high maintenance and everyone knows it, so there's no use denying it. Like he knows anything about me and my high-maintenance ways. (And yes, I am a little bit high maintenance. But not in a bad way. I just like to have things the way I like them.)

"Looks pretty high maintenance to me." He steps into the room, then reaches down and picks up the bottle of water the hotel has left on the desk. He opens it and takes a big drink.

"You owe me four dollars." Plus I wanted that water. But I'm not going to tell him that. Why give him the satisfaction?

"Don't you mean I owe your parents four dollars?"

I narrow my eyes at him then hold out my hand. "Give it to me."

"Fine," he grumbles, reaching into his pocket and pulling out a bunch of crumpled up bills.

"Figures that you don't have a wallet," I say.

"Figures that you would notice something like that, being that you're so high maintenance." He grins at me sweetly.

"I am *not* high maintenance! So stop saying that!"

"Then why do you have a million bags for a weekend trip to a wedding?"

I feel the anger building inside me—he's so damn arrogant I can't even stand it—and before I even know what I'm saying, I'm telling him. "Because," I say, getting ready to savor the look of shock that I know is about to cross his face, "I'm running away."

the trip jace

Saturday, June 26, 10:17 a.m.
Siesta Key, Florida

Peyton Miller hates me. And for good reason—I've been nothing but an asshole to her since we met. And even though I *knew* she was pissed at me because of what happened last night, even though I *knew* she hated me and probably wanted to beat me senseless with those ridiculous shoes she's wearing, I found myself getting up from my table and walking over to her while she was in the bushes.

I wanted to explain to her what happened last night; I wanted to explain to her all the reasons I had for being such an asshole. But when I got close to her, she started being such a brat that I figured it wasn't the time. Either that, or I just chickened out. Probably a combination of both.

Which is probably for the best, since there are a million fucking reasons that things are not going to work out between me and Peyton Miller, even before considering the fact that she hates me.

Some of these reasons are:

1. She is beautiful and she doesn't know it. This is a very annoying trait for a girl to have, because it makes you want them, while at the same time you can't even hate them for being conceited because they're not.
2. She is ridiculously smart—so smart that I sometimes cannot believe it. In fact, she is a horrible mix of beautiful and smart. One second she'll be tottering around in those stupid high-heeled shoes she always wears, and the next she'll be debating me over whether or not there should be universal healthcare.
2a. She is way too smart to put up with any of my shit and calls me out on it any chance she gets.
3. Right now she's trying to get rid of me, even though I'm trying to help her.
4. She broke my heart.

Number four is obviously the biggest one. She's the only girl who's ever broken my heart, and it's a very weird, uncomfortable feeling for me. I like to be the one doing the heartbreaking. Well, not really. No one ever *likes* to break someone's heart, but sometimes it has to be done. And if I have a choice between breaking a heart and getting my heart broken, well, call me selfish, but I'll take being the heartbreaker.

"You're running away?" I say now. I move into the room so she can't see the shock on my face, mostly because I know she *wants* to see the shock on my face. She wants to see me freak out like a little girl and ask her all kinds of questions. Which I'm dying to do, let's face it. But I don't want to give her the satisfaction.

Instead I head over to the minibar in the corner and start rustling through the contents until I find a Snickers. I rip open the wrapper and take a bite, then hold it out to her. "Want some?"

She wrinkles up her nose. "It's ten o'clock in the morning."

"So? It's never too early for chocolate."

"I don't share food with people."

"What, are you worried about germs? Because I think it's a little late for that after what happened last night, don't you?" I give her a grin.

"Get out," she commands, pointing toward the door. "Or I'm going to call security."

"Ooooh, good idea," I say. I plop down on her bed and take another bite of my candy bar. "And what will you tell them?"

"That an annoying jerk won't get out of my room."

I roll my eyes at her. "Relax," I say. "I'm going." I polish off the rest of the candy bar and drop the wrapper into the trash. I'm halfway to the door and trying to think of an excuse to stay, when she speaks.

"Wait!" she says. "You need to pay for that."

I reach into my pocket and pull out a few more bills, then

drop them onto the desk. "You should be careful," I say, "if you really are running away."

There's no sarcasm in my voice because I really am worried about her. She can't run away. She hardly has any street smarts. And I highly doubt her high heels are going to protect her from any robbers and miscreants that she might encounter out on the road.

"Yeah, well," she says. "You don't have to worry about me."

"Oh, I'm not *worried* about you. I just—"

She gives me a look, silencing me. Then she plops herself down on the bed. She bites her lip and pushes her hair out of her face, and then a second later, she's crying.

Shit. I hate when chicks cry. I never know what to do. You can never tell if they're crying about something that's actually important, of if they're upset because their jeans don't fit.

I move back into the room and sit down next to her on the bed, making sure there's a sliver of space between us. I cannot allow myself to get too close to her. If I'm too close to her, something might happen. Thinking about getting close to her and something happening makes me think about last night, about what did happen, after the wedding, after the champagne, after the two of us were alone. And then, of course, I think about how it ended.

"What's wrong?" I ask her gently.

"What's *wrong*?" Peyton yells and then sits up, grabbing for the tissues that are sitting on the nightstand. "What's *wrong* is that I'm supposed to be running away from home, and my friend, the one who was supposed to help me, she . . . she . . . she got caught and now I'm going to have to call my parents and tell them what happened!"

Wow. She's kind of hysterical.

"Why do you have to call your parents?" I ask.

She looks at me like I'm stupid. "Because!" She jumps up and starts pacing around the room, like she has so much energy that she can't take it. I'm a little disappointed that she's not sitting next to me anymore, but it's most likely for the best. I really have no self-control, and I probably would have tried to kiss her. It's one of my character defects. The lack of self-control, I mean. (Although I guess the fact that I want to kiss a girl who completely broke my heart and who hates me could also be considered a character defect.)

"Because why?"

"Because they thought that Brooklyn was flying into Florida, and that we were going to rent a car and drive to North Carolina, checking out colleges on the way, and then fly home to Connecticut together next week."

"But you were really running away."

"Right." She sniffs. "We were going to spend the summer in North Carolina. Brooklyn knows a boy there, and I . . ." She trails off, then shakes her head, obviously not wanting to tell me the reason she's going.

I shrug. "So why not just call your parents and tell them Brooklyn couldn't come and get you, and that you don't want to go by yourself? Tell them you need a plane ticket home.

They might be annoyed, but they're not going to be pissed. It's not your fault she bailed."

She puts her back against the wall and slides down until she's sitting.in a heap on the floor. "But then I'll actually have to go home," she says.

"So?"

"So!" She throws her hands up in the air, and I'm reminded of another reason why I don't like her. She's overly dramatic, even for a girl. "I was running away!"

"Yeah, I get it. But that plan's changed now. So call your parents. You can run away some other time."

She snorts. "Whatever," she says. "I should have known better than to expect you to understand."

"What's that supposed to mean?"

"Never mind," she says. "Just get out of here." Whatever it was that made her want to confide in me before is gone, and now she's back to being her old, bratty self. Reason number five things won't work out with us: She runs hot and cold. (Obviously I need to stop listing the reasons things won't work out. It's kind of depressing. And at some point, I'm going to lose count.)

"No, I want to know what you meant by that."

"Just that you've never dealt with anything hard in your life."

"I've dealt with hard things before," I say. But even as I'm saying the words, I know they're kind of a lie. My parents are together—happily in love. They're not rich like Peyton's parents, but they make enough money so that I can shop at Abercrombie once in a while and drive around in a (used) Nissan Sentra. I'm the starting forward on the school basketball team. I've never really had a problem getting girls, and I'm going to be valedictorian at my graduation tomorrow. (I have to give a stupid speech and everything, and my mom's all excited about it. I'm actually kind of dreading the speech. The whole graduation thing just seems so pointless, a big charade that's supposed to make you feel good about yourself, when everyone knows that in reality, high school is just one big sham.)

"Oh yeah?" Peyton asks. "Like what?" She smirks. "I'd love to know all these torturous things you've been dealing with."

"Like I'm really going to tell you." I stand up, because I'm starting to realize that this is pointless. Peyton hates me. And I'm not going to put myself out there for a girl who hates me, and who I don't even like. "Well, good luck."

"Thanks." She's still sitting there, her dress in a pool around her on the floor. She looks small and vulnerable, and I remember what it was like to kiss her last night, how her hair felt in my hands, how soft her skin was. What the fuck is wrong with me? I just said I was done with her, and now I'm thinking about kissing her again? I sigh.

"Listen," I say, kneeling down next to her. "Let me take you home."

She looks up at me, her eyes shining. "What?"

"I'll drive you home."

"You'll drive me *home*? I live in Connecticut."

"I know where you live," I say, rolling my eyes.

"You have your car?" she asks.

I nod. "Yes."

"And you'd drive all that way for me?"

"Not *for* you." I shake my head. "I wanted to check out a college up there anyway. This gives me an excuse." It's a lie, of course. But I can't let her know that I'm desperate to keep her with me, that once I leave this room, once we're apart, I don't know when I'm going to see her again, and that the thought is too much for me to take.

"But I thought you were going to Georgetown in the fall."

"How did you know that?"

"Facebook." She blushes, but points her nose in the air, all haughty. "What?" she asks. "I'm not allowed to look at your Facebook page? It's not like it's private or anything."

"I don't care if you look at my Facebook." I shrug. "And Georgetown's not definite." Another lie.

"So you'll drop me off somewhere along the way?" she asks. She pulls at the bottom of her skirt nervously. "Because like I said, I wasn't really planning on going home."

"No." I shake my head. "I'll drive you home, but that's it. I'm not getting involved in any kind of weird running-away plan. Your parents would kill me. Not to mention, I'd be kidnapping a minor."

She rolls her eyes, already wiping her tears away, already standing back up and smoothing down her dress. "Fine," she says, biting her lip. "But first I have to change." She crosses to the middle of the room and starts going through her suitcase, pulling out clothes and setting them on the bed until she finds what she wants, and then packing everything back up.

"Do you have to call your parents or anything?" she asks as she walks into the bathroom and shuts the door.

I try not to think about what she's doing in there, mainly taking off her clothes. "Call my parents?"

"Yeah," she yells through the door, "so that you can tell them you're not going to be home for a while."

"Oh, right."

"Are they going to be okay with it?"

"My parents don't run my life," I scoff. "They'll be fine with it."

And the lies just keep on coming.

LAUREN BARNHOLDT is also the author of *Right of Way, Sometimes It Happens, One Night That Changes Everything, Two-way Street,* and *Watch Me* for teens, and *Rules for Secret Keeping, Four Truths and a Lie, The Secret Identity of Devon Delaney,* and *Devon Delaney Should Totally Know Better* for tweens. She lives in Stow, Massachusetts. Visit her at laurenbarnholdt.com, follow her at twitter.com/laurenbarnholdt, and friend her at facebook.com/laurenbarnholdt.

Love. Heartbreak.
Friendship. Trust.

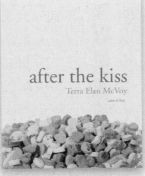

Fall head over heels for
Terra Elan McVoy.

Sweet and Sassy Reads

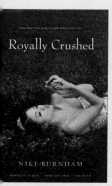

One book. More than one story.

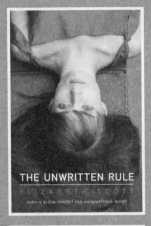

THERE'S A FINE LINE
BETWEEN *bitter* AND *sweet.*

bittersweet

SARAH OCKLER

AUTHOR OF *TWENTY BOY SUMMER*

EBOOK EDITION ALSO AVAILABLE

From Simon Pulse

TEEN.SimonandSchuster.com

SarahOckler.com